HEART TAKER: ALTERNATE COVER

MM COLLEGE HOCKEY ROMANCE

BAR DOWN 3

AVA OLSEN

CHAPTER 1

SILAS

Sitting in a hospital waiting room in the middle of the night was a universal experience. At one point or another, we all end up here.

Usually, I was waiting on someone else. There was nothing to do but wait. Wait and worry.

At least I had a stale cup of coffee to keep me company.

The emergency department was overcrowded and in bad need of renovation, the pea-green paint peeling from the walls. The longer I sat there, the more those walls closed in on me. Harried doctors and nurses scurried by as new arrivals crowded into the space, the sharp echo of watery coughs and someone puking nearby making me reach for my headphones.

I slid them over my ears, closed my eyes, and hoped that the music would distract me.

Hope was a word I was barely clinging to at this point.

I'd repeated this trip so many times that the triage staff knew me by name. First, it was because of my mom. She had inflammatory breast cancer six years ago. There was an initial misdiagnosis, a clinical "error" as her doctor claimed. When the truth of her cancer was finally brought to light, it was too late. The disease had spread, and she died in this hospital a couple of months later. Then there was my dad, who had a life-altering stroke eight months ago. He was only forty-nine. I rode with him by ambulance and stayed for hours in this very room, until the attending physician told me that my father would never make a full recovery. Dad was discharged and sent to a long-term care home and would probably be there for the rest of his life.

And now, I was back here again, this time with my younger brother, Josiah.

He was only fifteen and recently diagnosed with Crohn's disease. His bowel flare ups had him losing blood, losing weight, and making me fear the worst.

I couldn't lose anymore.

Not Josiah, not my dad. No more.

There was no way I could do it.

I'd been fighting like hell to keep what was left of my family. I was twenty years old on the outside, but on the inside, I felt like a hundred. Grief and loss made me grow up quick. When my mom passed, I skipped all the usual teenage shit—sneaking out, goofing off, getting into trouble—and became an adult overnight. I moved through days, months, and years like a zombie, the grief gradually getting less intense, but strangely enough, no less painful.

I reminded myself that if I could survive that, I could survive anything. Josiah was depending on me.

I'd grown up here in Sutton, Vermont, and had never been anywhere else, except the occasional bus trip out of state for hockey games. Hockey was my lifeblood, my one and only passion. My dream was to go pro, but lately I could barely keep up with my team, never mind playing good enough for the scouts to notice. I'd accepted admission to Sutton U, the local college, to save money, and it turned out to be the right choice, especially now that I was Josiah's legal guardian. He'd been through enough, and it was important that he stay in the same school with his friends. Plus, the partial athletic scholarship I received, thanks to hockey, helped pay for some of my student bills. Some, but not all of them.

In addition to my accounting classes, weekly practice and games, I worked thirty hours a week managing Verdant Ink, a tattoo shop in Burlington. It took me almost an hour to drive there, but the pay was good, I got to work with cool people, and they didn't mind my sarcastic mouth. Bonus, I got free tatts. My obsession. The pain of the needle was addictive; my way of dealing with stress and emotions I couldn't talk about. The loss that haunted my days and dreams. I needed release, since I had no time for a social life. Or sleep. I was always working.

Working or worrying.

Either way, I couldn't stop. I kept chugging along like a rusty car with a bad muffler, coughing, sputtering, but still moving. And I wasn't ready for the scrapyard yet…

Someone tapped my shoulder, startling me, and I opened my eyes, yanking off my headphones.

"Oh, hey, Cora."

Cora was a nightshift nurse in her forties, always kind and calm despite the chaos around her. The last time I brought Josiah here she told me that she had a soft spot for my brother, saying he reminded her of her own son.

"Josiah's resting in room 6A," Cora said to me with a warm smile. "You're good to go on back to stay with him for a while. He's being admitted for the night until we can get him rehydrated."

"Thanks," I replied with a nod and stood up.

Being a big guy, six-four, with long hair, a beard, plus the tattoos, most people gave me a wide berth. I looked older than my age, but I didn't see that as a negative. It was kind of ironic that I didn't mind looking older, just feeling it. On the ice, I was tough and aggressive, but off the ice, it was usually my mouth that got me into trouble. The only people who weren't intimidated by me were my family and my friends at Verdant.

I stalked down the packed hallway, trying to ignore the sound of a baby screaming and the acidic scent of vomit. The longer I walked, the less crowded and thankfully, quieter, it got. I turned right and stopped short at the doors that barred the entry, waving my hand in front of the sensor.

When the door finally creaked open, I kept moving until I hit room 6A.

It was one of the more private rooms here in the emergency department. Private. Right. Josiah was sharing it with four other patients, one of whom was coughing up what sounded like an entire lake's worth of water. I was greeted by the usual hum of machines beeping, and the metallic odor of blood and alcohol cleaner.

Without pause, I headed for my brother's side. Josiah's eyes were closed, his face pale, nearing on gray, and dotted with sweat, his blond curls sticking to his forehead. I tried to tread lightly—not easy for a hockey player of my size— but I wasn't as stealthy as I thought, and suddenly Josiah's eyes opened. They were a deep chocolate brown, like mine, but his were bloodshot and glassy. It wasn't only fluids he'd been given, but something for the pain.

"Hey bud, how're you feeling?" I asked as I plunked down in the one and only chair by the bed.

"Like shit."

"Language."

"Look who's talking." My brother gave me a wan smile. "Every other word out of your mouth is a curse."

"That's different," I countered and reached for his smaller hand.

It was colder than ice.

"I think I deserve to swear, don't you?" Josiah replied.

Yeah. Yeah, he fucking did. I nodded and squeezed his hand.

"Just here," I admitted. "But don't tell Dad."

"Deal," Josiah whispered.

My father was strict about stuff like that growing up, and he'd instilled a strong work ethic and a no-quit attitude in both his sons. Dad was nonverbal after the stroke, but his eyes told me he understood every word I said to him. He was going through therapy to learn to read, write, and speak again, but it was a tough battle, and writing—or speaking—one letter for him was like churning out a whole book.

Dad didn't care what the doctors said. He wouldn't give up. And I wouldn't either. Not on him, not on myself, and not on Josiah.

My brother had a baby face but the oldest soul; a disposition that was funny, kind, and sweet. Unlike me, Josiah was outgoing and bubbly, and he laughed. A lot. Or, he used to. Between everything that happened with our parents, and now this disease ravaging his body, the sunshine that was Josiah was starting to dim. Lately, he'd missed school days and outings with his friends, and worst of all, he became withdrawn. When Josiah was first diagnosed, he'd vent his frustration at being at home all the time. Now that his pain was worse, conversely, he was quieter, sometimes not wanting to talk at all. I couldn't let that happen. There were new treatments and surgeries, many of which cost a fortune, but I knew that something had to work.

Enough was enough.

I swallowed down the bitter taste of fear, like I'd done many times before, and forced myself to put on a brave face.

"They're keeping you in overnight." I smiled at him. "And then, tomorrow, when you're feeling better, we're going back to your doctor to talk about surgery."

"I can manage fine without it, Si," Josiah returned. "We can't afford it."

"I don't care what it costs, Jo. You need it. End of."

His condition was getting worse, the bleeding was happening too often, and I wasn't going to stand by and let his quality of life be destroyed. The surgery wasn't covered by our insurance. Meds yes, but surgery, no. Fuck that. I didn't care what it cost. Staring at him now, looking at how gaunt Josiah was, his cheekbones sharper than my blades, I made up my mind.

No matter what I had to do, Josiah was getting that fucking surgery.

I'd figure out a plan. I'd take a year off school and work full time. Fuck that, I'd take two jobs. I'd do whatever was needed. No matter what, even if I had to be ruthless, the surgery was happening. The only thing that mattered was Jo's recovery.

"You rest up and let me take care of things, okay?" I reassured him.

Josiah didn't say anything in response. Instead, his clammy hand squeezed mine.

Ruthless, it is.

CHAPTER 2

SILAS

A YEAR AGO—AGE TWENTY-ONE

was so tired that I was seeing double. Story of my life for the past year.

After finishing my shift at Verdant Ink, I ate a sandwich and grabbed a coffee, then hopped in my truck and headed to my next job. Given my skill for numbers, I worked as a bookkeeper for several local businesses, including a retail store and a café. All in, I clocked more than seventy hours a week, plus ridesharing.

And my day wasn't over yet. I had one more stop to make before I could head home.

Not that I saw much of that lately. But working my ass off was paying off.

Josiah's surgery bill was almost completely done, but I wanted it gone. Also, there was the mortgage on the house, and I needed money for my tuition, the part that wasn't covered by my scholarship.

After a year's leave, I was finally headed back to college. Back to Sutton U and to the Cougars hockey team. That was my plan. I found out recently that the team had a new coach,

Damien Banning, and I wasn't sure how that was going to play out. He'd started while I'd gone on leave and while I knew a bit about him as a player for Chicago, I knew next to nothing about him as a coach. Only that the Cougars kept climbing the college ranks and I wanted back in.

So many emotions hit me at once, heady anticipation, but also uncertainty about my future. Things only got worse when I got a terse email from Banning this week, telling me to report to the college rink for a tryout. Fuck me, I'd been so busy working that it didn't occur that I'd have to prove myself to the new coach one-on-one. But a lot had changed in a year. There were a bunch of new players, guys younger than me, and the pressure was on.

Whatever spare time I had, usually late at night or first thing in the morning, I spent at the gym and the local rink, staying sharp for the fall season. The dreams I'd put on hold hadn't dimmed at all. If anything, being away from school solidified that this was where I was meant to be.

I arrived at campus around eight p.m., the parking lot pretty much empty except for my truck and another SUV. Stepping inside the rink, the hallway was eerily quiet. I was running on fumes, caffeine, and anticipation.

It wasn't the first time I'd been back; I'd snuck in twice this week at the ass-crack of dawn to get uninterrupted ice time.

It was, however, the first time I knocked on Coach Banning's door.

"Enter!" a deep voice called out.

When I opened the door, I expected to see an old guy wearing worn sweats, like every other hockey coach I'd encountered. Certainly not a guy who looked only a few years older than me.

Duh, Banning only retired from the pros a few years ago, remember?

The sweats looked brand-new and the man wearing them

wasn't old. Older than me, for sure, but maybe late twenties? His raven hair was short but messy, like he'd ran his hands through it a hundred times, and his dark blue eyes met mine with surprise.

Surprise and irritation.

I glanced at the clock on the wall and realized my mistake. I was five minutes late for our meeting, and Coach was pissed. Still, angry or not, the pictures I'd seen online didn't do Damien Banning justice. I remember watching one of his last games and marveled at the intensity of his playing. He fought hard and played harder. Given the glare he was giving me, it appeared that he coached the same way.

Suddenly, my nerves began to rattle but I refused to give in to them.

"Coach Banning."

"That's what it says on the door."

"I'm Silas Moss."

He gave a curt nod. "The defenseman. You're late."

"I left work as soon as—"

"No excuses," he snapped. "If you want to be a part of this team, you show up on time. Always. Got it?"

I placed my fingers at my template and gave a mock salute.

"Yes, sir."

He shook his head. "You're giving me attitude already?"

I was exhausted and not in the mood to explain why.

"Are we going to get on the ice or sit here having a pissing contest?" I countered.

He leaned forward, the icy expression on his face telling me to shut the fuck up and do it now.

"There's no contest, pissing or otherwise," Banning replied. "I've already won. You, on the other hand, need to prove yourself."

"You've seen my admin note. You know the reason I've been off."

The gist of it anyway.

"I do," he replied as he studied me. "You have my empathy when it comes to your family matters."

"Thanks."

"But my priority is the quality of this team," he continued. "And given your year off, I have serious doubts that coming back is going to work."

What the fuck?

Before I knew it, I'd shot up out of the chair.

"So, that's it?" I snapped at him. "You're not even going to give me a chance? Why call me in here?"

He raised one dark eyebrow and slowly stood up, meeting me eye to eye.

I was more than furious.

You're not going to intimidate me, motherfucker.

"I said I have doubts," he replied calmly. "And losing your temper with me is adding to them."

"Then let's address it," I hit back. "I'm ready to play, and I can handle whatever you throw at me. Bring it on."

Banning motioned to my hockey bag. "You got all your gear?"

"No, I'm hauling around curling rocks." I rolled my eyes. "Of course it's all my gear. You told me to come prepared, and I did."

"Drop the sarcasm and go get changed," he demanded. "Meet me on the ice in ten minutes. And I don't mean fifteen."

Without delay, I grabbed my bag and headed for the door, slamming it hard behind me.

"He wants proof, I'll give him proof," I muttered as I stalked off down the hallway. "Fucking prick."

I was so fired up that by the time I stepped inside the drafty locker room I was shaking all over. The smell was still the same; rank as usual, but I ignored it and quickly got out of my jeans and leather jacket and into my gear.

Never mind ten minutes, I was out on the ice in eight.

Damien

So, that was Silas Moss.

I didn't know what I was expecting tonight, but it wasn't him.

Sarcastic motherfucker with a side of defense.

With his beard, long hair, and copious tattoos, he looked a hell of a lot more mature than the rest of the guys on my team. And none of them gave me lip like that.

No one dared.

I admired grit and determination, and Silas's gaze told me he had that and more. Of that, I had no doubt. Whether he was good enough for this team, however, had yet to be proven.

Still, I'd given my word. I'd test him and let the results tell me everything I needed to know.

As per his previous coaches, Moss had the hallmarks of a solid defenseman; good skating technique, quick stickhandling, and consistency when it came to protecting his zone. With his massive size, he was intimidating for anyone to face on the ice, and looking at my current roster, I needed a hardworking d-man.

But this one?

The major problem was his gap year. Time's not a hockey player's friend. You miss a month and it's a lot. You miss a year? Good luck in finding your way back. At first glance, it was obvious that Silas kept in shape, but working out at the gym and playing a regular college hockey season were two very different things.

Then there was the reason for his absence, the fact that he had guardianship over his younger brother. And what had he said about being late? He was at work. His file mentioned two jobs. I wanted my players focused on the game, and usually it was enough between hockey, classes, and their social life. But for Moss? He had a lot more going on than his peers, and it made me wonder about his focus.

To top it all off, there was his attitude.

Those smart-ass remarks he launched at me were amusing on a personal level, but I didn't need that kind of hassle as a coach. Very few people challenged me, especially my players. One knowing look and they backed off.

Not this guy. His gaze never wavered. He was a fighter for sure.

I looked down and realized that my hands were gripping the edge of my desk so hard my knuckles were white. Shit. A flash of warning teased the edge of my thoughts, but I ignored it. I was a professional, and I could handle a mouthy player.

Shaking off my weird mood, I did more research on his file and gulped down the rest of my coffee. Glancing at the time, I grabbed my tablet and phone from my desk and locked up my office.

When I finally made it to the ice, Silas was well into his warmup. I watched his form with my critical eye, but my gut had already made up its mind.

Silas skated up to me, sweat dotting his face, his dark brown eyes lit with a resolve I recognized. This guy was hungry for the ice.

"We're going to run a variety of drills so I can evaluate your skating, passing, and shooting."

"No shit."

"No talking either," I replied, biting back an unexpected laugh as I made a motion for him to zip it. "You want a chance; I'm giving you one. One. You ready?"

"Ready?" Silas scoffed. "I've been waiting for a year. Fucking right I'm ready."

At least one of us was.

CHAPTER 3
SILAS

PRESENT DAY—AGE TWENTY-TWO

"Rowland got the drop on you, Moss! How many times do I have to tell you, don't be distracted by his footwork, follow the puck. Run the drill again."

I stopped short and stared at Banning, frustrated as fuck, exhausted from practice, and fighting the urge to say *take my hockey stick and shove it up your...*

"Now!" Coach snapped and blew his whistle, motioning for me to get my butt in gear. "We have the college final coming up in two days. Head in the game or head out of this rink."

I nodded, biting back a snarky reply. He wasn't totally in the wrong, but I was pissed that he only seemed to notice my screw ups and not the good stuff. This extra practice time, one hour a week with my teammates Jace, Finn, and Axel, only proved that I still had far to go. I'd worked my ass off for months and months, but I was still not where I wanted to be.

September to December had me hanging on by my teeth, and shit, I hadn't played so hard or sweated so much in all my life.

The winter semester was much the same, and now April was here. I didn't feel any closer to my goal than I did that first day back. I assumed that I'd return from a year away from college, hockey, and socializing, and reenter everything full force, scoring a hat trick.

Not quite.

School was good and I was caught up on my courses. I always had a mind for numbers so that hadn't changed. And I'd finish my accounting degree no matter how long it took. That was the least of my concerns.

Socializing? I didn't have much time for that. The first semester was all about classes, follow up medical appointments for Josiah, visiting my dad, and working at Verdant. Now I made it to the occasional party, but I was still finding my footing. With teammates like Maddox and Finn, I found new friends. Finn for sure, both of us defenseman, both of us on Coach's shit list. Maddox, our first line goalie, was a prickly one, but I appreciated his snarky nature, and he seemed to appreciate mine. Not that there was any competition in that; Maddox won for sure.

The one thing I didn't do was sex. Not with any guy I went to school with, that is.

I'd hooked up with Darby, one of the tattoos artists who worked at Verdant, but he and I had an understanding. After closing, we'd give each other hands jobs or blowjobs in the alley behind the shop. I only had the inclination for casual and barely any time for even that. No one else knew that I was gay. Not my dad, my brother, or anyone in my life. Not that I expected a negative reaction from my family, but I was concerned about my hockey future more than anything. Even though our team had two openly queer players, like Dane, and two couples, Maddox and Kayden, and Jace and Axel, I still hesitated to come out. I figured I had enough against me; my age and my year off, without adding any more pressure.

There was also the fact that being around guys who

played hockey, or any sport—their drive, their competitiveness, their confidence—turned my crank like nothing else. Yeah, I had a type. Thankfully, none of the players on my team did it for me. I needed that kind of complication like I needed a puck to the head.

Besides, no one was bossy enough or crazy enough to put up with my shit anyway.

"Are you going to do the drill, Silas, or are you going to stand there growing your beard?" Banning commented.

I bit my lower lip. Hard. The copper tang of blood was painfully familiar. I'm sure I had permanent teeth marks on my lip at this point.

"I'm on it, *Damien*," I bit out, using Coach's first name and *really* pushing my luck.

The cacophony of the other players on the ice quieted to near silence. I didn't need to look at Coach to know that he was glaring at me. Hell, I could feel the bite of his frosty gaze, colder than the ice under my skates.

Banning had it in for me from the get-go, and I was determined to prove him wrong.

I had a knack for solving puzzles and reading players. But Damien Banning's problem with me was still a mystery and one I intended to figure out. One that I needed answers to. I'd given in to my curiosity and tried to learn more about him, but what I found online was nothing I hadn't already known. Five years ago, he played defense for Chicago, until his pro career was sidelined by a knee injury. An accident that could've happened to any player. But watching him skate now, it was hard to picture. He was eight years older than me, but he looked a lot younger than your typical hockey coach. And he certainly pushed me harder than any previous one I'd ever had.

I should've given him the benefit of the doubt. He was a coach, after all, and he was here to help players improve. But his expression was as clear as the blue line painted on the ice:

he didn't have faith in me. There was judgement and the verdict was "you're good, but not good enough."

Fuck that and fuck him.

Maybe his dream was gone, but mine was only beginning. Yes, I was facing guys that were all younger than me. But I had grit going for me. A ruthless core that never quit.

My teammates had hockey in their blood, like me, but they were living and breathing it. Me? I had other responsibilities that required survival.

Banning knew about my guardianship of Josiah. The parts I was willing to share, that is. I told him enough to let him know that I wasn't fucking around in my spare time. I was doing the best I could. Life wasn't fair, and I knew that if I wanted to make it to the next level, I'd have to forego everything but family and hockey.

"Moss!" Banning shouted again.

"On it!" I yelled back and skated over to face off with Jace.

I didn't let my temper get the best of me, and I focused on the drill. We ran it over and over, until I finally got the advantage and blocked Jace. After the danger zone drill, we played two-on-two, with me and Axel winning one-zip.

"Good job!" Banning shouted and motioned to the boards. "We're done for the day. Get out of here and rest up for the game. We have a championship to bring home."

"Yes, Coach!" all four of us called out.

I skated off with Finn by my side.

"That was a close call today, Silas," Finn muttered. "I've never seen Banning's face turn that shade of red before."

I chuckled and pulled one of my gloves off, wiping the sweat off my face with my hand.

"He's too easy to rile up."

"Yeah?" Finn raised one eyebrow. "Normally he's always cool. Nothing bothers him."

"Nah. Remember that penalty against Grainger College?"

"Oh, yeah. There was that. He lost it for sure."

"I don't blame him," I replied. "If you don't have passion for the game, there's no point, right?"

"Still, don't piss him off for no good reason."

"He doesn't want me here," I bit out. "I'm sick of it."

"He's trying to get the best out of you. If he didn't want you here, you'd be gone already."

I thought about that for a moment. Would I have been cut by now if my playing was subpar?

"Maybe."

Definitely.

"For sure. And stop thinking he has it in for you. He wouldn't offer this extra ice time if he didn't think you had potential."

My friend didn't see the way Banning looked at me. Finn was a sweet guy, scrappy on the ice, but often naïve when it came to everything else. Finn shouldn't be playing with guys like me; he should be protected at all costs. My teammate reminded me of my brother, and that soft spot in my heart that was reserved for the select few, warmed.

"Thanks," I offered. "I'll try to keep the negative shit out of my head."

"Exactly," Finn urged. "You need a mindset reset."

"Fuck, please don't go all sports psychology on me," I muttered. "You know I'm not into that woowoo shit."

Finn rolled his eyes, and it made me chuckle.

"It's not woowoo. It works."

"I'm not entirely sure it's working out for us." I sighed. "We're stuck here with extra practice."

"Jace is our top scorer and he's right here with us," Finn added and stepped off the ice first.

"That's because him and Axel weren't working together."

"They are now," Finn replied. "So, why's Coach still got them practicing with us? Huh? Well?"

Finn had a point.

"That I don't know."

"See? You're being paranoid for nothing. Coach doesn't have it in for you. He's trying to push you to be better."

Did I want to believe Finn? Yes. Did I? Not entirely.

"Look, I can admit that I didn't play the way I wanted to in the fall, and it wasn't easy coming back," I replied and followed Finn down the hallway to the locker room. "But I feel like things are clicking with the team, and I'm working hard. I want Coach to recognize that."

"We're playing for the national championship, Silas. What more do you want?"

I wanted it all. I wanted to be the best.

But there was more. Truthfully? I wanted Coach's approval. His praise.

Shit.

"You're right. I should listen to you and shut up."

"Don't do that." Finn chuckled. "You'd explode if you couldn't say something sarcastic every day."

I playfully nudged him with my elbow.

"Have faith in yourself," he added.

We entered the locker room, and it was damp and drafty as usual. I shivered but it was my nerves talking, not the temperature. A lot was riding on this final game of the season.

"I work my ass off, but, sometimes, it doesn't feel like I'm enough," I admitted. "I had a plan, but so far, I'm still not where I want to be. And what if going pro doesn't happen? I mean, I'm okay to go on and be an accountant—"

"An accountant that looks like a biker," Finn teased.

I gave him my tatted finger in response.

"You know you'll come to me when you need help with your books," I snarked.

"Me?" Finn asked, his eyes widening.

"Yes, you. When you go pro, you're not going to hand your money to a stranger, right? You need someone who knows what they're doing. Even if it's not me, you gotta do your research and hire the right people to manage your money."

Finn shrugged. "I'm sure if I get an agent, they'll watch out for me."

I sighed. "Finn, you're way too trusting."

"And you don't trust enough," he insisted as we headed for our cubbies.

I grabbed a towel and threw it over my shoulder, then reached for my shower kit. My cubby was the bare minimum, neat and tidy, everything in its place. I hated clutter. It made me twitch. Finn's cubby, on the other hand, was like my friend: overflowing with color and personality. He had neon stickers with funny slogans and jokes, a photo of him and his huge family taken at the farm in Nebraska, and a big stuffed cougar that sat on top, looking more like a teddy bear than a fierce cat. The sight made me smile, but also shake my head.

We were so different and yet we got along.

"You headed home after this?" Finn asked, running a hand through his messy auburn hair.

I nodded.

"You want to join us for dinner?" I asked.

Finn missed his family something fierce. He'd told me all about them, and about his girlfriend, their breakup, and the fact that he was demi. There were times I wanted to tell Finn that I was gay, to unburden myself to someone. But I didn't. I wasn't ready. Not yet. Not that I wasn't tempted to confess to him. Maybe releasing the secret would ease the pressure inside me. Pressure that was only going to get more intense from here on out.

"If Josiah's cooking, yes," Finn replied, breaking my musings. "If you're cooking, no thanks."

I threw my towel at his head, and he chuckled, ducking to avoid it.

There were too many smart-asses on our team.

CHAPTER 4
SILAS

GAME DAY

Game day nerves were normal but today, my heart was literally in my throat.

After knocking Langston College from the rankings, then crushing Grainger, we were ready to face off against the west coast finalists, Kallinger University, for the national win. Kallinger was a Seattle-based college with two of the top ranked players in the overall standings. Their forward, Matt Gross, was close to Jace's stats, and their goalie, Evyn Gerard, was phenomenal. Not to mention, two of their defensemen, Kai Strong and Niall Koskinen, were some of the biggest guys I'd ever played against.

Our opponents had size, speed, and scoring, plus, a rock-solid goalie. If we wanted to clinch this thing, there was no room for error.

We'd travelled to Chicago for the finals, far from our hometown crowd. Kallinger was in the same boat, so it leveled the playing field.

I'd had to arrange for someone to stay with Josiah, who was seventeen going on thirty, with an attitude to match. My sunny brother was back but there was an added sass to him that challenged me. Despite his surgery success, there were still issues with his health, and add in the teenage hormones... I wasn't fully prepared for raising a teenager, but I guess, no one is.

And I'd never been so far from home before. As I prepared to leave the house, I hesitated.

Until my brother rolled his eyes and nudged my side with his surprisingly sharp elbow.

"Stop acting suss and go already," Jo quipped. "I can manage on my own, you know. I'm not a baby, even though you got me a sitter for the next two days."

"It's not a sitter, it's your BFF," I insisted. "And I know you can manage, but you're still seventeen. These are the rules. Remember, if you don't feel good, you call me—"

"I know, I know."

Josiah was chafing at my protectiveness. Like any guy his age, he wanted independence. He also wanted to go back to playing hockey, which he'd given up. For now, that was a hard no. Much like me, Jo pushed back and stood his ground. I knew that he wanted to be with his friends, but I held firm. He was still dealing with a lot, coping with health challenges, medications, and appointments that most of his friends didn't even begin to understand.

"Now stop pacing and get moving, you don't want to be late for your bus to the airport," Josiah added with a smile. "And I'll be fine. I swear. River will make sure of it. Bring back lots of pictures and that freaking trophy so we can show Dad."

His confidence—in himself, in me—had me hugging my brother tighter than I ever had before.

Reluctantly, I let him go and headed for the door.

The rest of the day was a chaotic blur, getting to the bus, the airport, the plane ride, the hotel. It was like I was living in a dream-state at warp speed.

And after a restless night in a strange hotel bed, game day finally arrived.

Next thing I knew, I was sitting in another drafty locker room, tying my skates, and listening to the sounds of my teammates joking around as we pumped ourselves up pre-game. Looking down at my hands, I was surprised to find they were steady. I'd had Josiah's birthdate and initials tattooed on my right fingers, and anytime I felt myself wanting to give up, I curled my hand into a fist and remembered everything I was fighting for.

"Hey, Rufus!"

That shout came from Ethan Walker, one of our star forwards.

I'd had the word *Ruthless* tattooed on my chest recently, and Ethan thought Rufus was an appropriate, and somehow, hilarious, nickname for me. I'd warned him not to call me that. It made me sound like a dog or something. My clapback, of course, was ignored. Hockey players were weird and once they get something in their head, forget about it. Honestly, it could've been worse. Like Axel and Jace, who were tagged with *Hot 'n' Honey*. Or Maddox and Kayden, who were *Salty & Sweet*. If anyone called me any of those names, I'd be out of here.

"What do you want, Walrus?" I replied as I kept my head down, adjusting my laces until everything felt right.

Okay, so maybe I wasn't immune to mouthing off stupid nicknames either.

"Man, I told you, don't call me that," Ethan whined as our teammates snickered.

"Why?" I asked. "Those whiskers you call a playoff beard makes you look exactly like one. Maybe one day you can have a big boy beard like the rest of us."

There was more laughter and jeers, and Ethan shook his head. He was always styled, looking more like a model than a rough and tumble hockey player. His face was way too smooth for a thick beard, and his attempt at growing one had all of us razzing him hard.

"Bet you ten bucks you can't go the whole game without pissing off Coach," Ethan returned.

"Ethan," Dane St. Pierre, our captain, interrupted. "Not now."

"I'm going to play my ass off and no one's going to be pissed about anything," I countered as I stood up. "Am I right?"

There were shouts of "fuck yes!" and Ethan nodded at me. I knew that his comment was nerves talking. He was an outgoing, excitable guy, and when he was getting ready to hit the ice, he needed to joke around to ease the tension.

"But make it twenty," I added and reached for my jersey.

I proudly wore that number, and since I was as superstitious as any other hockey player, it was only right. That number meant a lot to me. It was the day of my mom's passing, the twentieth of July. Twenty was also the age when I took over care of Josiah. A lot had happened in two decades, but I was still holding strong.

I reached for my mouth guard and once that was in, grabbed my helmet, secured it, and then my gloves, and my stick.

One by one, we lined up outside the locker room, waiting for our turn to take to the ice. Most of the buzzing chatter from earlier was gone. There were nods of encouragement, and pats on the head. Even though everyone's expression was stony, I knew that inside, the fire was about to unleash.

The Kallinger Stars stepped out of their locker room, and my heart began to pump faster. There was quick eye contact with the opposing team, but nothing more. One of us would leave here a winner and the other would head home with regret. There was so much tension in the air you could practically taste the adrenaline. When "Thunderstruck" pumped out of the speakers, I shuffled my feet in time to the pounding drumbeat.

Kallinger headed for the ice first, and the roar of the crowd rumbled down the chute.

Everyone was ready to go. Everyone except Banning. Where was Coach?

I looked around and suddenly Damien appeared, stalking down the hallway in a three-piece navy suit, his tablet in hand, his raven hair slicked back, his eyes locked on us. The hottest flames burned blue, and Banning's gaze told me that my teammates weren't the only ones about to unleash fire. Coach moved like our cougar namesake, a predator ready to strike, his massive frame barely restrained by that tight, sophisticated suit. Not that I should be paying attention to what he was wearing, for fuck's sake. Still, I'd never seen him so dressed up before, but then again, there was a lot at stake with this game, for the team and for the school.

A final like this brought national media attention. Scouts for the pros would also be watching.

With my skates on, Banning came up an inch short of my height. His presence, however, loomed larger. I could easily picture him barreling down the ice full force and acknowledged that he must have been intimidating to play with, never mind against. He was certainly the most intense hockey coach I'd ever played for.

The closer he got, the quieter my teammates, until there was barely a breath among us.

My heart kicked up double, triple time. Game day nerves indeed.

As he drew near, his gaze hit mine and his eyes narrowed.

What did I do now?

I dropped my shoulders, lifted my chin, and offered him a cocky smirk in return. He had no reaction, not a flicker of recognition, which only irritated me further. Instead, he glanced at our captain and then scanned the rest of the team.

Whatever. I didn't need his validation. I was here to get that win, not to impress him.

He crossed his arms, the suit fabric stretching over his biceps.

"Remember what we talked about at our last practice," Banning called out. "Take advantage of their defensive weaknesses. I want to see aggressive plays, clear communication, and nothing less than your best."

"Yes, Coach!" we shouted in unison, shattering the calm.

"Good. Now get out there and bring that fucking championship home where it belongs!" he shouted.

There were more cheers as Banning motioned for us to get our asses moving.

The rink lights were low, the music was loud, and the crowd was feral. The excitement of playing in front of a packed rink never lost its appeal, or its drama, as, one by one, we skuttled onto the ice, getting warmed up.

Eventually, the music quelled, and the lights brightened, and suddenly the magnitude of this moment hit me. How far we'd come in a year. Making it to the finals was a big win already. And I knew there'd be players who'd get drafted within months, maybe a year. I doubted I'd be one of them, but I knew that soon, my time would come. Call it instinct or plain stubbornness on my part, but I knew it was going to happen eventually.

I was on the first line, along with Kayden, Dane, Jace, and Axel, with Maddox in net. The referee called up Dane and Kallinger's captain for the official puck drop.

Dane snagged the puck, and we were off. I didn't believe in omens, but I'd take it.

The game was fast; five minutes of play went by like it was five seconds. Axel got cross-checked by Gross—no penalty called—and Jace, who always managed to eek out an opportunity, couldn't get near Kallinger's goalie. Gerard was well protected. So much for their defensive weak spots.

With a line change called, I took my turn on the bench and grabbed my water bottle to cool down.

"This game is fire," Kayden admitted as he wiped his face with a towel. "Fucking hell, did you see the reaction time from Strong?"

"Yeah, their defense is on point tonight. Even Jace couldn't get a shot on goal," I muttered. "It's wild."

I didn't need to hear Banning pacing behind me to feel his stress. I could smell him, or rather his fancy cologne. He was probably sweating through that tailored suit with all his angsting. Unlike the rest of us, who smelled rank already, Banning was fresh, like a hot summer day. No doubt that scent was probably as expensive as that fancy-ass suit he wore.

Banning suddenly leaned forward between me and Kayden, his face close to mine, and I nearly slipped off the bench.

Jesus, jumpy much?

"Watch out for Gross," Coach warned us. "He nearly clocked Axel on the last play, and it looks like he's champing at the bit for more. He also has a habit of using his stick as a weapon when the refs aren't looking."

"Right," Kayden replied.

"Got it," I added, keeping my eyes strictly on the opposing team, studying and analysing every move.

The period flew by even though we ended it with neither team scoring. Right before the clock ran out, Gross slammed Finn into the boards with a telltale crunch. My teammate was shaken but, thankfully, okay since he was back on his feet quickly.

We started to push ahead during the second period. Axel and Jace did their magic, deke'ing around so many players it was difficult to keep track of them. And despite Kallinger's solid defense, they were no match for Jace's wicked slapshot.

Halfway through the period, he slammed it home and our team went nuts.

One goal for the Cougars and one period to go.

Intermission was a much-needed time out and had us guzzling down electrolytes in between catching our breath and comparing notes. We reviewed the plays, listened to more feedback from Coach, and hit the ice at full speed again.

Shit became real in the third period.

Seven minutes in, and despite our best efforts, Gross got the drop on our defense, specifically, on me. He ended up scoring, tying the game one-one. This was not the position we wanted to be in, but I had to hand it to my teammates; none of them showed any outwards signs of disappointment, except for a few chosen curse words.

When confronted with my error, I had a choice. I could either let it fuck with my head or keep pushing.

As if reading my mind, Coach yelled out. "Moss, get back in there!"

So, I did.

CHAPTER 5

DAMIEN

Ten minutes was a long fucking time in a hockey game.

In a final? With a one-one tie? Every minute felt like forever.

I wasn't surprised by Kallinger's comeback goal. Even though I was pissed at the result of that play, it was hard to find fault. Silas had done, well, pretty much what I'd have done in his position. I'd been on the other side of the ice as a d-man myself, and I understood the pressures that came along with it.

Silas was talented, but I still questioned if he was right for this team and the next level of play. For college hockey, he was good. For the pros? After two semesters of coaching him, I still didn't have a definitive answer. Good wasn't enough. And if he wanted to go all the way, only great got you there. Silas had a keen sense of awareness when it came to protecting his zone; he was aggressive, sometimes too much, and played hard. But something was missing. As to what that was, it was difficult for me to pinpoint. I didn't want to tell him "Sorry, you're too old" because I wasn't sure his age was the problem. No doubt taking a year off didn't help. But he'd stayed in peak physical shape, and his skating form over the last two semesters had improved exponentially.

It had taken him a long time to mesh with his teammates though. I saw the change recently, and had high hopes that I'd see him break out. That's why I'd given him extra practice time. Him and Finn. I wanted to see them both return at their best for their final year, but I had tough choices to make. New guys came in every fall, and competition at this level was fierce. My job was to take the best of the best and make them even better.

I got the sense that Silas was fighting something hard. Exhaustion no doubt. Silas had family obligations, and more responsibilities than any usual twenty-two-year-old would ever dream of. I respected that, but I also knew his mind was probably not always focused on the game. When I was his age, I'd been drafted to play for Chicago and with a contract in place and my ego pumped up, I was a cocky, wild brat. I lived like I played: full-on, full force, no thinking about tomorrow. Responsibility? The only one I had was to my team, and to winning. And to my then-girlfriend, who became my wife a year later, and my ex two years after that.

My focus was always hockey, first and foremost. From the time I was seven, that was it. I was Canadian by birth, born and raised in Belleville, Ontario, by a widowed dad. Hockey was a way of life, my family's obsession, and then, mine. My father coached, and my siblings played too. I had an older brother, Trent, who now worked as a physiotherapist in the league, and a younger sister Olivia, who, like me, coached university hockey. Except, she was off coaching in Switzerland and probably doing a better job. Then again, here I was at the national finals, so it was tough for me to find fault with that.

I didn't have reason to feel less than anyone else. Coaching hadn't been my end game. I anticipated playing hockey into my thirties and after that? Well, I never thought that far ahead.

Not until that fateful day that changed everything.

I didn't live my life on brash impulse anymore. I planned and plotted. Everything was done with precision, direction, and control. I'd reached the highest highs and lowest lows as a player, and I had no desire for a repeat as a coach. When I hit rock bottom, I decided rollercoasters weren't for me. I'd stay on steady, firm ground from here on out.

A loud whistle suddenly pierced the air, and I shook off my musings and focused on the game in front of me. I glanced at the clock and called for a time out.

We needed a goal, and we needed it now.

"Rowland, Lund, you've broken college records this semester. Now's not the time to stop."

A familiar refrain of "Yes, Coach" rang out.

I gave another round of encouraging instructions to the rest of the guys and paced the bench before the play was about to resume. Scanning the ice, I noticed Jace and Axel with their heads together, sharing words. Thankfully, they were both smiling and not arguing like they used to. There was still plenty of bickering between the boyfriends, but it was teasing rather than hostile. Like our goalie, Maddox, and our d-man, Kayden.

Given the way players were matching up on my team, it felt like I was a dating coach, not a hockey one. Not that they needed any advice in that area from me of all people. I sucked at marriage and relationships in general.

How could I give anything to anyone when hockey was my everything?

The crack of the puck hitting the ice snapped everyone into action, me included.

Eight nail-biting minutes passed.

Ethan and Colin were on fire today, but even their best moves were challenged. Sneaking past Strong, Ethan's shot got blocked by Gerard. Kallinger's goalie was consistently cool under pressure, but I expected nothing less.

The minutes ticked by, but no one came closing to scoring again, on either side.

Kayden made an aggressive play and nearly came to blows with two of Kallinger's forwards. Thankfully, Dane and Silas intervened, and the situation settled.

Then I glanced at the clock.

Two minutes remaining.

With no goal on either side, I made a line change.

Jace faced off against Gross. Kallinger's forward was fast, but no match for our center, who took control of the puck and blasted down the ice like the rocket he was. Jace was hitting his stride in this game, with his lethal combination of skating speed and skillful stickwork. Axel and Dane were aggressive, pushing hard, not letting anyone get the drop on them. Silas and Kayden too, taking hits and distracting the opposition so our guys could take the lead.

Axel deke'd around Kallinger's defense and nearly got a stick in his face from Koskiken. The ref didn't call a penalty, and I screamed my head off in response. Fuck, that could've been a bad outcome for Axel. I hated nasty behavior like that. But I also knew what it meant: desperate teams got sloppy and resorted to cheap tactics.

And then, as fast as I was angry, I was shouting for another reason.

Jace suddenly got boxed in, but he managed to sneak the puck to Axel, who took it down and dropped it, right between Gerard's legs.

The buzzer sounded off, the music blasted, and everyone from Sutton went crazy, me included. Axel's teammates crowded around him, offering hugs and smiles.

But the game wasn't over yet.

The last minute of play had me pacing even faster—my

heartbeat kicked up a hundred notches, my fists clenched tighter, my adrenaline ran hotter.

"Bring it home!" I shouted along with the guys on the bench. "We've got this!"

When the final buzzer blasted, I jumped up with my hands in the air and yelled as loudly and proudly as my players on the ice. Team Kallinger looked on in utter dissolution. I knew both sides, and while I celebrated our win, I nodded in conciliation to the opposing team. After I jumped back down from the bench and straightened my jacket and vest, that is.

Fucking hell, we'd done it. The Sutton U Cougars were national college champions.

For a second, it was like *I* was back on the ice, relieving those incredible highs. They were heady and addictive and made me want for things I could never have.

Never again.

Still, this was a big day for my team and for me. I'd take my wins now any way I could get them.

Confetti rained down on the ice, the music blasted, and the rink turned into a dance party. We lined up and shook hands with Kallinger's team. Both sides played a stellar game and deserved recognition.

Then the jumbo screen lit up with the Sutton U logo, and there were so many flashes going on in front of me, I could barely see.

I knew what was coming next. I fully expected to get doused by a bucket of water or Gatorade.

What I didn't expect was the champagne (presumably non-alcoholic). As soon as the initial shock of the win wore off, I got sprayed in the face. By Silas, no less.

Payback for sure.

My suit was drenched, my hair was a mess, and my eyelashes stuck together. But I couldn't stop smiling, which, for me, was a huge deal. Most of the time I used the stern coach approach, since players at this age tended to be cocky as fuck and needed guidance, not a friend. But, given the magnitude of this win, I let myself relax. A little.

I wiped my sticky eyes and met Silas's. His dark gaze was unnervingly direct, and I swallowed hard.

It's the intensity of the win. The shock.

For once, both of us were grinning like loons.

"Sorry about the suit, Coach."

I shook my head and removed my jacket. My vest was soaked through, and my white shirt sleeves were plastered to my arms.

"Don't lie, Silas. You're not sorry in the least."

He bit his lower lip and shrugged, giving me a once over.

"Maybe I am," he admitted and met my eyes again. "They're not for me, but I'd hate to ruin your best outfit. It suits you, pun totally intended."

His words almost seemed like… no. That was ridiculous. That wasn't flirting.

Jesus, where the fuck did I get that bizarre idea?

The players weren't the only ones who were dehydrated. I was obviously punch-drunk from the win, my adrenaline crashing.

A shiver ran through me, but hey, I was soaking wet and standing in a freezing cold rink, so…

"You played a great game," I finally managed to reply, my mouth suddenly dry. "I can't wait to see what you can do next season."

I didn't wait to around to watch Silas's reaction.

Shaking off my weird mood, I stalked off to greet the organizers, and then it was time for the winners to pose for pictures. I managed to smooth my hair back, slipped my uncomfortably wet jacket back on, and stood proudly as the photographer snapped away. I refused individual pictures, though, opting for one with the entire team instead.

The massive wood and silver trophy was brought out and there was more posing for the media. Then the guys took turns hoisting the mammoth trophy in the air and skating it around the ice.

My phone started buzzing, and when I saw the number flashing on the screen, I quickly answered it.

"Banning speaking."

"Congratulations, Coach."

It was Nora Renner, Sutton's President.

"Thank you, Nora," I replied. "But it's the players you should be talking to."

"I'll get to them eventually." She chuckled. "I'm sure they're too busy celebrating right now."

"They're having the time of their life."

And as I looked around at all the smiling faces, there was no doubt that the party was just getting started.

"I hope this means that you'll be coming back to Sutton in the fall," Nora continued. "Dean Chancer informed me that you haven't signed your contract yet."

David Chancer was the dean of athletics and the one who'd recommended me for this job in the first place. I played with him back in college, and once I moved to Vermont, Dave and I became fast friends again, in addition to colleagues.

"I'll sign it when I get back," I insisted. "I'm ready for another year. But I have a few additional clauses."

One year was all I was committing to at this point. I wanted to coach at the professional level, but I'd probably only get offered an assistant position. Still, I had a year to figure it out. I loved Vermont, and it had been a great place for me to land after a two-year coaching gig with Pemberton College in Washington. I didn't like my initial college coaching experience, but I knew it wasn't about them, but me.

It was my first job after leaving Chicago. I needed the income and the change of scenery, but mentally, I'd still reeled from early retirement.

Five years after I stepped off the professional league ice as a player, and I was ready to return. Coaching wasn't the same as being a d-man, but I'd found my footing again. I was ready for the next step in my career.

And with today's success, another goal accomplished, restlessness was already taking hold. I wanted more. There was another milestone to achieve, another high I needed to chase. One thing in my life hadn't changed and that was my unending desire to be the best.

You can take the player out of the game, but you can't ever take the game out of the player.

CHAPTER 6
SILAS

t suits you?

God, how lame was that line I'd spewed out? And to my coach?

Think before you speak.

Banning, of course, ignored my comment. Like I'd tried to ignore the way he looked when he peeled off that suit jacket. The guy hadn't played hockey for years, but his body was prime; his biceps nearly ripping through those white, now transparent, shirtsleeves. In my mind, there were all sorts of dirty jokes to be made about me showering him in sticky fluids, the least of which was champagne.

Thank fuck I had the good sense to keep my mouth shut.

It was the adrenaline rush from the win, pure and simple. Okay, not pure. Not at all. And not simple.

But to be honest, Coach was hot. There, I'd said it.

Hot and straight. At least, I assumed he was straight. I'd done a bit of digging around online and spotted pictures of him and his wife. Ex-wife. According to the hockey gossip, she'd cleaned him out of almost everything in the divorce and took up with another player only a few months after they split. Talk about a kick to the injured balls.

No relationships for me. No thanks.

And what did I care about him anyway? I needed to erase any thoughts about Banning from my mind forever.

Done. Phew.

Winning always made me horny, so I'd blame my inane wanderings on that. We had a championship to celebrate and everything in my body was primed to fuck or fight. Given that we were in Chicago, and had an overnight, I'd decided that a hookup was the best way to reward myself. In a city this big, there had to be plenty of gay bars, and I'd be ready to do some googling when I got back to my room. A sports bar would be ideal, but at this point, I wasn't picky.

"You got Coach so good," Finn teased me as we posed for pictures. "That suit is done."

I shrugged and smiled. "He knew it was coming."

And he did. I didn't feel bad. This was the way athletes celebrated.

The photographer motioned for us to squeeze in closer, and of course, instructing us to smile. Like we needed anyone to tell us to do that given this historic moment in our lives. We'd probably be grinning in our sleep from now on.

"There's gonna be a shitload of partying tonight!" Ethan yelled out.

"Fuck yes!" everyone shouted in return.

Then I remembered my plans. It was still doable. I could always go out with the team and then sneak off on my own afterwards. Our flight didn't leave until eleven tomorrow so there'd be plenty of time for slumber on the plane ride back.

"Damien!" someone called out, and my head shot up.

No one ever called Banning by his first name. Not students, not players, not even his colleagues. I'd done it during our last practice to get under his skin. But the minute I'd said it, I regretted it. It sounded too... personal.

And there wasn't anything personal about me and Coach.

Still, the fact that someone else called him by his first name had me strangely unsettled.

I followed the sound of the voice, and it belonged to a familiar-looking guy, headed in Banning's directing. But there was so much champagne in my eyes that everything was kind of blurry. What I could see was that the guy in motion was also wearing a fancy suit, and he had a nose that'd been broken a time or two. The stranger was a hockey player for sure.

"Who's that?" I nudged Finn. "I know him, but I can't put a name to the face."

Finn squinted and then his eyes widened comically.

"Are you kidding me? That's Selwin Kirkland, Chicago's best defenseman," he whispered.

I blinked again, not sure I believed what Finn was saying.

"Holy mother of hockey," Finn gasped. "He's going to speak at Sutton's firehall fundraiser next week. But he's also here. Now. Oh my God, he watched our game."

The chatter amongst the team turned from joking around to whispers of incredulity as more people recognized Kirkland. There were murmurs along the lines of Finn's and a lot of "fuck me's" in there too.

Kirkland and Banning hugged briefly, then headed back in our direction. Of course. They'd played together at one point and were obviously friends.

Both men strutted towards the team, and it was impressive to watch. Kirkland had a cool mullet and an easy smile.

But Damien—I mean, Banning—in that suit that molded to his body like a second skin, with those ocean blue eyes and that intense expression on his face? Fuck, there was no doubt I had to go out tonight and get laid.

Hearing Coach's praise earlier didn't help matters. It did funny things to my insides, or maybe I'd drunk too much of that sickeningly sweet champagne? Yeah, that was probably it.

"Guys, I'd like you to meet one of the league's finest, and my friend, Selwin Kirkland," Banning announced.

One by one, we lined up to shake Kirkland's hand. This day was getting better and better.

"You and Melnyk in the last period was something else," Kirkland stated when it was my turn to meet him. "Congrats on the title. I'll be keeping a lookout for you guys."

I was certain that I'd died and gone to hockey heaven.

"Thank you, sir," I replied. "I'm looking forward to your speech next week at the fundraiser."

He nodded and leaned forward.

"Call me Sel. Or Win. 'Sir' is for hard-asses like Damien." Kirkland chuckled and motioned over his shoulder.

"I heard that," Banning hit back.

"You were meant to," Selwin replied with an eye roll. "He's uptight, eh? So freaking intense."

"He wants the best out of us," I admitted, surprising myself. "We wouldn't have made it this far without his guidance."

"There's no one better," Selwin agreed with a grin.

The photographer snapped more photos of our team with Kirkland, and then we had interviews with several local media. It was completely overwhelming, but in a great way.

Finally, an hour later, done with the press and pictures, we cleared off the ice and headed to the locker room.

The first person I called was Josiah.

"I'm so proud of you, Si. I texted all my friends. Do you get to bring the trophy back home?" Josiah asked.

My brother sounded as excited as me.

"Yep, we all get our turn. Not sure when mine will be, but it'll happen."

"When you get here, we're heading to see Dad first thing."

"Definitely. I'm going to call the home now to tell him."

My father still had trouble speaking, but he was able to read and write a bit, and I got him a phone so he could text.

He still needed someone to assist him, but it was better than before. But a text right now wouldn't do. I called the home and had them put me on speakerphone so he could hear my voice.

"We did it, Dad! We won the college championship!"

I could hear shouts in the background, and what sounded like a muffled cry.

"Your dad is so excited for you, Silas, we all are," I could hear Mandy, one of his nurses, call out. "He's crying."

I blinked away tears myself. Fuck, I hadn't cried in so long —not since my mom's funeral—that I wasn't sure I remembered how. Swallowing past the gigantic lump in my throat, I took a deep breath and swiped a hand over my eyes. It'd been a rocky road to get here, so I guess tears were in order.

"I'll see you on Sunday to show you all the pics," I finally replied when I got my emotions under control. "Love you, Dad."

"Congratulations, Silas," Mandy replied. "We'll see you then."

I hung up and sat on one of the benches for a moment, taking a few deep breaths to settle myself. It was unusual for me to show that kind of emotion and I needed a moment to gather myself together. When I glanced around, though, I realized that the rest of the guys were the same, calling their family and friends, laughing and crying at the same time.

For the first time in six years, I allowed myself to feel joy. And I embraced it.

Calmer, cleaned up, and dressed up, the team headed back to the hotel for our post-game dinner celebration. I wore grey dress pants, a white button down, and tied up my hair in a bun. But as soon as the dinner was done, I was heading back upstairs to change into my jeans and leather jacket.

Dinner was raucous as usual, with the bonus of Kirkland's easy charm and ability to make everyone laugh. Finn got to sit beside his idol, but he hardly said a word all evening, which wasn't like him. Then again, if I was sitting in his place, I'd be starstruck too.

Once dinner was done, and dessert ordered, Coach paid the bill, and he and Kirkland said their goodbyes. I was relieved that Banning was headed out early, even though I was curious about where they were going. I'd overheard Kirkland mention a place called Moonbeam. I figured it was a VIP-only club filled with pro athletes and thirty-dollar drinks and turned my attention back to my teammates.

We finished up dessert, and I sat back and glanced around the table.

"So, where are we going?" I asked. "Ethan?"

"My frat has a chapter nearby. I texted their President and they've got a party going on tonight. Everyone's welcome."

"Do we need to rideshare?" Dane asked.

Ethan shook his head. "It's a ten-minute walk."

"I think that's a better idea than partying in our hotel rooms," Dane replied. "Or trying to find a bar that will let everyone in."

Then I remembered that not all the guys on the team were twenty-one plus like me. Back home, everyone drank at frat parties and the like, but bars and clubs were a no go, unless you had fake ID.

"Cool." I nodded. "I'll stick around for a while but then I'm heading for a club."

"Oh man, don't tell me that," Ethan whined. "I'm not twenty-one for another four months."

"Poor baby Walrus, afraid to sneak in?" I teased him.

"Not afraid," Ethan scoffed. "I've done it before. Not on a hockey trip, because if Coach finds out—"

I gave Ethan a playful shove.

"Hockey season is done. Relax."

"I want to be sure I've got a spot next year. Last thing I need is to be on Banning's shit list."

"Let's not even mention him, all right?" I countered. "Are we done here?"

"A little eager to get going?" Finn quipped.

"Damn right."

I wanted a couple of drinks to loosen up and then I'd find my distraction for the night. Or, for an hour. Hell, given how excited I was from that win, I'd probably come in record time. Hopefully, more than once.

Everyone headed back to their rooms to change into casual clothes and then we hit the street, the frat house, and the real celebration *finally* got underway. The chapter in Chicago was massive, with twenty-five brothers and a house that was more like a mansion than a college hangout. And the party? I lost track of how many students packed into the place; it was well over a hundred. We played drinking games and pool, then smoked on their rooftop deck overlooking the city.

But the longer the night wore on, the more frustrated I got.

Plenty of my teammates were hooking up, and now it was my turn. It was time to head on out. I scanned the room for Finn and found him and Kayden and Maddox talking with Ethan and several frat brothers.

Downing a last shot of vodka, I made my way over to my teammates.

"Hey, I'm taking off," I told Finn.

"Already?"

"It's after midnight, Finn, and I want to hit at least one bar before they close."

"Okay, you want company?"

I shook my head.

"Nah, but thanks. I need to be alone for a bit."

I'm sure some of the guys would be down for a gay bar, but I wasn't prepared for that conversation. Not tonight. Not even with Finn. The focus was our win, and I wanted to leave it that way.

"Be safe," Finn offered. "And text me when you're heading back to the hotel."

I nodded, gave my friend a hug, and said my goodbyes to everyone else.

Heading outside, I started googling local gay bars, trying to find one that wasn't too far or too expensive.

When the name Moonbeam popped up, I dropped my phone.

CHAPTER 7
DAMIEN

"You sure you're okay to stay here for a drink?"

It was the third time in ten minutes that Selwin asked me that question. I didn't care what kind of bar it was, if I could get a strong drink, I was good. I hadn't seen my friend and former teammate in person in over a year, and we had a lot to catch up on. Besides, it was a change from the usual sports bars or pubs back in Vermont. Moonbeam lived up to its name, with midnight-blue walls, velvet booths, and sparkling lights that lit up the ceiling and dance floor. And on a Saturday night, it was packed.

We'd snagged a couple of seats at the bar and settled in.

"If you want to go someplace else," he continued. "We can do that. it's fine."

I glared at my friend in response, and he laughed at my expression.

"I'm just checking," he replied with a grin and sipped on his negroni. "Not all guys are cool with queer clubs."

"You know me better than that."

"I do, but with that uptight expression on your face, it's always hard to tell," he quipped.

I rolled my eyes at his joke, reaching for my dirty martini.

"That's right, keep drinking. Let loose," he urged. "You took a team to the national college championship, Damien, you should be smiling. Hell, you should be dancing on this bar."

I shrugged.

"I'm happy, I am. It's just that—" I paused. "Again, you know me, it's never enough."

Selwin nodded.

"And besides hockey, how's life in Vermont?" Selwin asked.

"There is no 'besides hockey,'" I retorted. "It's what I live and breathe."

"You gotta make time for your personal life."

"Says the man who avoids relationships."

"I said personal. That could mean fucking. Or hanging out with friends. Doesn't have to be a romantic relationship."

I took another long sip of my drink and thought about that.

"Dave and I hang out sometimes, and I'm friends with the other staff in the athletics department. But other than a dinner here and there, I'm pretty much working. Or thinking about work." I sighed. "And sadly, there's hardly any fucking, and dating least of all."

Honestly, my libido was near to comatose. I'd had one hookup with a woman but that was over a year ago, and I hadn't met anyone that had me craving anything more. It was so unlike my twenties, when I fucked more than I slept.

"What do you do for fun?" he asked me.

I had nothing to say, so I took another sip of my drink. A long one, draining most of the glass.

"Seriously, Damien?"

"This is my first time out in weeks. No, months. I think?" I paused. "I can't remember."

"If you can't remember, it's too long."

"You didn't want to invite any of the guys with you tonight?" I asked, changing the subject.

"Not here." Selwin ran a hand over his mullet. "I'm still not out to anyone except you and a few of the guys I've known since college. I thought I'd be there by now, but nope. It's still scary to say I'm bisexual out loud. I have no idea how teammates, or the league, will take it. My agent tells me he's good when I'm good. As to when that'll be—"

"You gotta do it when it feels right," I replied. "Some of my players have come out recently. Things are changing, Sel. It's slow, but it's happening."

"There's so much more pressure on me now, you know? Once you hit the big-time spotlight, it's unnerving."

Boy, did I know it.

"Shit, sorry," Selwin started.

I waved him off. "That was a long time ago. It's old news. And I'm good with how things are now."

"But you want more?"

"I want back in the league. Coaching at that level's my ultimate goal."

"After today's win, I can see that happening. And speaking of today." Selwin waved at the bartender and motioned for a refill. "Let's get another round to celebrate."

I finally looked around the bar and noticed several guys checking out my friend, one man more beautiful than the next. Whoa. Since when did I notice if a guy was beautiful? Not since… no. I pushed that thought away.

What the fuck was in this martini?

"One more drink, but that's it," I added.

I was looking to get relaxed, not shit-faced.

"So." Selwin turned in his chair to face me. "Going back to your comment about barely fucking, why've you been living like a monk? Is that what happens when you move to Vermont? You eat cheese and maple syrup and stare at the green mountains?"

"Very funny," I replied and downed the remainder of my drink.

"The night's still young, maybe we can hit another bar and fix your problem."

I would've laughed at that comment had I not been choking on my vodka.

"There's no problem." I coughed and cleared my throat. "It's a dry spell. It happens. It's no big deal."

"Coming from you, wait, sorry, poor choice of words," he teased. "I'm shocked. You were quite the fuckboy in your day."

"Not when I was married."

"Before."

I nodded. "I was. But I'm not twenty anymore."

"No shit. Who is?"

"Every player I coach. God, I'm ancient compared to them. They can play all day and party all night. Which is what they're doing right now," I replied, shaking my head. "I'll be the only one on the plane tomorrow without a hangover."

"Not if you have more than one of those martinis." Selwin pointed to my drink. "Speaking of your team, they got you good after the game. That guy Moss had it in for you."

"Yeah, he did."

Thank God I packed another outfit.

To be honest, it wasn't the shock of the champagne that hit me. It was seeing Silas smile as he sprayed me with the bubbly. It was the first time in eight months that he'd cracked one. A genuine one. Once I saw it, I couldn't look away. And I couldn't help but wonder why he didn't do it more often.

Stop thinking about it. He's a student for fuck's sake.

"Anyway, we headed here so *you* could find someone, not me," I offered. "I'm too old for this scene anyway."

"Old? You're only thirty, D."

"Picking up someone at a bar isn't my thing anymore."

"Who are you right now?" Selwin replied with a concerned look. "I'm worried."

"I told you, I'm fine. I'm happy. Work makes me happy," I insisted. Shit, I sounded pathetic. "That being said, maybe it's time for a vacation. I'll be running a summer hockey camp this year, but I have a few weeks off in August."

"It's April, D. You need a vacation now."

Thankfully, our conversation was interrupted by the bartender. He placed our drinks down and gave me a smile that was near to blinding.

"One negroni and one extra dirty martini," he announced.

"Thanks, Quinnie," Selwin replied to the blond bartender.

"Um, I don't think I ordered mine extra dirty?" I added.

"You didn't, honey, but it's my pleasure."

I didn't miss the long once over or the fact that my face was now flushed as a result. The guy wasn't flirting, was he? Nah. Even if he was, that was about tips, not me. Fuck, not having sex for so long was screwing with my brain. I hadn't been hit on in, well, I couldn't remember that either…

"Sorry, Quinnie, but Damien's appallingly straight." Selwin chuckled.

"You are?" Quinnie's dark gaze met mine, and I shrugged. "Shame."

I took a long sip of my drink and groaned in appreciation.

"Damn, I should've been ordering extra dirty all along," I confessed.

"I know a filthy boy when I see one."

Quinnie winked and headed off to serve the next customer.

"What was that?" Selwin elbowed me.

"What was what? I was making conversation."

"It almost looked like you were flirting with him."

"Nope," I replied, the alcohol burning away my reserve. "He's cute, but not my type."

This time, it was Selwin's turn to choke on his drink.

"Cute? And what type? Damien, did you pop drugs while I wasn't looking?"

"Hey, I can appreciate a good-looking man," I insisted. "Besides, I've done my share of exploration. I'm not as straight as all that."

Selwin stared at me with his mouth open.

"Whoa, one mind-blowing revelation at a time," Selwin whispered. "How did I not know this?"

"Well, I… I mean… I—"

God, I was such an asshole. My friend was struggling with coming out and here I was holding back on him.

"Fuck, this is why I shouldn't drink," I added. "I'm sorry."

"You never said."

He sounded hurt, and I couldn't blame him.

"It was when I was in college," I admitted, the words all tumbling out. "Another player, a guy I roomed with on the road."

"Do I know him?"

I shook my head.

"Sometimes, he'd catch me jacking off and we'd, you know, finish together."

"That's not uncommon for straight guys."

"He jerked me off once."

Selwin pursed his lips. "That's less common."

"And we—" I paused, licking my surprisingly dry lips. "We had a threesome with a woman. I put it down to curiosity, I guess. It didn't happen when I hit the pros. I mean, yeah, okay, maybe there were times when I wondered about it, but by then I was dating Eloise, and we were exclusive. And then I was married and monogamous, so I didn't think about it again."

Why was I thinking about it now?

"And you haven't been curious since then?"

"I—" I hesitated, something in my gut telling me yes. "No."

"You paused, D."

"I'm thinking."

"Thinking about that threesome." Selwin chuckled. "It's okay, you know. You don't need to have all the answers."

"But I'm a control freak. I always need the answers."

There was no one I'd been lusting over lately. No woman, and certainly no man. No one had caught my attention.

No one made me feel anything.

No one except...

"So, another hockey player," he concluded. "That's your type?"

I could feel the heated flush stain my cheeks.

"Oh man, this is getting good." Selwin rubbed his hands together. "Maybe we came to the right bar after all."

"Please, I'm so rusty," I acknowledged. "I have no game to pick up women, never mind a guy."

"You don't need game. Just eye contact."

"People always think I'm pissed off."

"Well, you do give off that stern daddy vibe."

"Oh my God."

Selwin nudged my elbow. "You need someone younger, but experienced. A guy who likes a challenge. Like that defenseman, Moss. God, the body on him. And all those tatts? Ngh."

"Are you drunk?" I asked my friend.

"Not yet."

"Sel, he's my student," I hissed.

"So? That makes it hotter."

My pants were starting to get uncomfortably tight.

It's the alcohol. That's it. Nothing more.

"No. End of discussion. I need to finish this drink and go back to my hotel. Alone."

"Fine. I won't push."

"Thank you," I replied and paused. "Wait, why him?"

"Why not? I saw him looking at you."

"What do you mean?"

"Finish your drink."

I reached for the toothpick with the olives, set it aside, and downed the rest of the martini in one go. The salty brine and the burn of the vodka was so damn good.

"Are you ready?" Selwin asked me, his expression serious.

"Yes."

"He was watching you. Intently."

I shook my head with incredulity. "That's because he can't stand me."

Selwin rolled his eyes.

"Damien, for a former fuckboy, you're remarkably naïve. I don't mean glaring at you. I mean, undressing you with his eyes."

"What? No. He likes to push my patience," I stated, my voice cracking along with my calm. "And the feeling's mutual. He's always mouthing off, making some sarcastic comment or another, and I give it right back to him. That's all. You're wrong, buddy. So fucking wrong."

Selwin shook his head and motioned to Quinnie again.

"This news calls for another drink. And don't say I didn't warn you."

CHAPTER 8
SILAS

THE NEXT DAY

The plane ride home was quiet. No surprise, given that everyone on our team was hungover, me included. Even Banning had his sunglasses on and was passed out cold in his seat.

Huh. That was a first.

I'd thought about checking out that bar, Moonbeam, last night but decided that no, I didn't want to be anywhere near where Coach was. What he was doing at a queer bar was none of my business. And I sure as hell didn't want him to know mine.

Even with that, I couldn't help but wonder, had he picked anyone up last night?

Was he gay? Bi? Why was I so fucking curious?

Chill, who cares? I don't.

I'd blame my weird mood on being frustrated and exhausted. After all, I was up all night.

No, unfortunately it wasn't because I got laid.

I'd hit three bars and still, it was a total shutout. At the last bar, there was one guy who made serious eye contact, and I was stoked. Unfortunately, when he approached me, he talked my ear off when the last thing I wanted was conversation. Then he leaned over to kiss me, and I backed off. He had a confident air that should've had me saying yes, but kissing was way too personal for me, and never with a hookup. Hard no.

My rejection had him backing up faster than a hockey player near soft ice.

No one else caught my attention, and I was so annoyed with myself. Since when was I so picky? I reasoned it was because my adrenaline was crashing. By two a.m., I was done. All I wanted was my hotel bed and sleep.

I headed back to my room, broke, still horny, wiped, and dehydrated. I chugged a couple of bottles of water and threw myself down on my bed. I didn't even have the energy to jerk myself off. Finn was dead asleep in his bed, and I envied him. As tired as I was, sleep eluded me, and I lay there until I saw the sun peeking out from behind the heavy curtains.

I was a zombie throughout breakfast, grunting responses to my teammates instead of speaking in full sentences. Despite the euphoria from our win, my attitude was the same on the ride to the airport and on the plane. I knew there'd be a lot of school celebrations when we got back, so I needed to save my peopling for that.

We landed in Vermont in the afternoon, and the bus ride to Sutton took longer than usual given all the weekend traffic. I'd had a mind to stay in Burlington, to text Darby for a meetup, but I wanted to get home to see my family more than anything. We'd gone through enough hard times over the past decade, and when there was a celebration to be had, they deserved to share in it.

Moments before we disembarked from the bus, Coach got up and motioned for our attention. His hair was uncharacteristically messy, his black RayBans still perched on the end of his remarkably straight nose (for a former hockey player). Why I noticed all this was beyond me.

Must be the hangover.

For some reason, I was dying to see his expression. I'd never seen him less than put together and knowing that he was probably rocking dark shadows and bloodshot eyes like me made me want to laugh out loud.

Fuck, did I need a nap or what?

"The school's throwing a rally tonight, starting at eight, in honor of the Cougars win," Banning announced, his voice hoarse. "Go home and get some rest first. I'll see you guys on campus later."

Then he stepped off the bus and Jace took his place.

"And don't forget the black-tie firehall fundraiser next Saturday!" Jace added as we stood up and grabbed our shit. "Everyone's gotta be there."

Finn and I were due to help out at the event too, thanks to Coach volunteering us. Then I remembered that Kirkland was going to be there giving the keynote speech, and my mood improved exponentially.

I headed down the aisle and tapped Jace's shoulder.

"What do you need from me that day?" I asked him.

"If you and Finn can arrive at the venue at four to help us set up the silent auction items?"

"Got it."

"And you have to wear a suit," Jace reminded me with a grin. "No leather jacket."

I rolled my eyes and nodded. "I get it. I promise."

"You gonna crash out this aft?"

"Not yet. I've got to pick up my brother and go visit my dad first."

"That's cool. Are we going to meet them sometime? Are they coming to the fundraiser?"

"No." I shook my head. "I mean, my brother's seventeen. Jo's probably already got plans for next weekend that don't include hanging out with his older brother. And my dad, well, he's got health stuff."

"Oh, I'm sorry about your dad," Jace offered. "Maybe another time?"

"Maybe."

"Bring your brother to the rally tonight. He can hang out with us."

I nodded but left it at that. It was one of the rare times I mentioned my family. I'd confided in Finn, of course, who'd met my brother, and in Kayden, who'd made Sutton U bracelets for the entire team and, as per my request, several for Josiah. But I had a hard time talking about my situation with the rest of the guys. I wasn't sure they'd understand or maybe I was worried they'd feel bad for me. Or think I wasn't giving hockey my all. Either way, that's how I dealt with it, by keeping it to myself.

Like my sexuality.

I hated showing any kind of vulnerability and in hockey, you get used to staying stoic, and pushing forward, pushing hard, no matter what. There was no time for second guesses or doubt. Not from teammates or from myself...

I texted Josiah, stepped off the bus, and headed for my truck. The gray pickup was used when I bought it and it wasn't much to look at, but it was paid for, so it was all mine.

After picking up my brother, we drove straight to see my dad. The care home that he'd lived in for the past two years was set on the west side of Sutton and had views of the mountains and nearby lake. Since spring was finally here, the day sunny and surprisingly warm for Vermont, we arrived to find many of the residents outside. The home was once a hotel, refurbished to meet hospital standards, and had a lot of acreage, including a garden and terraces for residents and visiting family.

I spotted my dad right away. I got my size from him, along with brown eyes and blond hair, his now turning gray.

My father got around in a wheelchair most of the time, but he could use a walker when he wanted, and for short periods of time. He was fighting hard to get his mobility and his speech back, but I knew that it was going to take years. Watching him take tentative steps, the walker in front of him, his nurse by his side, I had an overwhelming feeling of pride. Pride and frustration. I wanted everything to be like it was for him in the past; to hear him laugh and joke around, to have him skate alongside me and Jo.

But wishing and reality were two different things.

Still, he was here, and that's what mattered.

When he spotted us, I waved, and though his mouth barely moved in response, his eyes brightened. He started in our direction, moving faster, much to the obvious concern of his nurse, Mandy, who kept urging him to go slow.

"Good afternoon, Silas, Josiah," Mandy greeted us. "Tobias is fighting fit today. Determined to outwalk me."

"I can see that," I replied and looked at my dad with a grin. "You'll be back on the ice with me and Jo in no time."

The *s* sound came out of Dad's mouth like a whisper, as he tried to say my name. It was faint, but I heard it. I bent over to give him a hug, and my father let go of his walker. His grip wasn't strong like it used to be, but it still made me happy. Jo leaned over and did the same.

"Let's sit down out here somewhere," I suggested. "I've got lots of pictures from the game to show you."

"Silas, why don't you and Josiah take your father over to the picnic table?" Mandy offered. "I'll go get his wheelchair in case he needs it coming back."

"Thanks." I nodded and glanced over at the nearby table.

It was only another ten steps or so to get there. Nothing for me and Jo, but a marathon for my dad. I stood on one side of him and Jo on the other, making sure Dad was steady enough but not wanting to intervene unless necessary. The determined look in my dad's eyes told me he was going to make it to the table, and he didn't want help.

Understanding his need for independence, I walked slowly, and looked over at my brother, who smiled knowingly at me in return.

It took us a few minutes to get what should've been a few seconds away.

When we reached our destination, I took hold of my dad's arm to steady him, and Josiah turned the walker around seat first. Once my father was settled at the head of the table, I sat down on one bench with Jo opposite me. I pulled my tablet out of my backpack and began to scroll through the media shots that the school had already posted.

"These aren't in any particular order," I started and placed my tablet in front of my family. "Have a look through."

Josiah began to swipe and tap on the pictures.

"Wow, cool shots. God, that first goal was something. Jace is awesome," Jo exclaimed. "And here's one of Axel."

After a while, my dad reached his right hand out and tapped the screen, then pointed a shaky finger at me.

"You like that one, Pops?" Jo remarked and turned the tablet back to me. "He's right, it's a good one. And is that a smile on your face, bro? I'm shook. Who knew you still had teeth?"

"Ha ha."

"The guy with the black hair, that's your coach?"

I nodded and swallowed hard. I'd talked about my teammates, but not so much about Coach, except to gripe about extra practice. But that was it. And with Josiah's immune system being more susceptible during the winter season, I hadn't allowed him to come to games to meet the team.

"Damien," I replied. "I mean, Banning. Coach Banning. You've heard me talk about him."

"You usually call him Coach. So, Damien, eh?" Josiah

looked at me inquiringly and then back at the photo of me dousing Coach. "He's pretty hot. For an old guy."

My dad's right eyebrow moved. Both of mine hit my hairline.

"What?" Josiah smiled innocently at us. "I only speak the truth. Like I don't notice attractive people? I'm almost eighteen. Please."

"Jo—" I started.

I guess it was time for us to have another one of those talks.

"I said, for an old guy."

"He's only thirty."

"Like I said." Josiah chuckled.

I was going to give him my finger but caught my father's disapproving gaze.

"Moving on," I insisted.

Josiah glanced at the tablet again, swiping. "Hmmm."

"What does that mean?"

"Nothing." Josiah grinned. "Only, you and *Damien*, I mean, Coach Banning, seem to have a glaring contest going on."

"Hilarious."

"OMG, is that Selwin Kirkland from Chicago?" Josiah squeaked.

"It is. Thank God we didn't know ahead of time. He stepped onto the ice afterwards to congratulate us and everyone on the team went nuts," I explained. "I got to shake his hand and talk to him. He's friends with Banning. They used to play together."

"That's so cool." Josiah paused. "Wait, you mean Banning, as in the defenseman for Chicago who wrecked his knee five years ago?"

"Yeah. That's him."

"How did I not know that *he's* your coach?"

"I think of him as Coach," I muttered.

I was such a liar.

"Now that it's spring and my health is stable, can I finally come with you and meet the team? Like, before you graduate?" Josiah smirked.

Sarcasm was a family trait.

"I think I can arrange that. In fact, we have a rally tonight. You can come for an hour."

"Yes!" Josiah turned to my dad. "Look at that. Si's going to be playing pro one day with guys like Kirkland."

My dad nodded and brought a shaky hand over to tap mine, then he motioned for the tablet, so Josiah put it in front of him. Dad slowly tapped on it, typing slowly. Once he was done, he looked up at me.

Proud of you. Both.

I smiled back at him. "I'm proud of you too."

CHAPTER 9

SILAS

After our visit with Dad, Josiah and I said our goodbyes and headed for home.

"Is there anything you want to talk about?" I asked Jo as we hit the highway.

His comment about Damien being "hot" had me wondering. And worrying. Josiah had several close friends, guys and girls, but he never mentioned crushing on anyone.

He would tell me, wouldn't he?

I wanted him to know that I supported him. Loved him no matter what. Then I thought about the fact that I hadn't even told him I was gay. I'd known for years and still, I kept silent. When would I finally stop hiding? Guilt gnawed away at my gut.

"Anything personal?" I continued.

"What do you mean?"

"Well, your comment earlier—" I paused, uncertain about how to phrase it.

"We talked about a lot of stuff this aft, Si, you need to be more specific."

I quickly glanced at him and then back to the road ahead of me.

Here goes nothing.

"The comment you made about Damien… I mean, Coach Banning."

Fuck, I had to stop doing that.

"Oh, that he's hot?"

I nodded, shifting in my seat. Nothing in life prepared me for having frank talks with my brother about sex and sexuality. Still, it was my job to ensure that he was a responsible adult in every way, and that meant, even if the conversation was difficult, I had to do it.

There was a pause of silence, and I worried that maybe I'd chosen the wrong moment to bring it up.

"Don't you think you should say something first?" he whispered.

"What do you mean?"

"I know."

"Know what?"

Josiah sighed.

"I saw a text, purely by accident, on your phone, a year ago. A text between you and Darby. I know you're gay. Or you're bi? Or pan? Whatever, it's cool."

That blush that burned my cheeks yesterday was back.

"I am. Gay, that is. I was going to tell you," I replied quietly. "I was, I don't know, waiting for the right time. It's not that I'm ashamed of who I am, but with hockey and your recent health stuff, I—"

"It's okay, bro. You don't have to talk about it. I know you're under a lot of pressure as it is. But I wanted you to know that I know. Not saying anything's been bothering me for a while." Josiah let out a sharp exhale. "Fuck, I feel so much better."

At least one of us did.

"Jo—"

"I know, language." He chuckled. "Anyway, it's good.

We're good. You're my brother, and I love you. I want you to be happy."

I bit my lower lip and nodded.

"And back to your question, I think I'm bi. Or pan," Jo stated matter-of-factly. "Pretty sure. I mean, I find girls and guys hot."

"Okay. You're not, I mean, we talked about this already, but, I mean, are you—" I fumbled for words like I'd never spoken before.

I gripped the steering wheel so tight I'm surprised I didn't wrench it from the dashboard.

"Si, we've had this talk. I already know all I need to about sex. And being responsible. Trust me. And no, I'm not sleeping with anyone. I'm not ready yet."

This time, it was my turn to let out a shaky breath.

"Good. Fine. You know you can ask me anything, and—"

"Can we change the subject? Please?" Josiah interrupted.

"Thank fuck."

"So, do *you* think your Coach is hot?" he returned.

I jerked the steering wheel, but thankfully, kept us steady.

"Okay, maybe now's a good time to exit the highway," Josiah pointed out.

And that's exactly what I did, taking the next exit, and the slower, but safer, route three to get home.

"No more talk about my coach," I insisted.

"Will he be there tonight?"

I nodded. "Of course."

"Yasss."

"Jo," I warned.

"What? I can't wait to meet him. And Jace and Axel, and Dane and the rest of the team."

"I'm sorry it didn't happen sooner."

"You were trying to protect me. I get it."

"How're you feeling this week? The new medication?"

Even with surgery, Jo would probably be on meds for the rest of his life.

"I'm fine. A bit lightheaded, and I had a headache yesterday. The pharmacist said that's common until I get used to it."

"If the rally is too much, you can skip it."

"No way. I'm not missing that for anything."

"You can only come for an hour," I reminded him.

"That's fine. I'm meeting up with River at Parker's house."

"What's going on there?" I asked as we entered the town proper.

"The usual Saturday thing," he replied. "Ya know, pizza, video games, smoking."

"Smoking?"

I hit the brakes a little too hard at the light.

"Kidding." He chuckled. "I'll leave that filthy habit to you."

"I'm only a part-time smoker. And I'm too young for gray hair," I quipped.

"And that beard."

———

Four hours and one nap later, I showered and got changed for the rally. This type of event was not my jam, but considering our big win, I had to be there. Hopefully, not for long. My social battery got drained quickly.

My brother, on the other hand, was excited as hell. He'd changed three times, finally settling for his baggiest jeans, a striped T-shirt, a blue button down—unbuttoned—and a black denim jacket. He wore—stole—my favorite pair of Doc Marten lace ups and added a trucker hat to complete the look. Josiah had style, which was more than could be said for me. I stuck to my usual denims, a plain white T-shirt, and my leather jacket. I gathered my hair up into a bun, ran some beard oil over my face, and decided that was good enough. Since Jo had my boots, I slipped on a pair of running shoes and headed for the front door. Then I remembered to grab my clean jersey and shoved it in my backpack.

We took a rideshare to campus, so that way, I could have a few drinks and not worry.

"When I turn eighteen, can I get a tattoo?" Josiah asked me.

Today was a lot. Me coming out to Josiah. And now this?

"It would be hypocritical of me to say no," I replied. "I'm good, as long as your doctor okays it."

"Yes!"

"Gray hair," I muttered to myself.

Ten minutes later, we pulled up to the campus parking lot and hopped out of the car.

Finn was already waiting by the main gates. The campus was the busiest I'd ever seen it, even rowdier than welcome week. There was music playing, lights flashing, and I swore I heard fireworks going off.

"Hey, guys." Finn smiled at us. "Wow, Jo, cool fit."

"Thanks." Josiah reached over and hugged my friend. "You look great too."

"Pfft, this old thing." Finn motioned to his black jeans and hockey jersey.

"Si, you should've worn your jersey," Josiah added.

"It's in my bag. I'll put it on later." I looked at Finn. "What's the schedule for tonight?"

"Well, everything's happening on the football field to start. The team's supposed to line up here, and then we'll all walk in together. Dane told me they'll be press and pictures. Then, the rest of the night's ours."

"Sounds good." I nodded. "Jo, are you okay taking a seat by yourself in the stands?"

He rolled his eyes. "I think I'll manage."

"Not appreciating the sarcasm at all," I quipped, and reached for the brim on Josiah's hat, tugging it down.

"Hey, don't mess with my cap." He chuckled and shoved my hand away.

"So, where's—"

I didn't finish what I was going to say because suddenly Damien stepped into my line of vision, and for a second, I couldn't breathe properly, never mind speak. My heart raced liked I was back in that game, chasing down the puck.

It's exhaustion. I need more than a power nap.

Yeah, I needed a fucking week to sleep off... whatever this was.

Damien was dressed casual like me, in black jeans, a gray T-shirt, and a bomber jacket. I cracked a smile when I spotted his battered combat boots. He looked different and it wasn't only the clothes, but I couldn't pinpoint exactly what it was. Then I realized that he still had his sunglasses on, and it was dark out. That must've been some night out he'd had in Chicago. My imagination began to work overtime as I pictured Damien in that bar, getting sweaty, and for reasons that had nothing to do with hockey.

Fuck, this is bad.

Damien finally removed his sunglasses as he walked up to us. His deep blues weren't bloodshot, but there were dark circles underneath. Then he offered a small smile, the corners of his eyes crinkling, which gave another shock to my system.

The closer he got, the more I fidgeted, until my brother elbowed me.

"Finn, Silas," Damien greeted us with a nod and then pinned me with his gaze. "Nice night for a rally."

Suddenly my palms were damp. I was used to him barking out orders on the ice, not making casual conversation. Was his voice always that deep and husky? Why was I noticing now? The longer I stayed silent, the more intense his stare became.

"Coach," I returned, my voice cracking. Ignoring Finn and Josiah's bemused stares, I cleared my throat. "This is my younger brother, Josiah."

Damien offered his hand to my brother and Jo readily shook his hand.

"Nice to finally meet you," Damien replied.

"It's a pleasure to meet you too, Mr. Banning."

Finn's phone rang. "It's Dane. I'll be right back."

He stepped away from us to take his call.

"So, did Silas give you the game highlights?" Damien asked my brother.

"Yeah, and all the pics and video clips. Your win was impressive. I've never seen anyone deke like Jace and that last goal from Axel? Unreal."

Damien offered his rare smile to Josiah. "Do you play?"

"Defense, like Si. But that was before I got sick. But I'm doing better now. I'm hoping to get back into it next year, for fun. I love it, but I'm not going pro like my brother."

Damien's eyes met mine, but I quickly looked away.

"Our season's officially over but there'll be a team gathering before we finish up the term. We make a day of it, with competitions and prizes," Damien replied. "You're welcome to join us, Josiah."

"Thanks, I'd like that," Jo returned and nudged me. "If it's okay with my brother."

"Uh, yeah," I finally replied, my mouth dry. "Why not?"

Suddenly, Damien's phone buzzed, and he glanced at it.

"Well, I better get going. I've got to find the president and Dean Chancer. I'll see you on the field shortly."

As soon as Damien walked away, I let out a sigh of relief.

For once, the season couldn't end soon enough.

Damien

What the fuck was I doing here?

Right. The rally.

I'd enjoyed my share of those when I was student. And I had to make an appearance at this one whether I wanted to or not. Unfortunately, I had the hangover from hell, with my head throbbing, my eyes dry, and my equilibrium so off balance I'm surprised I could walk a straight line.

More than that, I was on edge like I never was, and I blamed it all on those damn martinis last night.

Never again.

Selwin was going to get payback the next time I saw him. I didn't know how, or when, or what, but I'd think of something. Between the alcohol and that discussion about my personal life, ugh, I wanted to forget the whole damn thing.

Until I spotted Silas. Fuck, why did *he* have to be the one I noticed?

Like on the plane ride and on the bus. Normally, I slept or listened to an audiobook to relax. I'd tune everyone out. But not this time, and not him. When Silas walked past me, despite my sunglasses and my feigning sleep, I noticed everything. The stealthy grace of his walk, the intense expression in his eyes, and worst of all, the way his ass filled out those jeans.

I'm still hungover.

The campus was crawling with students and teachers, and the noise of chatter made my headache flare. But, out of the throngs of people, only one of them drew my undivided attention. Silas looked imposing as usual, with his height, his broad shoulders, and of course, those tattoos. Did he have them everywhere? I'd seen them on his chest and arms, but what about...

Get yourself under control, goddamn it.

My phone buzzed and I quickly glanced at the message. It was Dave asking me to meet him on the football field. He was already there with Nora.

Talk about a bucket of ice water.

Better than a bottle of champagne.

When I looked up again, I channeled my inner coach and put my stoic face in place. Not that it lasted.

Without knowing who the younger man standing beside Silas was, it was clear to me that they were siblings, and watching Silas offering a protective arm to his brother made me smile. Josiah was a few inches shorter, and not nearly as big as my defenseman, but then again, he'd been sick. My respect for Silas as a person wasn't in question. But I did wonder how he managed everything; a demanding school schedule, hockey practice, looking out for his brother, a part-time job. He worked hard, seven days a week.

But who was there for Silas when he needed a break? Not that I should be concerned. It was none of my business. Obviously, he was handling everything. Better than I ever could.

Instead of being rude and ignoring him, I made my way over and forced myself to be polite. Polite and proper. Even though Silas was staring at me like he'd never seen me before. Without his skates on, he met me eye to eye, and it was way too close for comfort. Neither one of us was known to give in first, so when he looked away, panic began to swirl in my gut.

"I better get going."

I said something else I'm sure, but I was too intent on getting the hell away from Silas to remember what. Something about inviting his brother to our team gathering?

Walk away, do it now.

I said my goodbyes and headed across campus, following the pathway and the students, to the football field.

The lights were glowing, the band was getting set up, and the stadium seats were already full. Dave stood near the goal post with Nora beside him. The two were in a very animated discussion given their wild hand gestures and it didn't surprise me. Both were strong willed and vocal about their opinions. Dave would probably be taking Nora's place one day and maybe that was the problem between them. I couldn't give a shit about rising in the college ranks myself.

Give me my skates and a rink, and I was set. College or the league, either way, I'd be content as a coach, not an administrator.

"Damien," Dave called out when he looked over and spotted me. "I was telling Nora about the summer training camp. She's pushing back on the extra items in the budget. Please explain to her that hockey is the most expensive sport ever, but it will earn itself out when we have top players vying for spots."

"Knock it off, Dave," Nora bit back, rolling her eyes. "I know all that. But I have a board to report to. I can't sign off on extras for a program that has yet to be proven."

"I should have brought my whistle for you two," I quipped, and Dave playfully nudged my arm. "Look, the first year of any program is always a test. I'm limiting summer camp to six students, and the fees, as outlined in my proposal, will cover the basic costs. The add-ons are to cover travel expenses for two pro players that have agreed to offer work-shops. But it's worth it. Think of the press coverage. And, if these students get drafted eventually, even better. We'll get interest from the league. Maybe even sponsorship money."

Nora pursed her lips and nodded.

"I'll agree to go to bat for it, but I'm not making promis-es," Nora replied. "If needed, you'll have to cut something out of your regular budget."

I'd worry about that if the time came. And I wasn't worried at all.

"And, if you don't get a minimum of four students signed up, the pros visits are a no-go," she added.

"Deal."

"Good." Nora smiled at me. "Now, we have a rally to launch. Let's get an early start on that positive press coverage."

Despite my hangover, I put on my best face.

CHAPTER 10

DAMIEN

A WEEK LATER—THE FIREHALL FUNDRAISER

'd been busy all week preparing the summer camp schedule; finalizing the email to the team, sending out the workshop invitations to the pro players and their agents, and working with the school's public relations office to get the press announcement ready. Which was going to happen formally at tonight's Hot Shots Firehall Fundraiser.

Keeping busy was good because with the regular season over, boredom was setting in. Any time after a long season or a big win was always a downer. Not only for the players, but for me too. And after the rally and the flurry of interviews with media about our championship win, things got quiet.

I had too much time to think and it wasn't all about hockey.

Ever since that night in Chicago, I couldn't get the conversation with Selwin out of my head. I couldn't get Silas out of my head. It had never happened to me before with any of my players. No way. I had strict rules about fraternizing with students or anyone I coached. To be honest, I'd never been so much as tempted before. Now I found myself hitting the gym every night to burn off this unsettling and out-of-league preoccupation. My libido, which had been all but dormant, was suddenly out of hibernation.

Only, it wasn't about a woman, but a guy.

I hadn't seen that coming. I hadn't seen *him* coming. And it was too late.

No, I could fix this. I needed a change. A weekend away. Selwin was right; a vacation was in order. I'd fly to New York for a weekend and resolve my problem. I needed to get laid as soon as possible. Or maybe there'd be someone here, tonight? Definitely. Why wait another week or two?

I needed distraction and I needed it now.

Adjusting my cufflinks one last time, I glanced at my reflection in the mirrored hallway. When I played pro, I wore a suit every game day. Now, I hardly ever wore one. This classic tux wasn't new, but it was dressier than anything I owned. Hopefully, it wouldn't get ruined like my last one.

Don't even go there.

Unbidden, a vision of me standing in a wet shirt in front of Silas popped into my head. Only, I wasn't the only one who was wet, and he wasn't spraying me with champagne…

No. Fuck, no.

I entered the packed ballroom, nodding at several of my colleagues along the way, and moving through the room with a determined stride. Determined to get to the bar, that is. No dirty martinis, though, extra or otherwise. That's what got me into this trouble to begin with.

Once I had a glass of red wine in hand, I headed for my table in the center of the room and joined the mayor of Sutton, Edwin Lane, along with Dave, Nora, and several local and state businesspeople. There was the usual introductory chit chat, and then the mayor and Nora took off into the crowd to meet with reporters.

After a fortifying sip of my drink, I gave in to temptation. I glanced around the room, looking for my team. Looking for one defenseman in particular. The Cougars had several tables at the front of the room, and it looked like every player was in attendance, including Silas. I did a double take, hardly recognizing him. I'd never seen him in a tuxedo before. Only, his tie was undone, and so were the top buttons on his white shirt. I could see the intricate floral tattoos that decorated his chest and neck. His long blond hair was tied up in a bun, and fuck, he was goddamn sexy.

Sexy? Get hold of yourself, Coach.

"Damien."

I startled at the sound of Dave's voice and nearly spilled my drink. Slowly, I placed the glass on the table and turned to look at my friend.

"Jeez, jumpy much?" Dave asked, shaking his head.

"Sorry, my mind's elsewhere." I paused, trying to think of a reason that had nothing to do with me lusting after one of my players. "I mean, I'm thinking about this announcement. You know me and speeches."

Dave's easy smile appeared as he took the seat beside me.

"Of course," he replied. "I still loathe the public speaking part of my job. It never gets easier."

"Exactly."

"No date?" he asked me.

"No." I shook my head. "But I was thinking of heading out once the dinner's over."

"You need a wingman?"

"I need a whole freaking team at this point."

Speaking of teams, I glanced around and caught sight of Silas again.

Fuck, stop doing that. Stop.

"Let's do it." Dave nodded and raised his glass.

I did the same and took another long sip of my wine.

"Are you sure?" I paused and lowered my voice. "What about Nora? I thought you and her, you know—"

"It's not for lack of interest. But she's my boss, she's off limits," Dave added then rubbed a hand down his face. "Okay, I shouldn't have said that out loud. That sounds hot."

"Hot, but potentially catastrophic."

Remember that.

"Thanks for the reality check, Damien. I can always count on you."

Hah.

"I think your boys are getting rowdy."

"What?" That snapped me out of my daze. "What are you talking about?"

"Rowland. It looks like the party's getting started at one of the Cougars' tables. They've got the rowing club there too."

I glanced over my shoulder and spotted the guys being their usual boisterous selves. Jace was talking loudly, waving his hand in the air and then clutching tight to Axel, leaning over to give his boyfriend a kiss. And yes, there were several students I didn't recognize, presumably the rowers.

"Nothing unusual going on there," I replied. "But that reminds me. I better go over and give them the news about the training camp before I give my speech."

"I'm going to grab another drink before dinner starts," Dave added. "You want anything?"

"I'm good for now, but thanks."

Dave wandered off while I emptied my glass, reached up to straighten my tie, and took a deep breath. Standing up, I put on my iciest, most professional mask, and made my way around the various tables until I reached my target.

There was an empty seat near Axel but as I was about to sit down, a napkin hit my chest. I glanced up and realized the napkin was thrown by the one person I was trying to avoid. I was annoyed, but also grateful for the distraction.

"Silas," I bit out and glared at him.

"Nice fit," Silas commented. "But where's your whistle?"

Everyone at the table laughed at his comment.

"I don't think you want me to tell you where you can find

it," I retorted, making all the players laugh harder. "Are you done now?"

He held his hands up in mock surrender.

Ignoring the urge I had to keep bantering with him, I went straight into my pitch about the summer training camp and got a few interested questions.

Once I was done, I wished them all a good night, stood up, and headed back to my table.

Done. See, I can handle being around him. It's no problem. I'm fine.

Okay, my hands were shaking, and I was sweating something fierce, but it was pre-speech nerves. It had nothing to do with Silas.

I was halfway to my table, safety in sight, when someone tapped my shoulder.

A shiver ran up my spine, and I didn't need to turn around to know who was standing behind me.

"Hey," I managed to whisper as I turned to face Silas.

With more and more people crowding into the ballroom, there was hardly any room to manoeuvre, never mind a proper distance. We were standing way too close, and when I got jostled, I accidentally reached for Silas's arm to steady myself.

"Sorry."

I yanked my hand back.

"No worries. There're too many people in here for my liking."

I smiled at his put-out tone.

"Was there something you needed?" I asked, swallowing hard. "I mean, about the program?"

"Is it really open to any of us?" he asked me.

"Of course. I've already sent out invites to several pro players for the workshops. That kind of mentorship is what's going to set this program apart."

"I want in, Damien."

Goddamn it, he shouldn't call me by my first name. I liked it way too much.

"You need to apply like everyone else, Silas," I stated, crossing my arms, needing some kind of barrier, any kind.

"I will. But I'm telling you, I want in," Silas repeated, his eyes imploring mine. "I need this. I think it's going to give me that edge that I've been missing."

The blunt way he spoke, his ambition, it made my blood race. Fuck, I needed to get gone.

"It means three days a week," I insisted. "It means a lot of time, commitment, and hard work."

His deep brown eyes never wavered.

"I can handle it."

I didn't know if I could.

Silas

"I've got to prepare for my speech," Damien announced with a clipped voice. "Enjoy your dinner."

I watched him stalk off into the crowd, his back rigid, his hands fisted, while I stood there like an idiot staring at him. Something was up. He seemed nervous, which wasn't like him. Was it due to the event? Giving speeches was part of Damien's job, but with all the press tonight there was added pressure.

I was feeling the pressure too, but mainly in my pants.

Jesus, I'd nearly swallowed my tongue when he'd tumbled forward and grabbed my arm. The guy was intense, in more ways than one, and I wasn't immune. That tux he had on was cut perfectly for his form, but I still preferred him in that three-piece suit, soaking wet, over anything else.

Go back to your table and cool off.

Right.

Stop thinking about your smoking hot coach.

The sooner this dinner was done, the better. I'd been here

since four and wearing a suit for hours was killing me. Not literally, of course, but still, how long was this event going to last? I was already itching to rip this jacket off and the button down too.

When I made it back to our table, Ethan was halfway through telling one of his ridiculous frat stories and everyone was hanging on his words. I didn't know if he was bullshitting or telling the truth, but knowing Ethan, it was probably a mix of both. I wasn't paying attention at that point because I was too busy replaying Damien's words in my head and wondering why I was so hung up on them.

On them, and him.

I needed more than a drink to get me through this night.

"Who wants to hit a bar once the auction's done?" I asked. "All those twenty-one and over raise your hands."

Four of my teammates put up their hands, plus one of the Sutton U rowing team.

"You're gonna get laid tonight, right?" Ethan smile was as cocky as ever. "Pick up a hot girl that'll blow your mind and your—"

I shook my head.

"Not exactly."

I don't know if it was the fact that I'd come out to my brother recently, the alcohol in my veins, or the excitement over summer training camp, but suddenly, I was done hiding.

"I want to tell you guys something first," I continued, glancing at Finn.

"Go on," Finn replied with a smile.

"So, the thing is… I'm gay," I blurted out.

No one at the table stopped talking. Or stared. Or did anything to suggest they were shocked by this news.

"Okay," Finn replied and took a sip of his drink.

"Okay?" I repeated.

"Yeah. That's cool."

I looked around the table to find nothing but smiles.

"Right." Ethan leaned forward. "So, you're going to pick up a hot guy to blow your—"

"Ethan," I warned.

"What? You came out to us. Can't I say that?" He looked around the table. "My next question is, do you get laid with that beard?"

"It won't be a problem," I countered with a dirty grin.

"I want to come with you," Ethan urged. "Please, please, let me be your wingman. Please."

"You?" That comment came from Jett, one of the rowing crew, who gave Ethan an incredulous look. "Yeah, right. You look eighteen, never mind twenty-one."

"Hey! I'm in my twenty-first year, fuck you very much. And I'm goddamn hot. I'll have guys climbing all over me."

"Okay, first of all, that's way too much ego talking," I replied with a chuckle. "Second, do you *want* guys all over you?"

"Sure, I can handle it. I'm a master flirter. I've got your back."

"Jesus, why does that scare me?" I muttered.

"You're worried that all the sexy guys will want me and not you." Ethan smirked.

"Fuck off."

"I only call it as I see it."

"Stop talking!" Jett called out.

Ethan placed a napkin over his right hand and held it up in Jett's direction in a discreet, but meaningful way.

"Wait, are there gay bars in Sutton?" Ethan asked. "Is that where we're going?"

"Not that I know of. And *we're* not going anywhere. I usually go to Burlington."

"Ooh. Give us the dirty deets. Come on, spill."

I turned to Finn. "Please, make him stop."

"Like I have control over Ethan's mouth?" Finn rolled his eyes.

I glanced at Ethan. "You're not coming with us, no matter where we go. If we go."

"But it'll be so much more fun if I'm there."

"You're being annoying."

"And?"

This time, instead of a napkin, I grabbed a roll and lobbed it at Ethan's head.

CHAPTER 11

SILAS

The rest of my night didn't go as planned.

I got back home after midnight to change out of my suit and into my jeans and found my brother sitting on the bathroom floor, sweaty and pale, holding his stomach. He'd been sick most of the evening. It sounded like it was a reaction to something he ate, or maybe it was the new meds. I made a note to call his doctor, then I texted my teammates and told them we'd go out another time.

I heated up a bowl of bone broth since it was good for the stomach and offered it to Jo along with a bottle of Gatorade. Thankfully, Josiah managed to keep that down and he fell asleep an hour later. I cleaned up the bathroom, threw his PJs in the wash, and made myself a sandwich.

By three a.m. I was still wired, so I checked my emails and immediately opened the one from Damien about summer training camp. The fee was two thousand dollars. I lived frugally, no new clothes or anything, unless it was hockey related. It would mean taking on an extra shift at Verdant or possibly another job, but I'd manage. I filled out the form and paid for the deposit with my credit card right then and there.

I was confident that I'd get a spot since no one else on my

team had applied this fast. Who else was applying in the middle of the might? Only me. My teammates were probably partying at Ethan's or fast asleep.

Tired, but restless, I did some prep work for my upcoming finals and logged off two hours later. Next thing I knew, I woke up at the kitchen table with a sore back, the smell of coffee, bacon, and toast teasing me.

I sat up and blinked, and my brother smiled back at me.

"You okay?" I asked him.

"I'm better," he replied. "What about you? Falling asleep in that chair is not smart, bro."

"At least I slept."

I sat up, stretched, and shoved my hands in my hair, which was a tangled mess. Glancing at my phone, I realized it was already ten. Shit. I had to be at the tattoo shop by noon.

Josiah placed a mug of coffee in front of me and a stack of toast piled high with crispy bacon.

"Thanks. Did you eat yet?" I asked him as I took a grateful sip of java.

"Toast and a banana," he said as he sat down beside me. "I think it was that stupid burrito I had at River's last night."

"You're sure it's not your meds?"

He shrugged. "Doubtful."

"You know what the doctor said, you have to watch certain foods."

"I know, but sometimes I can't help it," he replied. "I want to be normal like everyone else. Eat what I want, when I want."

He'd missed out on a lot so I couldn't blame him. I'd be the same.

"Take it easy today, plain foods, and lots of liquids."

"Yep."

I reached over and ruffled his hair. "And no bacon."

"Ugh, no kidding. I made it all for you."

"Thanks. I've got to be at work by noon. You'll be okay?"

"Yeah, I've got a project to finish for English. I'm going to work on that and play some video games."

"Speaking of school—"

I started and took another sip of coffee.

Shit, I should've discussed the camp with Jo before booking it.

"Banning's offering a summer training camp in June and July, three days a week. I'm hoping I get a spot, but we should talk about it."

"What's there to talk about?" Jo replied. "I'm in school until mid-June, so it's a couple of weeks. And if you want to do it, go for it. It sounds cool. I'm going to start a summer job anyway."

What? "Where?"

"The local driving range."

"The one River's grandfather owns?"

"Yup."

"That won't be too strenuous for you?" I asked.

"All I can do is try. If I get a flare up, I'll find something else. Something remote. I've been working on a graphic design course online."

"All right. But you tell me if it gets to be too much," I insisted.

"Stop worrying."

"Not gonna happen."

"You better hurry up and eat," Jo insisted. "You don't want to be late."

I quickly ate my breakfast, downed another mug of coffee, and hit the shower. Once I was dressed, I grabbed my backpack and keys and headed for my truck.

The drive to Burlington was the relaxing kind, no traffic jams. With the windows down and the tunes blasting, it was just me and my music. The only time, except for sleep, that I had entirely to myself. I wondered how many more drives like this I'd experience. Once I got drafted, I'll probably live in a big city, and all this would be a distant memory. My mind began to whirl at full speed. I'd have to move my father with me, and Josiah too. Then again, my brother only had a year of high school left, and then hopefully, college. If his health continued to improve, he'd be moving out on his own soon.

When I arrived in Burlington an hour later, the parking lot near Verdant Ink was almost full.

After I opened the shop, I disinfected each station, I made sure the room supplies were stocked, did some inventory, and checked the bookings.

I was replying to emails at the front desk when the door opened, and familiar faces appeared. Henny and Coulter were the co-owners of the shop, a couple in their thirties who were as colorful as their tattoos. Coulter carried a tray of coffee, and Hen, a box that I recognized from a local bakery.

"Maple cream donuts and blueberry Danish," Hen announced with a flourish and popped the box on the counter. "You look like you need both, Silas."

"And coffee," I muttered.

"No question." Coulter chuckled and placed the tray beside the box. "Help yourself."

"Thanks," I replied with a yawn and grabbed one of the cups.

"Partying too hard?" he asked me. "I remember those days."

"You mean, last week?" Hen quipped.

Her husband gave her a knowing look, raising one pierced eyebrow.

"What?" She laughed and stuck out her tongue. "It's the truth."

"I was at that fundraising event for the firehall last night," I replied. "When I got home, I found out Jo was sick, then I was up doing school stuff until the early morning. Fell asleep at the kitchen table. Do not recommend."

"You should've texted," Hen insisted. "You're entitled to a sick day."

I shook my head.

"Nah. I need to keep busy or I think too much."

"Tell me about it," she replied with a smile. "What's the calendar like?"

"Fully booked today, Tuesday, and Thursday."

"Awesome, we better get ready then." She started walking past me and paused. "Oh, by the way, Darby's going to be late."

I nodded but said nothing in response. I didn't think Hen or Coulter knew about me and Darby hooking up occasionally, but gossip in this place wasn't unheard of. Not that I was worried. If it didn't interfere with the shop, no one here would care.

"Jo turns eighteen in September, and he's decided he wants a tatt," I announced.

"Cool," Coulter replied and grabbed a donut from the box.

"You okay if I bring him in for a consult?"

"Of course, you don't need to ask. His first one is on the house."

The phone rang, and I got busy with bookings and answering questions. Clients arrived, then another one of the shop's tattoo artists, Zephyr, came in for his shift, followed by Darby an hour later.

Darby looked like he'd had the roughest night of any of us. His long black hair was tied back in a messy braid, and his green eyes were bloodshot. When he walked up to the counter, I finally noticed the swollen lips and beard burn.

At least someone around here got lucky last night.

I thought maybe I'd feel… something, anything, but I didn't. No jealousy or anything like that. Why should I? We didn't have any kind of arrangement, only a casual one.

"Morning," he muttered and plucked out a Danish, shoving it in his mouth with gusto.

"Afternoon," I corrected.

Darby swallowed a bite and sighed. "Man, I should've cancelled my bookings today."

"Hungover?"

"No." He smirked. "I didn't get any sleep."

"Was it worth it?" I asked.

"Oh, yes."

I chuckled as Darby stalked around the desk to head down to his station.

"What are you doing later?" he asked.

I looked over my shoulder. Darby looked like he had barely enough energy to work, never mind fool around.

"I've got to get back to Sutton. Jo was sick last night."

Truthfully, Jo was okay now. But I wasn't in the mood for a hookup. Not today.

"Right. Of course." He sighed. "I don't know how you do it."

I stopped typing, turned around, and crossed my arms. "Do what?"

"Look after a kid at your age. Or at any age."

"He's my brother. And not so much a kid anymore."

"Good. You need to make time for your own life."

His comment pissed me off.

"I'm doing exactly what I need to for my family," I replied. "I have a life. I have school and hockey."

Maybe to Darby that wasn't much, but it was all I needed.

"Relax, Si, I'm just saying—"

"Your first appointment is arriving in ten," I snapped. "You better get ready."

My phone buzzed in my pocket, and I pulled it out, expecting Josiah.

Instead, it was a text from Damien. My irritation morphed to anticipation.

Banning: I got your application, but at three in the morning? Hockey players need sleep LOL.

Silas: Sleep is for other people.

Banning: Congrats, you've got the first spot for the camp.

"Oh my God!" I shouted.

Everyone in the shop came running out of their stations, concerned looks on their faces.

"Sorry," I offered with a wave of my hand. "I, uh, I got accepted to a hockey training camp this summer. I'm a little pumped."

"Phew. I've never heard you yell like that before," Coulter replied with a grin. "I thought for sure something was wrong."

I chuckled. "Nope, for once, everything's right."

My colleagues headed back to their work, and I typed out a response to Coach's text.

Silas: Thank you.

Banning: No thanks needed. And you won't be saying that a month from now when I'm working you hard.

My heart kicked off like crazy. Probably too much caffeine.

Silas: Are you kidding? Anything you can give, I can take.

Fuck, I didn't mean to write *that*.
Delete. Unsend.
Did Damien read that before I unsent it? Holy shit.

Banning: I'll remember that. Don't forget our team gathering is next week.

Silas: Wouldn't miss it. See you then.

"Silas, does training camp mean you're only available part time this summer?" Hen walked out of her station, snapping on her gloves.

"I can work Tuesdays, Thursdays, plus Friday evenings, and the weekend. Probably a few hours short of full time."

"That's means you're on the go seven days a week."

"Yeah, but you know I need the income, Hen."

"It's not that. You can have all the hours you need. I worry about you, that's all."

"I appreciate your concern, but I'm good. I can handle it."

"All right." She paused when she spotted the phone in my hand. "Is hockey the only reason you're smiling like that?"

"Of course," I replied quickly. "There's nothing else."

My pounding heart told me I was a liar…

"It's not someone you're hung up on?" she teased.

"Me? No. No way. Of course not." I scoffed and put my phone in my back pocket. "Pfft. Never."

"The longer you talk, the more I don't believe you. But that's okay, we all have secret crushes at some point."

"Secret crushes? You're supposed to tattoo the ink, not inhale it," I snarked.

"One day, Silas," she announced as she walked off, calling out over her shoulder. "One day you'll be like the rest of us. It'll hit you before you even know it."

"The only hits that happen to me are on the ice," I called back.

My ass began to vibrate. I mean, it was my phone again. Was Damien texting me?

Why did that make me breathless? I was lightheaded too.

Eat a donut, you need carbs.

Banning: And a reminder, don't bother clearing out your stall.

Silas: Right. Of course. Thanks.

I was about to ask him how the press coverage for the camp went after the fundraiser, but the door of the shop opened, and I had to get back to work. Damien's introductory speech that night had been one of the few I listened to. His words and delivery were so eloquent, but also mixed with his dry sense of humor. Not many people could combine both. I could listen to him talk all day and night. My hand itched to ask him questions, but I stared at my phone instead.

Exactly. He's all that. He's got his shit together. You're his student. Why would he want to talk to you?

Two of our returning customers stepped inside, so I put my phone back in my pocket and did what I always did.

I got down to business.

CHAPTER 12

DAMIEN

MAY—LAST TEAM GATHERING

Lacing up my skates always gave me goosebumps.

It didn't matter how many times I'd done this, hundreds, thousands—every time was like the first. I guess when you loved hockey like I did, that wasn't surprising. Whether playing or coaching, if I could get out on the ice, I was in my element. It had taken two surgeries and two years of rehab to get my knee to ninety percent mobility. It wasn't perfect, but it was enough. I still went to physio twice a month and kept up my regular gym routine to maintain my flexibility.

I always preferred to be with my team, on the ice, during every practice. But there were also times when I was nervous. Sometimes, when I stopped short near one of my players, or when I got near the boards, my right knee pinged, like I was preparing for the worst. It would probably always be that way, and no surprise given the severity of my injury. There was rehab for my leg and plenty of therapy for my mind too.

After tying my laces, I ran my hands over my Sutton U sweats, double-checking that my shin pads and knee protectors were properly in place. I stood up, grabbed my stick, and shuffled down the hallway until I reached the ice.

The team was already warming up, laughing, and joking around as usual.

I took a moment and looked up at the new banner that hung from the ceiling.

National College Champions.

Nothing usual about that. I still couldn't believe it. Maybe that's because, despite the win, I didn't get a flood of offers to coach elsewhere. My ego took a hit. When you win that big, you expect big things.

Okay, I got several inquiries, but all from universities or colleges. Not from the league.

Not what I'd hoped.

Hope would have to wait. My job was to get that camp underway and angst about the next steps of my career later. Okay, I was angsting about camp too. All week, in fact. Not that I was concerned about it being a success. Not at all.

It was the fact that I'd be spending a lot of one-on-one time mentoring a certain d-man who kept me awake at night. A player that was getting under my own defenses far too readily.

There was no mistaking Silas's form on the ice, after all he was one of the biggest guys on the team. Like a magnet, my eyes followed every movement. Then I spotted his brother Josiah, decked out in a Cougars jersey, skating alongside him. The young man was far too pale and slim for his height, but then I remembered he'd been dealing with a serious health condition. I didn't know the details, and it was none of my business, but it had required Silas to take a year off school to take care of him. And it was clear to me that Silas was a very protective older brother. The sight of them skating together made me smile. Their bond was undeniable and reminded me of my own siblings. Silas had his eyes glued to his baby brother, gently passing Josiah the puck, and watching carefully as his brother took a shot on goal. Silas slid around the back of the net and headed back my way.

Too late, Silas spotted me, and the icy aloofness I was known for, slipped.

Shit.

I stepped out onto the ice and ignored the urge I had to skate over to him.

Get it together for fuck's sake.

"Okay guys," I called out. "Our final ice time for the season. Are we ready?"

There were shouts and cheers.

"Good. Before we get started, let's welcome our guest today, Silas's brother Josiah. I expect nothing less than your best behavior." I motioned to Josiah. "Welcome, Josiah."

Everyone clapped loudly and Jo eagerly waved back.

"Okay, it's competition time," I added. "Who's up for it?"

There were shouts and whistles this time.

"That's what I want to hear," I called out. "We'll start with fastest skater, then hardest shot, stick handling, accuracy shooting, and finally, the passing challenge."

The guys were fiercely competitive, even amongst each other. There was a lot of laughing and trash-talking, but all of it good-natured.

And an hour later, we had our winners.

Jace won fastest skater, no surprises there. Hardest shot went to Dane. Stick handling, Ethan. Axel won the passing challenge. And the last one, accuracy shooting, to my shock, saw Silas come out on top.

I had Josiah help me pass out the prizes. Each winner got a gold medal and a fifty-dollar voucher from the local sporting goods shop. When it came time to hand out Silas's prize, Josiah motioned for me to offer it to him. Instead of refusing, I slid the silly medal around Silas's neck, and when I caught a whiff of his musky sweat, I tripped over my feet.

Silas's hand suddenly grabbed mine, steadying me. It was

the fundraiser all over again. Once again, my knees were about to give out on me.

"You okay, Coach?" he asked.

"Fine, yes, great," I muttered and pulled my arm away. "Sorry. I guess I hit a rough patch or something."

There was no problem with the ice; I'd tripped over my tongue.

Silas offered me a questioning look, which I ignored. And shit, my hand was burning, but I figured it had to be from the cold. It had nothing to do with Silas touching me. I needed to layer up more the next time I came out here. Gliding around the ice at a leisurely pace wasn't the same thing as playing hard like these guys.

Shaking off my unease, I skated backwards and held my hand up.

"I want to thank every one of you for playing your very best this season. We had an ambitious goal, and we achieved it. Many of you are returning next year and you know what that means. The pressure's on to keep our top spot. For now, I hope you get to enjoy some much-needed rest this summer. Have fun, but not too much," I warned and paused as players chuckled. "For those of you joining the camp, fair warning: it's going to be intense. But I'm sure come the fall, it will mean great things for you and for the team. Thanks, guys, you're good to go."

Players came up to me, one by one, to shake my hand before they headed off the ice.

Everyone except Silas. He skated over to his brother and gave me a wave before heading for the boards.

Relief and disappointment hit me, but instead of sitting with it, I put on a practiced smile and watched all the players leave until it was just me and the echo of my breathing. I did a few gentle laps around the rink and tried to shake off this weird mood that had been building since that final game.

More questions whirled in my mind, questions I shouldn't even be asking.

The answers that came to me didn't help matters at all.

Silas

"That was rude, bro."

"What?" I turned to Josiah as we headed down the hallway.

"You didn't shake Coach's hand like everyone else."

"I'll see him in camp in a few weeks, Jo."

What else could I say? I didn't dare think about Damien, never mind touching him again. Bad enough I'd grabbed hold of him when he'd tripped. The electricity that sparked between us was as heady as it was the night of that fundraiser. And it was getting out of control. I was more than eager to get the fuck out of here. What would've happened if he'd fallen on top of me? The vision of the two of us, him lying over me, melted what was left of my brain.

"You're acting weird, Si."

I muttered a few choice curse words as we headed for the bench outside the locker room.

"I'm tired."

I didn't want to lie to my brother, but my thoughts about Damien, he didn't need to know.

Josiah sat down on the bench and began to untie his skates. "Is that all?"

I nodded. "I'll change real quick and then we'll go grab a bite, okay?"

Jo nodded and pulled out his phone, tapping away.

When I stepped inside the locker room, I didn't offer small talk. Six of us: me, Finn, Ethan, Colin, Sean, and Dane were staying on for summer camp, and everyone else was busy cleaning out their stalls. I headed for mine and quickly changed.

I was a funky mess by now, but showering could wait until I got home. I grabbed my backpack, Jo's, his boots, and duffle bag, then made the rounds of the room, saying goodbye to the guys.

"It was great skating with your brother," Jace offered with a grin. "Hopefully he can catch some of our games in the next season."

"I hope so."

When I stepped back out, Jo had his skates off and was sitting cross-legged on the bench with his feet under his thighs, perusing his phone.

"That was fast," he said as he glanced up at me.

"I'm starving," I replied and dropped his boots.

Jo waved his hand in front of his face. "You smell rank."

I ruffled his blond curls.

"It's no worse than your toxic bedroom."

I got a raspberry for that comment.

After Jo changed into his boots, we headed down the hallway towards the exit.

"Thanks for letting me join you today," Jo said quietly.

"Of course. I should've done it sooner. But with the winter season, I was worried."

"I know."

I could've invited him in the fall, but I was getting used to the routine of school and practice again. And I guess I wasn't ready to answer questions about my family.

"You need to use the washroom before we head out?" I asked.

"I'm good."

That was a relief. I noticed that Jo didn't need as many bathroom breaks as he used to. The surgery plus medication was finally offering him relief. Too often, Jo had to plan out everything in advance and made sure he had access to a washroom. Crohn's was a literal pain in the ass. The teenage years were rough for anyone, but for someone with a chronic illness? Try tough times a hundred. But my baby brother was strong, and nothing was going to stop him.

"You want to grab a bite at Boots 'n' Burgers?"

We didn't eat out often, but this was a special day. To see Josiah on the ice again was something I'd never forget, an event worth any sacrifice.

"Oh yeah. Can I invite River to join us?"

"Sure."

Josiah got busy texting his friend as we exited the rink.

The sky was still light; the horizon painted with pink and orange streaks from the sunset. Sutton was beautiful at any time of the year, but I liked it best in the spring when the mountains were bright green, and everything felt new and fresh.

"River's busy," Jo muttered.

Josiah's face looked sad for a moment and then he shoved his phone in his pocket.

"Everything okay with you two?"

Josiah nodded. "Us, yeah. Him? Not so much. His parents have separated."

"Shit, I'm sorry."

"His mom moved back to New York a week ago," Josiah whispered. "River might be moving with her in the fall."

I put my hand on my brother's shoulder. River was his bestie since grade school.

"You want to talk about it?"

"No. Not yet," Josiah admitted with a shake of his head. "But thanks."

"We haven't discussed what's going to happen if I get drafted. You and Dad moving with me."

"I want to finish high school here and then go to college. I'll be eighteen soon and I can take care of myself. And Dad. You've already given up a lot of your life for me, Si. It's time to focus on you."

"I haven't given up anything."

"You know what I mean. You don't have a life outside of hockey, work, and school. You need to have fun too."

"I have fun," I insisted. "Hockey's fun."

"I mean going out with friends, dating—"

"I go to parties with the team. And I don't need to date," I replied vehemently. "Not at all."

"If you say so."

"I do."

"Are you looking forward to training camp?" Josiah asked, and I was grateful for the change in subject.

I nodded. "It's gonna be hectic, but I'm excited."

"Banning was watching you today."

I stopped short and stared at my brother like I'd never seen him before.

"What are you talking about?"

"He was staring at you the whole time we were there," Josiah replied with a shrug.

"He's a coach, it's his job to watch the players."

"You know, you're alike."

"No way."

What the fuck did me and Damien have in common except hockey?

Josiah ignored me and kept on talking. "He's focused and intense. Dedicated."

I didn't need to hear a list of Damien's attributes; I knew them already.

"Next topic, please."

"You were doing the same."

"What?"

"Staring at him."

"Where else am I supposed to look?"

Josiah smirked at me.

"He's not as ancient as I imagined either."

"Again, thirty's not old." I insisted.

"That's what I said," Josiah replied with a grin. "Old, but not that old."

"For that, you're paying for lunch."

CHAPTER 13

SILAS

THREE WEEKS LATER—FIRST WEEK OF TRAINING CAMP

Summer bloomed in Sutton and while the town was packed with tourists, the campus had thinned out.

I didn't mind at all.

In fact, since classes were done, I'd taken extra shifts at Verdant and played hockey at the rink twice a week with Finn. But I hadn't seen Damien since our team gathering. I knew he was around somewhere, but his office door was always closed. Probably best that it was.

Not that I was tempted to go near him. Why would I need to do that?

Today, though, I was nervous like I never was. Our first day of hockey training camp and I was already screwing up. First, I slept past my alarm. Then, when I was well on the road to campus, I realized I forgot my phone and had to drive back home to get it. And finally, I spilled my coffee—iced, thank fuck—all over my jeans.

By the time I arrived at the rink, I was late, wet—not in a good way—and irritated at myself.

When I spotted Damien talking to Dean Chancer in the parking lot, things only got worse.

Coach had his back to me, but he was wearing his usual Sutton sweatpants, and for some reason, I couldn't stop staring at his ass. This time, however, he wore a tight T-shirt instead of his usual jacket. Of course he did, it was hot outside, a balmy seventy-one degrees, so duh, naturally he didn't have a jacket on. With his hands on his hips, I could see the long lines of his powerful back, and the way his biceps strained against those sleeves. Presumably hearing the rumble of my truck, Damien looked over his shoulder and spotted me. He had those black sunglasses on again, and I couldn't read his expression, though I did see his lips press together, like he was holding back his temper.

I was late and Damien was going to ream me out good.

I couldn't fucking wait.

My cock started to fill in my jeans and wasn't that what I needed right now? A boner for Banning. I nearly laughed out loud at my train of thought and mistakenly hit the brakes too soon.

After realizing what I'd done, I quickly pulled into a nearby spot and parked. I took a sip of what was left of my coffee, did a quick countdown to deflate my horny dick, and reached for my duffel bag.

Feeling calmer, I stepped out and slammed the door.

Every step closer to the entrance, to Damien, had my heart taking off like a sprinter on the starting block.

"Dean Chancer," I acknowledged as I walked past the two men. "Coach Banning."

"Moss," Damien hissed and crossed his arms over his chest. "You're late."

"I apologize. It won't happen again."

"You know my rule. Either you're committed to this camp or you're not," Damien bit out. "Make up your mind and fast."

"I'm here, aren't I? I said it won't happen again," I bit out and kept walking, ignoring Damien's molten glare.

I didn't know what was hotter, him dressed in that T-shirt and sweats, or his attitude, all riled up, that sharp mouth aimed at me. Even with his sunglasses on, I felt the burn of his gaze on my back.

"Ease up, Coach," I heard the dean whisper behind me.

"I know how to do my job, Dave."

I left their comments, and my frustration, behind and pushed the door open. The cool, damp air of the rink wafted over me, and I finally felt myself settle. Once I had my skates on, once I hit the ice, I'd be good.

The locker room was empty of course. It was weird to see only six stalls with stuff in them. I quickly changed, got my skates and helmet on, grabbed my stick and headed for the ice. The rest of the guys in the camp were already warming up, Dane, Finn, and Ethan at one end of the ice, and Sean and Colin, the other.

"Ten minutes late, bro," Finn announced when he spotted me. "Coach's been waiting on you and getting angrier by the second. He was pacing up a storm behind the boards."

"I know," I muttered. "He was standing in the parking lot with Dean Chancer when I pulled in. I got warned."

"You know how he is about being on time."

"It was an accident. My stupid alarm. It won't happen again."

"Better not," Finn added. "Go get warmed up before Coach comes back."

I did some easy laps, my usual stretches, and a bit of one-on-one with Finn.

By the time I was loose and limber, Damien reappeared with his jacket on and his sunglasses off. I got the full impact of his blue glare, but it had the opposite effect he intended, making my heart race for an entirely different reason.

Fuck, not this again.

Instead of letting my reaction worry me, I decided to push my luck and offered him a cocky smile in return. His pissed-off gaze said he wasn't impressed by my attitude, even though I swore he was fighting a smile.

When he stepped onto the ice, gliding over to join us, I braced myself for whatever he was about to throw at me.

"Training camp day one," Damien announced and pointed at me. "First rule, if you're going to be late, don't bother showing up at all. Understood?"

I nodded, feeling my cheeks unexpectedly heat.

"Second rule, this isn't time for you to socialize. We're here to work and work hard. Most days will go something like this. After your warmup, we'll spend two hours on drills. We have a short break, in the lounge, and then we'll review strategies and plays for another hour. After lunch, we have a scrimmage, followed by Q&A. On Wednesday afternoons, things will look a bit different. I'll rotate working one-on-one with each player while the rest of the group practices. Any questions so far?"

Finn raised his stick.

"Go ahead Finn," Damien urged.

"Have you confirmed the visiting pros?"

Damien nodded. "I have. More news on that next week."

"Cool."

"Anything else?" Damien asked.

Silence.

"All right then, I've got some new drills that I want to try out today. Ones that will challenge the way you play. We're going to do a bit of role reversal, with defensemen playing offence and vice versa. These exercises will get you thinking about the game in a holistic way. I want you to see the bigger picture so you can take advantage of an unexpected play. Hockey is about action and reaction. Things don't always go to plan, so you gotta be ready for anything. That means, a defensive player needs to be able to take the puck all the way if the situation warrants it and that an offensive player can protect our zone as needed."

There was something about the way Damien talked, the passion in his voice when he spoke about the game, that I didn't get with previous coaches. Maybe part of it was because he was a player in mindset too. Sure, most coaches provided guidance and instruction, but they tended to favor the star players and leave the rest of us to fend for ourselves. But with him? It felt like he was talking directly to *me*. I wanted to be the best and I knew that with hard work, I'd get there.

"Silas, you're first up with Dane."

Not surprising. Damien was going to make me work my ass off as punishment for being late. Like I told him in that text exchange weeks ago, anything he could dish out, I could take.

An hour later, however, played out, wrung out, I was about to eat my words. Damien had pushed me harder than ever before. Not that I'd ever admit that to him.

"Do it again, Silas," Damien called out. "And this time, don't hesitate when you get near the net."

I didn't get a chance to respond given the high-pitched whine of his whistle in my ear.

And this was only day one?

I grabbed hold of the puck and made my way down the ice again, exactly as he'd instructed. My slapshot wasn't like Jace's or Dane's but I managed to hit it hard. Hard and accurate. This time.

My teammates clapped behind me, and I raised my stick in response. I don't think I've ever sweated so much as I did this morning.

When Damien finally called for a break, I downed a whole bottle of water in record time. Then another. My breathing came in fits and starts, like I'd been running a marathon, but at full speed. I used the bottom of my jersey to swipe the perspiration that rolled down my face.

"Towels are on the board," Damien called out as he stared at me.

I followed his line of sight.

"Oh, thanks."

I was so tired that I hadn't even realized. I'd left mine in my bag, since I was already late and was rushing like mad to get to the ice. I skated over and swiped one of the white towels draped over the boards, breathing in the smell of bleach. My hair was soaking wet too, but I didn't dare take my helmet off yet. This was a break, not the end of the day.

"Take fifteen, guys," Damien called out.

Everyone but me skated off the ice. I waved at Finn, still trying to catch my breath.

"That includes you, Silas."

I turned around at the sound of Damien's voice.

"I'm good right here," I panted. "I don't dare pause or sit down."

"Afraid you might not last the day?" Damien challenged as he drew closer.

I would've skated backwards, anything to keep the distance between us, but I was already up against the boards. Where the fuck was I gonna go? Thankfully, I had the towel in my hands to distract me.

"Not at all," I replied as I wiped my face again. "I'm just getting started. I don't wanna break my stride."

"You did very good. Despite the late start."

I ran a hand down my beard. "Sorry. My stupid fucking alarm."

"I don't accept excuses."

I knew that. I bit my lip, holding back a sharp response. Instead, I nodded.

"You're going to have to work at this pace for the entire camp, you know that, right?"

"Yeah."

"If you want to get drafted, you can't ease up. Not for a play, not for a second."

"I get it," I bit out.

"I don't think you do. There are younger players hot on your heels, guys with just as much talent and drive."

"Don't tell me what I already know," I snapped. "And I don't care about anyone else. I don't think about them. I focus on me and I'm going to make it."

Damien stared at me for a long moment, and I shivered at his turbulent blues. How could one look say so much and affect me like no one else? Why did this man get to me when nothing else did?

"I'm not questioning your ambition," he added, standing toe to toe with me. "But temper it with realism. Don't make the mistake I did and make playing your entire reason for being. Because if your plans don't work out, if something doesn't go your way and shit happens, you have to find a way to deal with the situation you find yourself in. Hockey doesn't last forever."

"Life has already kicked me in the balls one too many times," I replied bluntly. "I know how to defend myself. And to pick myself up when I fall."

Damien nodded and started to skate backwards.

"As long as you have a plan," he returned. "Don't get blindsided by the potential for fame and big money. It's great but it's fleeting. You can easily lose sight of everything."

I saw the pain on Damien's face before it turned into an icy mask again.

"Is that what happened with your knee injury?" I asked him. "You didn't lose hockey, but yourself?"

CHAPTER 14
DAMIEN

"Yes," I replied without hesitation. "For a while."

Silas was blunt but spot on. Years ago, I would've avoided the difficult questions.

Not anymore.

Instead of heading for the boards, and taking a break myself, I glided forward again.

"It wasn't only losing my job, the one thing I loved to do, it was everything else that followed," I admitted, not knowing why this was all spilling out of me, and to Silas of all people. I didn't like to talk about my injury or the aftermath it caused. Even though my therapist insisted that I had to. Staying silent meant giving my fears power. If I wanted to move on, I had to own my past. "I didn't realize that some people in my life were only there because of my job, and the money and fame that came with it. Going from a pro player in the best season of my career to never playing again in the blink of an eye was shocking to say the least. You find out real quick who your true friends and family are."

Silas wiped his face again, put the towel aside, and skated towards me.

"I'm sorry."

I shrugged. "It's life. Sometimes you're dealt a shitty hand. And despite the pain, you gotta find a way to keep going."

"Don't I know it," Silas returned. "My mom passed away when I was thirteen. Cancer. Then a few years later, Josiah got sick, and Dad had a major stroke. I've been working my ass off to keep our family together ever since."

"I didn't know," I replied. "I mean, not all of it. I'm sorry, too. I lost my mom when I was six, so I get it. That kind of loss changes you forever."

Silas nodded. "Trust me when I say that I know what's important in life. Going pro isn't going to change that. And even if it doesn't work out, I've got a plan. Hockey might be my ultimate dream, but it's not the only one."

I had dreams too, but none of them seemed within reach anymore. Or maybe I was too busy working to think about it. I thought Eloise and I would have kids one day, a family to call our own. But that shattered too when she left me. I didn't want to put my heart out there again, not for anyone, for what? Only to get it crushed again? No thanks. I'd been so fucking naïve when I looked back. Did she even love me? Or had she been playing me the whole time we were together? So much of our relationship depended on my career, my money, and my celebrity.

I'd never make that mistake again. A broken heart wasn't worth the pain.

I glanced at Silas, so young, and yet much more mature than I was at his age. He had his priorities in line, even if they came with a side of sarcastic attitude. The guy had a lot riding against him, but he kept on fighting. Every day that passed, I admired him more and more.

"That's good. At least one of us has their shit together," I finally replied, my voice hoarse.

The longer I stared at him, the harder my heart raced, and my hands began to tremble.

"You're an amazing coach, Damien. And that's something to be proud of."

Why did he have to keep using my first name? I liked it way too much. No, more than that. I was becoming addicted to it.

"I've had four coaches since I started playing, and none of them pushed me like you do," Silas continued. "I mean that in the best way. You challenge me. That's what I need. Other coaches ignored me because I wasn't a star player. They didn't want to spend the time to help me get better. They didn't see me or my potential. But you do."

I was paying *too* much attention to Silas and that was the problem.

"Thanks. But you've gotta admit, we had a rocky start," I confessed.

I wasn't sure if Silas was the right fit for the team last September. I still wasn't sure or maybe that was envy talking. He had a shot and mine was done. Shit, I hadn't realized I was thinking that way. And I was glad he'd proved me wrong.

"I'm still part of the team. The team you took to the championship. And I think it only gets better from here."

I nodded, touched by his words. Why did Silas make me feel like I was standing under a spotlight? His chocolate brown eyes never wavered from mine and having all that attention on me was heady.

Oh God, where the fuck were the rest of the guys? This break needed to be over. Now.

"I think you're right," I replied, swallowing past the lump in my throat. "But we won't get there if we don't get to work. If you want to become the best, you need to improve your communication. Especially with your defensive partner."

"I think I'm doing a pretty good job right now," he pointed between us.

Silas gave me a wicked grin, and I forgot that we were talking about hockey.

"With your teammates," I corrected. "On the ice."

"I'm here to learn, Coach. Teach me all your tricks."

"No tricks," I replied as I plucked one of the pucks with my stick. I passed it to Silas, and he skated off with it. "It's all about eye contact and body language."

"Oh, like when I'm trying to hook up with a hot guy?" he announced, then skated up to me, in the face off position.

What did he say?

"Damien?"

I couldn't speak.

"I came out to the team at the fundraiser," Silas continued, skating off to circle around the net and then back to me again. "I meant to let you know as well. Not that you'd have any issue with me being gay, I know that much by now. It's more like FYI."

"Well… um… thanks for telling me."

My gaze clashed with his, and fuck, what else needed to be said? Every rational thought in my brain was gone. Zapped. Selwin's teasing about the way Silas looked at me reverberated in my head, but I shut that shit down.

Don't go there.

"You were talking about eye contact and body language," Silas continued, staring at me. "Tell me more."

My mind veered off hockey and went straight to sex. Fuck, Silas wasn't the only one who was sweating hard. I pulled one glove off and wiped my face, willing myself to calm down.

I looked around but the rest of the guys were still nowhere to be seen.

"Uh, yes." I shoved my glove back on and forced my body to move. "Don't… don't get so involved in chasing the puck that you ignore what your teammates are signalling."

That sounded right, but who knew? I was surprised I could speak at all.

"Are you okay?" Silas asked me, skating closer.

I nodded.

"I'm good. Everything's great."

"Sometimes I'm too blunt. Did I startle you by coming out like that?"

"You didn't," I insisted. "It's fine."

You're fine, but I'm not. I wish I had courage like that.

My confession to Selwin had cracked open the door to all the "what if" scenarios about my sexuality, and I wasn't sure I'd be able to close it again. Or, that I'd know what to do if it turned out I was bi.

Silas and I stared at each other for a long moment, neither one of us looking anywhere else.

His gaze burned through my reserve and the only question that kept replaying in my head was why now? Why him?

"Hey, Coach!"

I jolted and turned around to find Dane on the other side of the boards.

"Yes?"

"Someone's waiting by your office. A woman named Eloise. She said she needs to talk to you."

Talk about timing. What the fuck was my ex-wife doing here?

"I'll be right there. You get the rest of the guys and continue with the drills."

Dane nodded and stalked off.

"Eloise… is that your wife?" Silas asked as he slid beside me, shoulder to shoulder.

Too close. The smell of his sweat had my heart thumping harder.

"Ex, yeah." I paused and stared at him. "Wait. How did you know that?"

"I read up on your time in the league. Sounded like you two had a nasty split."

"You could say that. Eloise loves the spotlight," I admitted. Silas knew more about me than I knew about him and being vulnerable normally made me hold tighter to myself. For some reason, though, I kept on talking. "She only contacts me when she wants something. Money, usually."

"That's cold. And it confirms why I don't do relationships."

"For once, we agree on something."

Me and my big mouth. Why was I unloading all this to one of my players? The word "inappropriate" came to mind but it was too freaking late.

Do something. Change the topic.

I pointed to his head.

"Can I borrow your helmet?"

"You need protection that badly?" He smirked.

"You have no idea."

Leaving a chuckling Silas behind, I headed for the boards, put my guards on, and wandered down the hallway to my office.

Sure enough, Eloise was standing there, leaning against the wall in one of her designer pantsuits, her phone in hand, her face an unreadable expression. Her brunette hair was shorter now, styled in a chic bob, and conversely, her nails were longer and painted a vivid coral red to match her lipstick. There was no doubt she was a beautiful woman, but outward appearances didn't tell the whole story.

During the divorce proceedings, and to this day, Eloise harped on the fact that I was the sole cause of our breakdown. I disagreed. Sure, I played my part. I was in a deep depression after my accident, and there were many times when I couldn't communicate with her about how I was feeling. I owned that. But to be fair, she only ever asked me *when* I was going to go back to hockey, not if. Like I hadn't wrecked my future along with my knee. I was the one who was in constant pain, enduring surgery after surgery, and I was the one who had to deal with the fact that my career as a player was done. Yes, I was a cold asshole at times, but I was hurting. The shock of the injury lasted long after I was carted off the ice. It was months and months of denial, anger, and finally, therapy. Unfortunately, her concern was never about my health, it was about losing her status as a WAG, and the bank balance that came with it. Six months after I shattered my knee, when she finally realized I'd never return to the ice, she was done. With me, and our marriage.

And I thought I was cold…

"What are you doing here?" I launched the first shot.

"Nice to see you too, Damien."

"I wish I could say the same. My question stands, what do you want?"

She pushed off the wall and stalked towards me, a cloud of her signature scent, Black Orchid, hitting me. I'd never been a fan, and I felt like I was choking.

"I have news I wanted to share. In person."

"I'm honored," I snarked.

She put up her left hand, and I was blinded by the huge diamond on her ring finger.

"Rick and I are getting married."

"I can see that." I sighed in relief. "Congrats."

Rick Platt, her boyfriend, now fiancé, played offense for New York. He was a cunning forward with a killer instinct and a wicked slapshot. When Elois left our marriage, she moved out of our house and into Rick's. In hindsight, I was pretty sure they'd been having an affair long before we split, but I didn't care to dig into it. My lawyer thought I was nuts, but I didn't want to go down that route. All I wanted was Eloise out of my life for good.

"This doesn't mean you're off the hook when it comes to

alimony," she reminded me. "At least, not until I'm officially married."

I gritted my teeth. "Of course not."

"But I wanted you to know before it hits the press."

"You could've called."

Eloise shrugged and crossed her arms.

"I was in Maine visiting my brother, and since I was headed through Vermont on my way back to New York, I figured it made sense to stop by," she added. "And I was also curious to see where you'd ended up."

She glanced around the dimly lit hallway. The forest green paint on the walls was peeling and the usual musty smell of the rink couldn't be denied. Her eyes told me she was slightly less than horrified at the humble surroundings, even though her face didn't move an inch.

"This is quite the departure from the league," she muttered. "But I guess any job's better than nothing, right?"

"I've got to get back to the ice. I'm running a summer training camp."

"Sounds boring as hell."

"It's not. But then again, you never understood the sport, did you? Just the attention that came with it."

"So?" she snapped. "I'm not the only one who enjoyed the spotlight."

Did I enjoy the accolades? Hell yes. But it wasn't the reason I played. And it wasn't any of her business anymore. I'd had enough of this conversation.

"I hope you and Rick will be happy," I offered.

"We are. He's renewing his contract with New York for another two years."

"Good for him. He deserves it," I replied.

"Don't be jealous because your hockey career is over."

I shook my head, which was now throbbing like a motherfucker.

"I've got a new direction in coaching. One that I'm very

good at. One that I enjoy. We won the national college championship. I'm very proud of that fact."

Eloise reached into her pocket and pulled out a huge pair
of sunglasses, sliding them onto her nose.

"I'll send you an invite to the wedding," she stated.
"We're buying another home upstate and we'll have the cere-
mony there."

"Thanks, but I think I'll pass."

She sighed dramatically. "Can't you at least be happy
for me?"

"I am, I said so," I insisted. "Can't you do the same for
me? Maybe this isn't as glamorous as the pros but it's still
hard fucking work. And I'm damn good at my job."

"Your leg looks better. I could hardly see any limp."

"I've worked my ass off in physio for years."

She nodded and pursed her crimson lips. "I better get
going."

"Next time, a call will suffice," I replied curtly. "*If* there
needs to be a next time."

"You're still an asshole, Damien."

"Tell me something I don't know."

CHAPTER 15
SILAS

Did I stick to practice like I was told to? Yes, but my concentration was shot to hell.

My curiosity about Damien's ex had me wanting to follow him off the ice. My defensive instincts pinged loudly and that didn't make any sense at all. Damien didn't need my protection. The very idea was ludicrous. Still, from everything I'd read, and what Damien said, his ex-wife sounded like a narcissistic puck bunny.

Why was she here, now? Did she want him back?

"Banning looked shook up when he left," Finn offered as he nudged my arm. "What's that about?"

"His ex-wife is here."

"Shit, that can't be good."

"Exactly. And before that, I came out to him."

"How did he react?"

"He's fine," I replied as I took a sip of water. "No worries. Just like I expected."

"Banning's cool."

"He is."

Damien was a lot more than that. He was brutally honest in his opinions, he worked as hard as his players, and he was fierce as hell when it came to hockey. All in, he was the most intriguing guy I'd ever been around. Smart, sharp, and sexy. It made me wonder why the guy was still single. *If* he was single. Not that I should be assuming or wondering about my coach at all.

What type of women did he go for? Or what type of men, for that matter? I thought about that queer bar in Chicago and more questions rattled around inside me like a pinball machine. Once I started, I couldn't stop. It was foolish, but I couldn't help it.

Finn nudged me again. "Dude, why's your face purple?"

Jesus, so much for keeping these crazy feelings about Damien under wraps. I downed another gulp of water, hoping—no, praying—that it would calm me down.

"It's the workout. Hardest one we've had in months. Even leading up to the finals."

"I know. Coach was all over you this morning."

I choked on a mouthful of water and nearly showered my friend.

"Seriously, Si?" Finn chuckled and glanced at me with a knowing smirk. "What's going on?"

"Nothing."

Nothing except my dirty imagination. All I could picture was Damien and me getting sweaty, minus the hockey equipment. Okay, maybe a jersey was involved in my fantasy. That would be hot too…

"Earth to Silas?"

"I'm fine." I cleared my throat. "Promise."

"Then let's get back to it."

I nodded and placed my towel and water bottle on the bench behind the boards. Dane and the rest of the guys rejoined us, and we played a quick game of three-on-three.

I didn't see Damien's return so much as feel his presence nearby, and I couldn't help the shiver of awareness that snaked up my spine, goosebumps popping up all over my skin. It took everything in me *not* to look over at him. I could pretend my reaction was due to the cold air but that would be total bullshit. But this recognition of him, or whatever the hell was going on, was disturbing as fuck. I wasn't in sync with other people that way, except when it came to hockey. Outside of the rink, my teammates, and my family, I was a loner at heart, and I fully accepted the fact. I didn't need or want anything from anyone else. So why did I feel this connection to Damien? Okay, he was smoking hot, but so what? I noticed plenty of guys and that was nothing more than sex. I wasn't curious to "get to know them," not even Darby. I was satisfied with getting off and getting gone. But Damien? I wanted to talk to him, to tell him stuff I didn't talk about with anyone.

Even worse? I wanted him to do the same with me.

No. No way. That line of thinking was asking for trouble I didn't need.

How about you refer to him as Coach or Banning instead? Keep some of that distance you're so good at maintaining with everyone else?

Right. Exactly. I would do that.

"Time for lunch, guys. Leave your sticks on the bench," Banning called out, and we all came to a sudden stop. "Meet up in the lounge."

Coach—see, I could do this—stalked off before anyone could reply. We skated off the ice and headed for the locker room, quickly changing out of our gear and into jeans and sweatshirts, and headed for the equally drafty breakroom, or the lounge, as we preferred to call it. With two couches and a couple of chairs, the space was small and cramped when the entire team was here. Given there were only seven of us now, Banning included, it was a perfect fit. There was a table set up against the far wall, and on it, trays of sandwiches and wraps, bowls of fruit, and desserts, along with bottles of Gatorade, juice, and water. I was the last one in line and snagged two turkey wraps, an apple, and an orange Gatorade, and then plunked myself down on one of the couches.

Of course, there was only one seat left, and I was sitting directly across from Damien… Banning. Then I noticed that he had the same exact lunch as me.

"I think you forgot something," Damien muttered and pointed to my plate.

I stared at him, confused.

"You're going to need more than two wraps to keep you energized for this afternoon," he added with a smirk.

"I'll grab another one in a bit," I replied. "Make that two."

I took a big bite of the first wrap and groaned loudly in appreciation. The soft tortilla was stuffed with smoky bacon, thick slices of turkey, tomato, and a ranch dressing that tasted homemade.

Banning raised one eyebrow.

"What? It's damn good," I stated.

Banning shifted in his seat and then finally began to eat. My eyes caught on his mouth, and the way he licked his lips after taking a mouthful of his sandwich. The guy made everything, including eating, look sexy, and I couldn't look away from his lips.

Stop eye-fucking your coach…

I forced my gaze back to my plate. Until I heard Damien's rumbling groan. When I glanced up again, he was halfway through his wrap.

"See?" I smirked knowingly.

"Eat, don't talk," Banning grumbled in response.

Despite his snarky comment, I caught the humorous glint in those stunning eyes, like we were sharing an inside joke. The joke was all on me at this point. If Damien knew what I was thinking right now, he'd tell me to get out of this rink, and this team, for good.

Thankfully, Finn sat beside me and began to chatter away, distracting me.

Once everyone downed enough food to refuel, Damien set up his laptop and a mini projector so we could watch replays of past games. Our games and pro ones too. We spent over an hour reviewing the plays and bouncing ideas off one another. From forechecking, to maintaining puck possession to power play execution, it was all on the table. During the regular season, I'd often stay silent when it came to these types of discussions. I played by instinct, not analysis. But this camp wasn't about watching from the sidelines or doing our usual. Damien demanded that we *all* participate, even me, even if it meant forcing myself outside of my comfort zone.

I thought I'd be bored as fuck, but it turned out to be the total opposite. Being in a smaller group was helping me focus.

It also made me aware of Damien in a way that was fucking intense. I wanted more of his attention and not all of it was about hockey. Fuck me, this hard-on I had for him was getting out of hand.

Hockey was a high-risk sport. My reaction to Damien, even more so.

I needed to find a guy to hook up with. Any guy. Anything to take my mind off *him*. This weekend, it was happening. Then everything would return to normal.

When we hit the ice again in the afternoon, I had a ton of adrenaline to burn. But I wasn't as focused as I was in the morning. My gaze tracked Damien's every move. And because of that, I missed a pass from Ethan and got razzed for being slow on the uptake. At least no one suspected the reason why I was so distracted.

"What do you think of the camp so far?" Dane asked me when we took a breather.

I turned to our captain.

"It's good. Harder than I expected, but more time on the ice is never a bad thing, right? I'm learning a lot."

"I think this fall is going to be a banner season for us."

I nodded. "I feel it too."

We were halfway through our scrimmage when Damien's phone rang. He started skating away as he answered it, but he didn't get far.

"Silas!" Damien called out and motioned for me.

I skated over to the boards and noticed Damien's tense expression. "What's up?"

"It's your brother," Damien replied and offered me his phone.

A wave of panic washing over me as I frantically pulled my gloves off and reached for the phone.

"Jo?" I answered.

"Sorry to interrupt your practice. I tried your cell but when I couldn't reach you, I called the office at the rink. Didn't realize they'd put me directly through to your coach."

"It's all right, what's going on?"

"I had a fainting spell. One moment, I was gathering up the golf balls at the driving range, and the next thing I knew, I woke up in the lounge in the clubhouse with River beside me. Thankfully, he drove me to Burlington General."

"Shit, are you okay?"

"Still waiting to see a doctor. I've been bleeding more than usual, and I went to the bathroom several times today. I think I'm dehydrated. I need you to come down here. River had to head back to work."

"I'm leaving now. You're in emergency?"

"Yeah, and thanks. Sorry about this."

"Stop apologizing, Jo. I'll be there as fast as I can."

I hung up and passed the phone back to Damien with a shaky hand.

"I've got to get to the hospital," I stated, my voice hoarse. "Jo passed out at work."

"Is he going to be okay?"

"I think so. I hope so," I replied with a sigh. "He has Crohn's disease. Jo had surgery two years ago and he was doing better, much better. But he started a new medication recently and it seems like it's not working. Or maybe it's the side effects? I don't know."

"That's a lot to deal with at his age. Fuck, at any age." Damien stared at me. "Thanks for telling me. We're almost done today anyway. Go take care of your brother."

"Thanks, Damien."

He nodded. "Of course. Let me know how he's doing. Text me later."

"I will."

I made a beeline for the boards, changed in record time, and was back in my truck on the way to the hospital not ten minutes after Jo called. My phone buzzed with notifications, and I tried my best to ignore the guilt that threatened to swamp me every time I thought about missing my brother's call for help.

When I pulled into the hospital parking lot, my phone pinged again.

I tapped on it, assuming it was Josiah. Instead, it was a text from Damien.

> Damien: Despite the late start, you did good.
> Keep it up.

It wasn't a major endorsement, but I'd take it.

CHAPTER 16

DAMIEN

Dane and the rest of the guys kept asking why Silas left early but it wasn't my place to tell them what was going on. I said he had a family emergency and left it at that. Admittedly, I was distracted the rest of the afternoon. My mind should've been focused on my job. Instead, I was worrying about Silas and his brother.

Like I would be with any of my players.

Right. Sure.

My inability to get my head in the game didn't begin to describe how fucked up I was. I looked out for all my players but there was something about Silas that was different. He challenged me like no one else and made me feel things I had no business feeling. The professional line was blurring again.

No, that wasn't right. I had no idea where it was anymore.

Like this morning, and then during lunch when Silas made those porn-worthy moans as he ate. Did he even realize what he was doing? The rational part of me said no fucking way but the teasing glint in his eye told me I needed to be very careful.

It was only day one. How was I going to make it another six weeks?

After another hour on the ice, I called it a day. When all the guys headed off to the locker room, I texted Dave and suggested we head to Burlington tonight. I needed a drink, a good meal, and a distraction. When Dave replied that he already had plans, I let out a groan of frustration. I thought about asking someone else, but I realized that I didn't have anyone to ask. I was friendly with several teachers at the college, but they were off on their summer vacations. It was time for me to expand my social circle. I'd been putting all my energy and time into this team, and there was nothing left.

Fuck it. I'd go out by myself. Lots of people did the same. Flying solo wasn't anything to be ashamed of.

I tapped on my phone and began searching for bars in nearby towns. Nothing stood out. One place was rated tops for "date night." Uh, no thanks, I didn't want to be surrounded by couples in love. I wanted to sit and enjoy a beer and maybe watch a game. Or listen to live music, that'd be cool too. Someplace I'd never been to. Maybe I'd even practice my flirting with a stranger. Not that I had any game when it came to that anymore, but it was worth trying.

Suddenly I was typing "gay bars," surprising myself. If Selwin could see me now, he'd be laughing his ass off. Then again, he'd be the first to cheer me along and he'd also love to be my wingman for the night.

What am I doing? I had no freaking clue.

Questions about my sexuality had haunted me since Chicago. Was it finally time for me to find out if my previous experience with a guy was a one off? There was only one way to find out for sure. I searched for queer bars near Burlington and found a few. One was a dance club, so I gave that a hard pass. But the second one I found was a pub with great reviews for the atmosphere and the food. That sounded perfect. I could grab a meal, and it would be an easy drive to get there. It was far enough away from campus, too, so it was unlikely I'd run into anyone I knew there. I could get some answers, and who knows? Maybe I'd get lucky too.

Then maybe this intense attraction I had to Silas would finally get the fuck gone.

Resolved, I headed for my office, locked up, and exited the rink to a deserted parking lot. The drive to Burlington gave me enough time to think. Probably too much. I was tempted several times to turn back. Nerves got the best of me, but I kept on driving.

When I finally arrived at my destination, Unicorn & Ale, I sat in my car for almost twenty minutes, unable to move. The bar was one of several historic buildings on this stretch of road in the town proper. Outside of the rainbow flags hanging near the door, the place looked like any other storefront in the neighborhood. I watched people walking in and out of the place, laughing and talking.

Why couldn't I go inside? Why was I so nervous?

> Damien: SOS personal shit.

I only had to wait a few seconds for Selwin to respond.

> Selwin: You're lucky it's off season. What's happening?

> Damien: I'm about to venture into a gay bar in Burlington.

> Selwin: R u serious??

I snapped a picture of the place and sent it to him.

> Selwin: Damn, I wish I was there.

> Damien: I don't know if I should do this. Part of me says go for it and see what happens, the other part is scared as fuck.

Selwin: That's normal. And wouldn't you rather find out if it's something you want to explore rather than holding back? I know you. You're not a middle of the road kind of guy. It's all or nothing.

Damien: True. Ever since Chicago, things are different. My personal life was stuck in sleep mode but suddenly I'm awake again. And I think it's time I figure myself out.

Selwin: Only do it if it feels right. Also, this sudden need to explore your sexuality, it wouldn't have to do with a certain defenseman you coach, would it?

I gripped my phone so tightly; I'm surprised I didn't break it. My hands were shaky, and it took me forever to type out a response.

Damien: What? No. I told you, he's my student.

Selwin: He's hot AF and an adult. An adult who eye-fucked you. There was no mistaking it.

Damien: I can't go there. Come on, Sel, I need to think of my career for fuck's sake. Imagine if Dave found out? Or worse, the college president?

Selwin: Who says anyone needs to find out?

Damien: I'm heading inside.

Selwin: Text me later. I need to hear ALL the details.

Damien: I doubt they'll be anything to report. Except me making an ass of myself LOL.

Selwin: I doubt it. Remember, eye contact
and a smile. That's all you need.

Damien: If only things were that easy.

Selwin: Have a beer first, remember to relax,
and don't overthink it.

My jaw clenched so tightly that at this point I was in danger of breaking a tooth...

Damien: Telling someone to relax has the
opposite effect, you know that right?

Selwin: The younger guys are going to be all
over you. You'll be fighting them off.

Damien: I doubt that. And I want to ease into
this, not jump without a parachute.

Selwin: Stop using your brain and think with
your dick. Remember him?

Damien: It's been years since I did that.

Selwin: Welcome back.

I shoved my phone in the pocket of my jeans and finally eased out of the car. Either it was warm for June, or I was stress-sweating because my button down stuck uncomfortably to my skin. Rolling up the sleeves, I checked my reflection in the driver side window and decided I looked fine. Maybe a bit tired and anxious, but hey, it was what it was. I popped a breath mint, ran an agitated hand through my hair, and stepped up to the front door of the bar.

When I ventured inside, I was greeted by the noisy hum of conversation and the enticing smell of greasy pub food and beer. Music was playing, but thankfully, at a level that didn't shatter my eardrums. Two guys in their twenties stood ahead of me in line, holding hands and trading lingering kisses.

And I thought it was hot outside…

The couple was greeted by a host and seated at one of the booths that lined the walls. Since I spotted a couple of empty seats at the bar, I made a beeline for the last stool.

The bartender, a dark-haired guy with big dimples and a cropped tank top, leaned over and gave me a welcoming grin.

"Hey there, what can I get you?"

"I was thinking a pint of a local IPA," I replied. "What do you recommend?"

"We've got a new one for summer called Golden Hour. It's very smooth with a hit of citrus."

"Sounds great."

"I'm Kolt," he offered with a tip of his head.

"Damien."

"Haven't seen you in here before," he added as he gave me a long once-over. "Not that we've been opened that long, but still."

Nerves that usually took flight during games suddenly washed over me. I was feeling all kinds of awkward and I'm sure it showed.

"First time," I replied and hoped like hell I wasn't blushing. "I live in Sutton."

"Ah, the college town. Are you a teacher or something?"

I nodded. "I coach hockey."

"Cool." He tapped the bar. "I'll be right back."

So far, so good. I managed to make normal conversation, and I didn't trip over my tongue.

Looking around, I noticed plenty of attractive guys, although no one caught my attention. Shifting awkwardly, I realized I didn't even know where to begin. Maybe I couldn't do this. What *was* I doing?

I was about to get up and bolt for the door when Kolt returned with my beer.

"You want a menu?" he asked.

I could at least stay for a bite. I had to eat anyway.

"Sure, thanks."

I took a grateful sip of the crisp IPA, feeling my nerves settle. Slightly.

"So, what brings you here tonight?" Kolt asked as he passed me a paper menu. "Meeting a date?"

"Unfortunately, no. I'm trying to break my usual rut of working, working, and oh yeah, working."

Kolt's knowing smile was cute, but I didn't feel any spark. This would've been a perfect time to try out my flirting skills. Unfortunately, they'd retired along with my hockey playing days.

Kolt placed his forearms on the bar and leaned in. "Well, you've come to the right place. Great food, friendly staff—if I do say so myself—and lots of sexy guys to talk to."

I took another sip of my beer before I responded.

"Not sure about the last one," I confessed. "I'm pretty new to that, too."

Kolt didn't look in the least surprised and nodded.

"There's a first time for everyone."

"Not exactly," I muttered. "But close."

Kolt gave me a wolfish grin.

"Sorry," I whispered. "I don't know why I said that out loud."

"Sure you do. It seems like you want to get something off your chest. Go for it, I'm a good listener. It's part of the job."

I took another sip of beer and nodded.

"I was talking to a friend recently and I realized some things. A lot actually," I confessed. "There's nothing like having a sexual reawakening at thirty."

"Awesome," Kolt replied. "What's your type? Maybe I can help you out."

A vision of Silas immediately popped into my mind, and I was speaking before I could stop myself.

"Athletic, tatts, and an attitude that challenges me."

Kolt chuckled. "That sounds remarkably precise."

I shrugged. "I'm sure lots of guys fit that bill."

"Right," Kolt added as he leaned in closer. "So, tell me about this guy you're crushing on."

I shook my head.

"I'll need another beer first."

CHAPTER 17

SILAS

fter a couple of bags of IV fluids, blood tests, and a follow-up appointment with his gastro specialist, Josiah was given the all-clear to head home. He looked a lot better than when I'd first arrived. This visit was, thankfully, a lot shorter than past ones, and a couple hours later, we headed out of the hospital.

"The doctors said you might need to try a new medication. I know it's a pain but maybe it's for the best."

"I wanted to have a normal summer."

"It's still going to happen," I insisted as I unlocked the truck. "It was one day."

I slid into the driver's seat and glanced over at my brother.

"So, you won't stop me from going back to work?" Josiah replied.

"No. Why would I do that?"

"Because I passed out. And it could happen again."

"I know. It's scary and there are a lot of unknowns. But you need to keep trying."

Josiah finally gave me a smile.

I was overprotective by nature, but my little brother was

growing up. And if I wanted him to be happy and independent, I needed to let go a bit. He couldn't stay at home, isolated. And wherever he worked, driving range or not, it was important that he at least try if he was able.

"I'm starving and there's nothing at home to eat. Can we stop and grab something on the way back?"

"Take my phone and order whatever you want," I replied. "Tell me where to go."

Josiah got busy typing.

"There's a new place a few blocks from here that we've never tried. It's looks like a nice pub. You want a burger?"

"Sounds good."

I started up the truck and pulled out of the lot.

"Done," Josiah added. "Pick up at 25 Walnut Street in fifteen."

Josiah placed my phone back on the handset and tapped on the screen so I could see the directions.

"What did you order?"

"A grilled chicken and rice bowl for me and a medium burger and fries for you."

"Perfect."

"Did you miss much practice today by leaving early?" Josiah asked.

"Nope," I reassured him. "I told you; we were almost done for the day."

"Was Banning annoyed that I called his phone?"

"Not at all. He understood," I replied. "And he wanted me to pass along his best."

"You like working with him, don't you?" Josiah remarked. "I can tell by the way you talk about him."

"I do," I muttered and left it at that.

"Liking Damien" was an understatement. I was already counting down the hours until our next session. Three days a week? I could play five or six days and never get enough.

And it wasn't only about hockey. It was about being around *him*.

Fuck, forget it. Forget him.

I couldn't. Damien had asked me to text him, and as soon as we stopped to pick up the food, I'd type out a quick "we're good" and leave it at that. Not that I was anxious to message him or anything, but I didn't want to be rude after he was so kind.

I followed the directions to our dinner pick-up and even though the address was located on one of the busiest stretches in the city, I managed to snag a parking spot nearby. I glanced at the name of the restaurant, Unicorn & Ale. Huh, this was a favorite of Darby's. I'd heard him talk about it at work. It was a queer-owned pub that opened a few months ago. I'd yet to visit the place, but I'd heard good things.

First, I grabbed my phone and texted Damien.

> Silas: We've left the hospital. Josiah's feeling much better.

> Damien: That's great news. Is he able to return to work? Summer jobs are a big deal at his age.

My stomach flipped over when Damien responded right away. It was late evening, and I figured he'd be busy. Or that he wouldn't reply at all.

> Silas: I encouraged him to keep going if he's able. It won't be easy. He might have to switch meds again. But he's a fighter.

> Damien: Runs in the family. See you Wednesday.

> Silas: Can't wait.

Can't wait? Ugh, that sounded so freaking needy. Ignoring

the flutter in my belly, and my suddenly sweaty palms, I shoved my phone in my pocket.

"I'm gonna head inside to grab our order," I announced. "You okay waiting here? You need anything else?"

"I'm fine," Josiah insisted. "I'm going to call River."

I grabbed the green elastic from my wrist and pulled my hair up into a messy bun. Sliding out of the truck, I debated taking off my leather jacket since it was so warm out. Nah. I was only going to pop in and grab our stuff, so it wasn't worth it. I'd leave it on.

I walked quickly to the front door, and when I stepped inside, I was immediately drawn to the cozy pub vibes. Next time I was in town, I'd make sure to stop by for a beer and a bite. And maybe I'd get lucky too.

As I scanned the place, I took in the polished wood bar at the back of the room, and my gaze landed on a familiar, if surprising, figure.

What the fuck was Damien doing here?

He was chatting up the sexy bartender for one thing. A flash of heat and unwarranted jealousy burned in my gut.

It's not your business.

The last thing I needed right now was a run-in with my irresistible coach. Thankfully, the host spotted me, and I quickly showed him my phone so I could grab my order and get the fuck gone.

When I looked up again, it was too late. Damien spotted me, his eyes widening.

Shit. There was no ignoring him now.

Instead of standing there, staring back at him like an idiot, I stalked over to the bar, my heart racing faster with every step.

"Hey," I offered.

"Funny meeting you here," Damien replied, his voice hoarse.

"I'm picking up dinner for me and Jo on the way home."

"Me too. I mean, obviously I'm having dinner."

I glanced at his half-eaten plate with a nod. Burger and fries, a man after my own heart.

"Looks great. It's my first time here."

"Me too. The food and the beer's amazing."

We stared at each other for far too long, something heady flashing between us. It wasn't all me and it wasn't my imagination. Damien's eyes drifted lower to my lips, then back up again, catching my gaze. I knew interest when I saw it. And fuck, it took everything in me *not* to lean forward and brush my mouth against Damien's ear. I wanted to feel him tremble, to tease him, and taste his skin.

Was it smart to eye-fuck my coach? Absolutely not.

Was I going to do it again? Absolutely yes.

Until the bartender spoke and startled me from the trance I was caught in; namely, Damien's vivid blue gaze.

"Hey, I'm Kolt. Can I get you anything?"

"Silas." I turned and greeted him with a nod. "I'm waiting for a pickup order."

"Nice to meet ya. You two know each other?" Kolt asked as he glanced at Damien.

I replied "yes" at the same time Damien mumbled "sort of."

"Sort of?" I quipped and placed a hand over my heart. "Ouch, what happened to 'See you Wednesday'?"

"You work together?" Kolt asked.

"Yes," I replied and left it at that.

Kolt started to chuckle, and I no idea why. What was so funny about that?

"I figured you were an athlete. I'll go check on your order," Kolt added and walked away, leaving me alone with Damien.

Well, as alone as we could get in a crowded bar.

"Sorry to interrupt your evening," I muttered as I leaned against the bar top, facing Damien again.

Instead of doing what I wanted, sitting my ass down on the empty bar stool next to him, I decided to stay standing as I was. Damien looked relaxed for once, far too tempting, and sitting next to him in the cozy atmosphere of the pub was only going to make matters worse.

If only he wasn't my coach, if only I had more time, if only, if only...

"Nothing to interrupt," Damien responded and reached for his beer, taking a long sip.

"He's cute."

"Who?"

"The bartender."

"Oh."

"Not my type," I added. "But he seems like a nice guy."

"He is. I was nervous when I first sat down and—" Damien's eyes implored mine. "I don't know where to start. You're probably wondering why I'm here."

"Not at all. It's none of my business," I reassured him. "I'm trying—and failing miserably—to make small talk. I'm sorry if I interrupted your evening."

"You didn't. And I think I should probably tell you that—"

I shook my head. "It's okay, Damien. You have a right to a personal life."

"I haven't had one in a long time," Damien confessed and worried his lower lip. "And... I'm trying to find some answers as to why."

First, that queer club in Chicago and now here. It didn't take a huge leap in logic to parse out that he was trying to come to terms with questions about his sexuality. My gaze locked on his full lips, and damn, why did he have to be so hot? Hot and unavailable.

Why did he have to be my freaking coach?

"I think I'm bi," he whispered. "But I haven't explored that for years."

Say what?

Did that mean… I stood there, gaping, unable to speak.

"Forget I said anything," Damien replied quickly and took another sip of beer. "Tonight, this discussion, it never happened."

"I'm sorry, you… wow, you shocked me. It normally takes a lot to do that."

"I shouldn't have said anything. It's not exactly appropriate conversation given our roles."

I stared at him and shook my head.

"Considering what I told you about myself, I can assure you I'm a safe person to talk to. I'm an adult. So, knock off the appropriate shit. It doesn't apply in our case."

"I think it does," he bit back. "If anyone from the school ever found out that you, I mean, that you and I—"

He paused, biting his lower lip.

"That what? We're talking, not fucking in the middle of the football field. Or the rink."

"Silas," Damien hissed, his cheeks flushing a bright shade of scarlet.

I couldn't help but chuckle, way too satisfied with teasing Damien. Me, making the unshakeable Coach Banning lose his cool? It was intoxicating, addicting. And his response was too fucking adorable.

Adorable? Since when did I even use that word?

"What? I like talking to you, okay?" I admitted. "Most guys my age are too busy partying or pulling stupid pranks. I sometimes feel ancient compared to them. I know I'm twenty-two but trust me, I've got years of responsibility behind me. I'm not your average student."

"I know." Damien sighed. "I do. I think that's part of the problem."

"Like I said, we're having a conversation." I pointed between us. "Nothing wrong about that."

Damien looked like he was about to reply, but he was

interrupted by Kolt returning with a friendly smile and a bag that I assumed was my order. Damien did his best to stare at his glass and avoid eye contact. Maybe I *had* overstepped the boundary between us, but I assumed it worked both ways. It wasn't often that I vibed with someone so easily. I felt like I could talk to Damien about anything and everything.

Then I remembered why he was here. He was probably looking to hook up with a guy.

Not me. Never me.

Use your fucking brain.

He had plans, and so did I.

Kolt offered me the bag, and I nodded. "Thanks, Kolt."

"I love your tatts. Are they done locally?" he asked me.

"Verdant Ink. I work there part-time. They've got tons of cool artists. Drop by sometime."

"Thanks, I'll check it out. I moved here a few months ago so I'm still finding my way around."

"If you ever need a tour guide, I'm game," I said to the bartender and turned to Damien. Fuck it, if he didn't want to look at me, that was his problem, not mine. "I've got to hit the road. See you Wednesday, Damien."

"Yep."

Damien nodded but didn't so much as glance my way.

Despite my jacket, and the warm atmosphere in the pub, I was freezing cold.

CHAPTER 18
DAMIEN

THE NEXT DAY

There was no one in the school gym when I arrived at six a.m. During the regular semester it was packed, and because of that, I tended to choose late evenings for my workouts. In the summer, however, the place was a ghost walk. And mornings were my preference, since exercising early always started the day right. Hitting the weights forced me to focus on my body and to forget about work for a while. Inevitably, afterwards, I always gained clarity to whatever puzzle or problem I was dealing with at the time. And like any former pro athlete, I was used to the routine. Working out was as necessary to me as eating right and drinking plenty of water.

And I needed a workout today more than ever.

I couldn't stop replaying my conversation with Silas. Fuck, I'd told him things I didn't even talk about with Dave, who I considered my closest friend here in Sutton. What was up with that?

After Silas left the pub, I finished my dinner, alone, and headed back home, alone. I was too caught up in my head to try and attempt to make a connection with anyone in that bar. Not that I was giving up. But I didn't know what to do with these intense feelings for a man that I could never have. A man so far out of my league we were playing in different games.

Doing my best to put last night aside, I warmed up on the treadmill, a brisk twenty-minute walk, and then headed around the corner for the weight machines. First up was a couple of sets on the chest press, then I focused on my legs. After that, I did a few reps of seated cable row.

I was halfway through my second set of reps when I heard a door open. I paused momentarily, distracted by the sound, then continued with my workout. There was the familiar beep and whirl of a treadmill starting; someone was warming up. I kept going with my reps, until sweat trickled down my face and neck, and my muscles began to burn. I knew not to push it too far with my right leg, though. There was a fine balance between staying flexible and risking another injury.

I finished my set and reached for my towel, swiping my face. The echo of footsteps getting closer meant my solo time in the gym was done.

When I dropped the towel on my lap and looked up, there was Silas sitting on the rowing machine opposite me. He was wearing tight black shorts, all those stunning tattoos across his chest and arms on display, his hair tied up in that messy bun that was my new obsession. I wondered if his hair was as soft as it looked and how it would feel against my skin. Shit. Was I hallucinating or was he looking back at me with the same intent? And why was it that everywhere I looked lately, there he was? I'd spent months seeing him at practice and games but now everything felt different. It was getting harder to keep any distance between us.

My professional line was already way past gone.

"Hey," I managed to whisper, my voice cracking.

Jesus, I sounded like a nervous teenager with a first crush.

He glanced at me and his expression turned wary. "I can come back later if you prefer?"

"Don't be ridiculous," I replied and reached for my water bottle. "I'm halfway done anyway."

"Early riser?"

"Always. My mind spins twenty-four-seven. You?"

"Same."

I nodded and swallowed hard at the sight of him. Normally, I saw Silas when he was padded up, on the ice. Or in a suit for game day. All he had on now were those thin shorts, exposing long, hard thighs lightly dusted with blond hair. My formerly slumbering libido was wide awake and into this view. My eyes roamed over his chest, lower, and I couldn't help but let out a laugh when I saw the word he had tattooed across his taut abs.

"Ruthless?" I stated with a raised eyebrow.

"Fucking right," he stated with a wicked grin.

Suddenly, I was back in that bar, wanting to see that smile and more. Wanting to talk to him again. And wanting to know more about him but also, seriously unprepared for what was going on between us.

Get up and walk out of here. Do the right thing.

"I don't see you that way," I confessed.

Silas shrugged, placed his feet in the pedals, and reached for the handlebar on the machine. "It's a reminder to never give up. Not on my family or myself. And that I'd do anything for them."

"Anything?"

"Yep."

I admired his tenacity and loyalty more than I cared to admit. But it was more than admiration; his drive turned me on. Just like when it came to hockey, a lot of people talked a good game, but very few could play it. And some would argue that responsibility wasn't sexy, and when I was younger, I probably thought that way too. But now? A person who kept their word and gave their all for the ones they cared about? Who never gave up? It was the most attractive thing ever. I liked it. A lot.

What was worse? I liked him. More.

"Why the rowing machine?" I asked, curious.

"Full body workout," Silas replied as he began to glide back and forth, his biceps straining with every pull. "Plus, there's a competition in the works with the Sutton Crew come September. We've agreed to a soccer match, but I have a feeling they'll convince us to get in those tiny fucking boats they use. And I want to be prepared to kick their ass at their own game."

I chuckled at his competitive comment. "Ruthless indeed."

"Fuck, yeah." He panted as he moved faster. "You good? You need me to spot you?"

"I don't want to interrupt your workout," I replied and took a sip from my water bottle. "Maybe in a bit."

"Once I'm done on this machine, I'm all yours."

Mine? I nearly spewed my mouthful of water all over the floor.

Imagining Silas standing beside me in nothing but those indecent shorts had my blood pressure spiking to dangerous levels. I downed another sip of water and wiped my face again. Instead of standing there like an idiot, gawking at him, I finished my reps and moved on to another machine, determined to ignore him and my crazy reaction.

It was a lot more difficult than I thought. Being in a gym with a hot guy was never a problem before. In fact, I was always so intent on getting my routine done that I didn't notice anyone else, man or woman.

God, how much had changed.

Silas's stamina was something to watch, and dirty images of him doing a much different kind of workout bombarded me. My face flushed, but thankfully, I could blame it on the exercise. I willed myself *not* to get a boner and headed for a nearby bench to do chest presses. That didn't help matters at all. I was still too close to Silas, so close that I could hear him grunting. Did he sound like that when he was fucking? Would he scream or moan? Then I was hit by the scent of his sweat and bodywash. He didn't smell like fancy cologne, and I was a fan. Would he taste as good as he smelled?

I shoved my face in the towel again and used it like a paper bag, breathing in and out slowly to try and calm myself down.

"Are you okay?" he asked me.

I slowly dropped the towel only to find him standing directly in front of me, his crotch in my line of sight. The bulge in his shorts had all my attention. I licked my lips and tried to speak but I couldn't make a sound.

"Damien?" he repeated.

A shiver wracked my body when Silas called me by my first name. Why him? Of all the goddamn people in this town, why did it have to be one of my students?

Instead of staying where he was, he quickly rounded the machine to stand beside me and that didn't help matters at all.

Finally, my tongue cooperated. "I'm fine. I needed a break to catch my breath."

"You shouldn't be in the gym by yourself, especially when you're doing bench presses. That's dangerous."

No, dangerous was being in the same room as this man.

"I know. I wasn't thinking."

No shit. The only part of me in working order right now was my dick.

Silas crouched down, and eye to eye, he was far too close.

"Lie down," he demanded.

"What?"

"I said, lie down." When I didn't move, he let out a chuckle, the sound low and deep. My gut told me he knew exactly where my mind was at. "On the bench. I'll spot you."

"Oh. Right. Yes."

He walked around to stand behind me and that wasn't any better. I could feel his body heat and prayed that I'd get through this next set without making a fool of myself.

I stretched out on the bench and reached for the weighted bar. I did several reps, pushing up and lowering slowly, trying to focus on my breathing, which was way too fast. I'd lifted a lot heavier, but every rep had my arms shaking and my lungs seizing up.

"One more set and then break," Silas murmured.

I completed my set and he helped me secure the bar back in its resting place, his fingers accidentally brushing mine. There was no mistaking the shock of desire that ran down my arms and lit up the rest of my body, or the way his brown eyes widened. He stepped back and I felt the loss like I'd been stung.

"You need water," he added, his voice hoarse. "You're flushed and your breathing's too fast."

He'd noticed? Of course he did.

"Maybe I'm coming down with something," I replied.

Yeah, this former fuckboy, now coach turned monk, was suddenly feverish for dick. Not just any dick. Silas's. This had disaster written all over it, and yet I felt so fucking alive. For the first time in forever.

Silas stalked around the machine and bent over to pick up his water bottle, and I nearly lost it. First, he'd tempted me with the frontal view, which was spectacular, and now the back view, which was even hotter. His high, round ass in those thin nylon shorts was downright sinful and so was the raging hard-on that I was now sporting. I leaned forward to try and cover it up, bracketing my forearms on my thighs. Those shorts of his left nothing to the imagination. Did they need to be that tight? Did he always walk around here like that? He must've had everyone in the gym lusting after him.

No kidding. He's twenty-two. Think of all the guys he must draw. Guys that were younger and sexier than me.

I shoved the towel in my face again and this time, bit down on it.

"Can you return the favor?" he asked.

I looked up so fast that my neck made a popping sound. "What?"

"Can you spot me?"

"Oh, sure, give me a sec to hydrate."

I made a show of gulping down more water when in reality, I was buying time so my erection would go away. While Silas added more weight to the bar, I took a few deep breaths. After a minute, my problem deflated, and I slowly got up. Silas took my place, sitting on the bench.

"Wait, I forgot to wipe it down," I insisted, and offered my towel.

Silas shook his head and leaned back, grinning at me. "I don't mind your sweat at all."

Wait, what? Was he flirting with me?

"I broke one of the cardinal rules of the gym," I muttered.

"Come on, Damien, you and I both know that some rules are meant to be broken."

I stared down at him, and my breath caught when I saw the heated interest in his eyes. No, that couldn't be right. I was imagining things.

Suddenly nervous, I licked my lips.

"How was the rest of your night?" Silas asked me.

I was too preoccupied by the sight of him laid out before me like an offering to answer right away.

"Um, it was uneventful. I finished dinner and headed home. You?"

"Same. Me and Jo stuffed our faces, and he crashed out. But I didn't sleep well."

"Why? What's going on?" I asked, concerned.

"I'm distracted," he admitted. "By a guy. Can't get him out of my head."

Oh. Oh. I didn't want to hear about this.

"A student in one of your classes?"

That was my pathetic attempt at finding out who Silas was crushing on. Instead of waiting for his answer, I walked around to stand behind the machine, trying to get some distance between us.

"No."

I swallowed hard and tried to calm my racing heart, but it was no use.

"Someone you work with at the tattoo shop?" I suggested.

Silas reached for the bar and shook his head. "Nope."

"Well, if it's someone on the team, I can't say I'm surprised. Seems like all my players are matching up. And I'd offer you advice but unfortunately, I have none," I quipped. "My track record is nothing to brag about."

Silas began his chest presses and watching him work out unlocked a new kink.

"It's not… a teammate," Silas panted as he lifted the bar up and down. "But he is… a hockey fanatic. Older… smart… sexy… intense."

I didn't want to hear anymore.

"I'm pretty sure he's interested too… but there's a problem," Silas added. "Well, several of them."

Even though I wanted to walk away from this conversation stat, I didn't.

"Why don't you start by telling him how you feel? I'm sure the rest can be worked out."

Silas placed the bar on the rack and looked up at me.

"Damien."

"Yes?"

"I did."

CHAPTER 19

SILAS

What started as me working out my sexual frustration in the gym turned into an unexpected confession to Damien about the fact I was crushing on him. Except for hockey, I didn't like playing games, and I always used the blunt approach when it came to the men I was attracted to. It saved a lot of time and there were no complications. If there was mutual interest, and we hooked up, we both walked away satisfied.

Only, lately there was only one man I was hung up on.

And fuck the fact that he was my coach.

I wanted Damien, and like always, I was ruthless when it came to the things that mattered to me. And Damien mattered. Earlier, when I brushed my hands against his, I knew that he felt the spark too. I wanted to reach for him, to pull him onto my lap and stroke him off. Fuck, I wanted to watch him come all over me and watch us come together. I didn't have a thing for sexual fantasies about the gym until now. Did I always walk around in here with no shirt on? No. Was I going to show off in front of him? Hell, yes.

I knew in my gut, the only thing I trusted in, that he and I would be explosive together. Under his tightly wound exterior beat the heart of a passionate player. And it was clear from everything I'd learned about him that he wanted to explore his sexuality. And me? I was happy to reverse our roles and do the teaching.

"Damien?"

He paced beside me, hands on his hips. "I think I should leave."

"Tell me I'm wrong. Tell me I'm the only one feeling this and I'll go."

"I don't know what to... I mean, you—" Damien shook his head. "You and I should... fuck."

"Exactly, you and I should fuck," I teased and stood up to face him. "But we can start with a kiss."

Damien's eyes locked on my mouth and there was no stopping the way my pulse kicked up, all the blood in my body rushing south as my shorts grew tighter. And God, he smelled better than good, like sweat and sunshine, and I wanted to lean down and taste every inch of him.

"Don't deny what's going on here," I added, stepping closer. I didn't miss the flare of heat in his dark blue gaze. "Give me a chance."

"Silas, this isn't the time or place," he whispered.

I licked my lips. "So, name one."

"This is crazy. If anyone found out—"

"They're not going to," I insisted. "What happens between us is our business."

"Christ, you're relentless."

I shook my head and pointed to the *Ruthless* tattoo on my abs. Close enough.

"I know what I want, and I go after it."

Damien twisted the towel in his hands.

"Text me later," Damien finally replied. "We can meet up and... talk about this."

It wasn't a date, but I'd take it.

"You're not going to ghost me, are you?" I teased, swiping

a hand down my face and then my chest, watching the way his eyes tracked my hand.

"I wouldn't do that."

No, he wouldn't. I was starting to think that I knew Damien more than any man I'd ever met. There was a warning in my brain that told me to put a stop to this, that he and I would turn out to be more than I could handle. But life was boring without taking risks.

I was about to say something flirty in response when I heard a door slam. We weren't alone in the gym anymore.

"I need to finish my workout," I stated reluctantly.

Damien nodded. "I'll leave you to it."

He walked past me, his arm brushing mine. The indelible spark that passed between us was not a fluke.

Before he could take off for good, I reached for his bicep, his skin hot and slick. I didn't want to let go and what was even more satisfying was that Damien didn't pull away.

"Don't forget your stuff," I reminded him, motioning to his water bottle and the set of keys lying on the floor.

"Oh, yeah," he replied, sounding breathless. "Thanks."

I dropped my hand slowly, fighting every urge I had to pull him closer.

Then he was gone, leaving me staring at my stunned reflection in the mirrored wall.

What are you doing? Fucking around with your coach could screw up your life exponentially. And his.

I couldn't help myself.

I want him. I'm going to be the one to break his icy control.

Instead of ruminating about Damien and reckless choices, I got back to my workout.

Ten minutes turned to twenty, then thirty. I was drenched in sweat by the time I was done with my full circuit, tired but feeling calmer than when I first walked in here and spotted Damien. I thought nothing could compare to him in a tailored suit but seeing him in shorts and a tank top rivaled for top spot in my spank bank. The only thing better would be getting him naked in my bed. Probably a hotel out of town if we wanted to be careful.

I hit the shower, but I ignored my hard-on. Unlike our locker at the rink, where we had a communal shower room, the ones here were stalls. I had privacy and time to rub one out, but I wanted to wait. Damien was worth it.

Once I was cleaned up, I headed for my truck and was on the road to Burlington.

Verdant wasn't busy, but most Tuesdays rarely were, so I spent most of my time confirming upcoming appointments and taking care of the monthly bookkeeping. Until Darby rolled into work.

"What are you up to later?" he asked, stepping into my personal space and giving me a flirty grin.

What we'd had was fun, but I wasn't interested in a repeat. Not anymore.

"I've got plans."

I'm going to kiss my coach... fuck, the very idea had me so horny I had to hide my hips behind the counter.

"Are you seeing someone?" Darby added.

"Define 'seeing.'" I chuckled. "It's brand new. I don't know what it is yet."

Ain't that the truth.

"Who is he?"

"I can't say. He's not out."

"Ugh, please don't tell me you have feelings for a DL guy," Darby warned.

I didn't know how to describe what was happening between me and Damien. We hadn't done anything yet, and I was already consumed with thoughts about him. I'd never felt such a pull towards a guy before, like if we didn't touch soon, I'd go out of my freaking mind. Bad enough I'd wanked off to fantasies of him last night until I came all over my sheets. Seeing him in the light of day only made the wanting worse.

"Doubtful," I replied.

Sex I could handle, feelings for a guy... I had no clue.

"Well, if you change your mind," Darby continued, "and you need a distraction, let me know."

I glanced at him. "We're better off as friends, don't you think?"

Darby gave me another long look and finally stepped back.

"That works, too," he replied. "For what it's worth, I hope this guy treats you right."

"Like I said, I have zero expectations."

"If that's true, why don't you want to hook up with me anymore?"

"I don't... I don't know."

How could I explain it? I wanted Damien. No one else.

Darby gaped at me. "Shit, you really like this guy."

I swallowed hard and nodded.

"I guess I do."

Darby tapped the counter. "Like I said, I hope things work out. Relationships are hard. I wouldn't even know where to begin."

Honestly, I had no clue either.

The familiar buzz of the front door opening had me looking up. I greeted a returning customer and handed them off to Darby.

Then I pulled out my phone and texted the source of my distraction.

Silas: What did you do?

I smiled when my phone pinged a second later.

Damien: Me? Don't you mean what did you do?

Silas: You teased me with that gym outfit, Coach. I thought nothing could top the game day suit, but I changed my mind. You should wear shorts year-round.

Damien: I'd prefer not to freeze my balls off in the winter LOL. And look who's talking. Do you always wander around the gym half naked?

Silas: I'm proud of this body and I work hard for it. But no, only in front of you. As soon as I spotted you, the shirt came off. Did you like it? Tell me.

Damien: Yes, I did. More than liked. And you're bossy. Normally that's my role.

Silas: We're not talking about hockey, baby.

Damien: Fuck. We're skating on very thin ice. Pun intended.

Silas: We're both skilled players.

Damien: I don't know about me.

Silas: Never mind a phone call, how about meeting someplace nearby when my shift is done?

Damien: Did you want to drop by my place? My house is a short drive from campus. We need privacy to talk.

The office phone rang. I needed to get back to work.

Silas: Send me the address. I'll be there around nine.

I pocketed my phone and got on with my shift. But I was flustered, unable to focus on any one task at a time.

Thank fuck I wasn't the one handling the needles around here.

———

Six hours later, I logged off, locked up, and got in my truck. I tapped on my direction app and entered Damien's address.

What do you know?

It turned out he lived only a few blocks from my house.

The sun had set earlier, but the sky remained vivid with shades of orange and violet, a dramatic contrast to the lush green mountains. God, I loved the long June days in Vermont. I just wished I had more time to actually enjoy them...

I pushed aside my longing, and headed for the highway. The roads were empty, but unlike my usual drive home, I was filled with nervous anticipation.

Damien's place turned out to be a rustic log cabin, nestled at the end of the street and surrounded by a huge piece of property and lots of trees. A familiar black SUV sat in the driveway. I pulled up next to it and parked.

Stepping out and glancing around, I was relieved to see that his neighbors were a long distance away.

My nerves were running high but the closer I got to Damien, the more confident I felt in my decision.

I walked up the gravel driveway to the front door, and before I even had a chance to knock, the door swung open. Damien greeted me with his usual intense expression, wearing a plain white T-shirt, faded jeans that were snug in all the right places, and my personal favorite, bare feet. His outfit said relaxed, but his rigid posture told me otherwise.

"I thought maybe you'd changed your mind."

I shook my head. "No way."

"Are you coming?" he asked, his cheeks turning pink. "I mean, are you coming inside. Inside my house. Not coming as in... Jesus."

Watching my normally unflappable coach blush and stumble was completely irresistible.

"I knew what you meant." I chuckled as I watched him let out a breath, his shoulders dropping slightly. "But it's good to know where your mind's at."

"Trouble."

"Nah, Silas is fine."

He motioned for me to enter the house.

"Wow, nice digs," I commented.

Most people would probably find the space dark, with natural wood walls and a stone fireplace, but I loved it. The house had an open floor plan, not big at all, but the living room had floor-to-ceiling patio doors that led to an outdoor deck and a view of the sparkling lake beyond. The Vermont countryside didn't get any better than this.

"I think you're the only person who agrees with me," Damien replied. "Everyone who's ever visited tell me it's too small and I should paint the wood walls."

"No paint."

"Right? I like the natural color. And I know it's not huge, but it's cozy. Massive homes aren't for me; they have too much echo."

"I agree. Jo and I share our family home, a three-bedroom bungalow, and it's big enough. If I lived on my own, though, I'd probably get a smaller place and spend the money on a cottage instead."

"Smart. Do you want something to drink?" Damien offered.

"Not right now. Maybe later?"

Damien nodded and glanced outside. "You want to sit out on the deck?"

"Love to," I replied. "Can I take my shoes off?"

"Go for it."

I slipped off my running shoes and my aching feet met cool hardwood.

Damien turned and headed for the patio doors. My gaze followed the long lines of his body; from the broad shoulders to that fine ass, and finally, the thick thighs that I was dying to see without the denim. I wanted to wrap them around my waist, or even better, my head.

Maybe I should've taken him up on his offer for a drink, because damn, I was fucking thirsty, and it was all for him.

Being in Damien's home was… different. I never did this with my hookups. Usually, I preferred a bar bathroom or an alleyway. I couldn't bring someone home, and I didn't want to. Not in my personal space. Oddly enough, that was too, well, personal. And I never stuck around long enough for them to invite me to theirs, so it didn't matter.

I should be freaking out, but I wasn't. Not with Damien.

What did it mean? I had an inkling, a trickle of awareness that there was no going back after this. But still, I didn't have a clue as to what I was doing.

Except what felt right.

I stepped out of the house and onto the deck, which ran the whole length of the house. There was a barbeque at one end, along with two red Adirondak chairs and a firepit at the other. There was no wind tonight and the surface of the lake was like a gilded mirror, almost too perfect to be real.

Damien leaned on the railing, and I slid up beside him, our shoulders brushing, sparks of electricity racing over my skin.

"Incredible view," I commented, staring out at the lake.

"I'm quite taken with it," Damien replied.

Only, he wasn't staring at the lake, but at me.

"Fuck, I can't believe I said that out loud," he whispered.

I reached down and rested a reassuring hand on his hip. Wanting—no, needing—to touch him. Any part of him. All that desperation I felt earlier came rushing back, adrenaline coursing through my body. My jeans were too tight, my cock hard and aching.

"Is this okay?" I asked.

I recognized the fight in his gaze. He was holding on tight to his control. Feverishly, I wanted to be the one to break it.

"I should say no," he started, and my stomach dropped out. "I should definitely say no... but I won't. I can't."

Suddenly, I was the one who was nervous.

"Damien."

He closed his eyes and shook his head.

"You saying my name like that gets me every fucking time," he admitted.

When he opened his eyes again, there was desire in those vivid blues, and all that heat was aimed at me. He slid his hand to my waist, and I did the same, pulling him in tight, letting him feel how much I wanted him. And when his hard cock brushed against mine, despite the layers of denim between us, it took every ounce of my control to go slow.

Then, I didn't need to.

Damien moved first.

CHAPTER 20

DAMIEN

I hadn't kissed a guy in years, so I should've been nervous. And I was, from the moment I saw Silas in the gym this morning to the second he stepped into my home.

But once he touched me, something inside clicked. I didn't have time to think, I wanted to feel. And there wasn't any hesitation in the way I reached for him.

Kissing Silas didn't feel like a mistake, but the best damn thing that had happened to me.

Nothing this good could be wrong. And if it was, it would be worth whatever chaos would come after.

The second my lips touched his, that first heady taste, my nerves fled along with my concerns. I don't know if it was me, him, or the impact of the two of us coming together, but it was on. I slid my tongue deep in his mouth, and hearing Silas's groan of pleasure had me rubbing my hips against his, desperate for friction. His hands moved up my back, sparking trails of fire along my skin. When he reached my neck, his grip turned possessive as he brought me even closer, manhandling me, until my back hit the railing. And fuck, that move was a total turn on. It made my cock ache so hard, so fast, that I was in danger of coming in my jeans.

We ate at each other's mouths, all eager tongues and lusty moans. The rough scrape of his beard against my lips heightened my pleasure, and I barely recognized the feral groan that rumbled out of my chest. Silas leaned back briefly, licking his lips and staring at me like he couldn't quite believe what was happening.

That makes two of us...

One taste of him was only a tease, and I needed more.

"Don't stop kissing me," I growled, chasing his mouth.

His responding chuckle was deep and dirty. "Is that an order, Coach?"

"Goddamn right it is."

The words barely left my mouth when he reached for me again, kissing me senseless. One of Silas's skillful hands slid down my chest, his thumb teasing my nipple, goosebumps erupting all over my skin. Since when did that touch feel so freaking good?

"Take this off," Silas demanded, his voice hoarse as he pulled at my T-shirt.

I broke the kiss and we both reached for each other, him yanking up my tee, me nearly ripping his in my rush to touch his skin. I flung his shirt aside, and ran my hands along his taut pecs, tracing those sexy floral tattoo designs. I was going to lick every single one.

When his hands found my nipples again, I shivered and moaned, crying out as he tugged and teased.

"Even better than I imagined," he confessed. "So fucking hot."

My stomach flipped and my pulse kicked up another hundred notches.

"That's you," I replied as my hands slid over his shoulders and down to his biceps. "I don't have the definition of a twenty-two-year-old."

"Don't even start," he stated and took one of my hands, pulling it down to cup his hard cock. "You do this to me,

Damien. You. I've been in this state since Chicago. You're the sexiest man I've ever had the pleasure to kiss, bar none."

Silas reached for my belt loop and tugged me close, his lips brushing mine.

"Lean back and let go," he whispered.

"What?"

Silas dropped to his knees in front of me.

"Silas, oh fuck, I—"

"This is all about you," he confessed, his hands reaching for my zipper. "I'm going to suck your cock until you scream so loudly; you won't be able to speak tomorrow."

"Fuck."

"Maybe later," he quipped with a wink.

He pushed my jeans and briefs down my hips, and I barely registered the cool night air as he leaned in, delving his face into my pubes and letting out a filthy moan, licking a heated path up my V-line. I was starting to understand the whole obsession about beards because when he rubbed his face against my hip, it set off a million fireworks on my skin, in my belly, hell all over my body.

"You smell so fucking good, Damien. And you taste even better," he whispered as his tongue teased my skin. "Fuck, you are one gorgeous man."

I flushed hot all over.

"Silas."

I lost all train of thought when he looked up at me with those soulful brown eyes. Instead of wanting to take control, I put my hands on the wood railing behind me and held on tight. Silas reached into his pocket and pulled out a packet of lube, ripped it open with his teeth, and poured it on his hand.

"I want to swallow your cum," he moaned.

My dick jerked hard in response.

"I've been tested recently and I'm negative," he continued and kissed my belly. "I assume you are too since you said you hadn't been with anyone in a while?"

How could he even make conversation at this point?

I stared down at him and nodded.

Silas let out a wicked grin and took hold of my cock in his slick, callused grip. Oh God, this was even better than my first experience with a guy. That had been hot too, but fast, because we worried someone might catch us. This time, however, Silas and I had *all* the time. My eyes rolled back in my head, and I gripped the railing like a lifeline. My erection was so painfully hard at this point, it would probably only take a couple of strokes before I unloaded.

And shit, he knew how to stroke me off, with firm, rough pulls that had me pumping my hips, needy for more. Judging by the smug look on Silas's face, he knew exactly what he was doing. He was younger than me, but far more experienced when it came to pleasuring a man.

"Take your hair down," I insisted.

Silas reached up with his free hand and pulled the elastic from his bun, the messy blond waves tumbling around his face. Without pause, I let go of the railing and reached for him, sliding my hands through his hair and groaning with delight at how silky it was. Stray tendrils teased my skin, making me shiver. When he locked eyes with me, I was completely and utterly seduced.

"I've been thinking about this every day and night since Chicago," Silas growled, tugging faster. "Jerking off to fantasies of you and me together. But fuck, Damien, reality is so much better."

He leaned forward and gave the head of my dick a teasing lick.

"So much better," he repeated. "Can't wait to taste your cum. I want you to give it all to me. Don't hold back."

"Fuck."

That was the only word I could say as I watched Silas take the head of my cock into his mouth, lips stretched wide, the warm, wet heat of his mouth making me shudder.

"Jesus, look at you," I moaned as his tongue teased my sensitive dick, the pleasure so intense that my head fell back.

All I could see around me were the explosions of brilliant stars in the sky. Or maybe I was dreaming. Either way, I was floating to another dimension. Who needed a bedroom? The best sex of my life was happening right here. There was something innately primal and thrilling about having sex outdoors. I'd had my share of adventures with past partners, but nothing felt like this.

I looked down again, mesmerized by the view as Silas swallowed my cock, inch by inch. His mouth was incredible and when he took me all the way down, deep throating my dick? I didn't think the pleasure could get any better, but I was wrong. So wrong.

"Don't stop," I moaned loudly, a savage pleading in my voice. "Please, please, don't stop."

Silas made a humming sound and the resulting vibration on my dick was so fiercely good that it had me hanging on to my climax by a thread. With one hand at the base of my cock, he began to bob his head, sucking me harder, faster, wrecking my control. I was going to come embarrassingly fast.

"Shit, I'm close," I whispered, my balls drawing up tight. "What… what are you doing to me?"

Provocative groans I didn't know I could make echoed loudly in the stillness of the summer air. And it wasn't only me. Instinct took over as I gripped Silas's hair tightly, pumping my hips, fucking his face. He reached frantically for his zipper with his free hand, and when he pulled out his dick, I realized he wasn't wearing anything beneath those tight denims. Shit, that was hot. All the while he was sucking me down, he jerked himself off with rapid strokes.

Oh God, Silas was going to come. Because of *me*.

And I was going to unload my cum in his throat.

My balls pulled up tight, my climax within reach. He

never let up, his hand and mouth moving in skillful tandem, like making me come was the only thing he wanted.

I was the only one he wanted.

That knowledge pushed me right over the edge.

"Oh God, I'm coming!" I shouted.

My orgasm erupted like a flash of wildfire, and I came hard, unloading in his mouth. Coming was always good, but this blowjob completely ruined me, stealing my breath and whatever brain cells I had left. I think I might have fallen were it not for the fact that I had the railing behind me for support. My knees were done for, and no, it didn't have anything to do with my old injury.

Sex with Silas was intense, carnal, hot as fucking hell.

He finally pulled off my dick and seeing my cum drip down his chin was too much for me to take. Another jolt of pleasure rolled through me, another spurt of cum leaked out of my cock.

"Damien," he moaned, running one hand over his mouth and beard, then lowering it to cup his dick, using my cum to stroke himself off.

I stared down at him, panting hard, barely able to speak.

"Come," I demanded, my voice hoarse. "Come all over me."

Silas jerked hard, his forearm rigid, as pulses of creamy cum shot from his dick. Seeing and smelling his release was more intense than I expected. My chest tightened as I gazed at his face. He didn't look away from me, and something more than lust flashed between us.

I was in so much trouble with this man. So much.

I didn't care. No, not that. As a player and a coach, I relied on my training, but more importantly, my instincts. Ignoring them led to no good. All I had to do was look at my relationship with Eloise. Somehow, I knew deep down that she loved my image more than me, but I never wanted to admit it out loud. In the end, I didn't have to. Her leaving told me everything.

My gut told me that Silas was different.

Whatever this was between us, it was right. And he could be trusted.

Then again, this was sex, not a relationship. I was getting ahead of myself.

Funny though, nothing about me and Silas felt casual. I was long past the days of meaningless hookups. The yearning for more, for a meaningful connection both in and out of the bedroom, hit me like I'd been cross-checked. It should've been warning enough to put a stop to this. But for once, I wanted to be selfish, to enjoy what I had and not question it.

Like me, Silas was breathing hard, his skin glistening with sweat. When he offered me a naughty grin, I was helpless to return it.

"I think I'll take that drink now," he mused.

"You and me both."

CHAPTER 21
SILAS

Damien offered me his hand.

It was a simple gesture, no big deal, and yet it was a huge shift for me.

Normally, I'd be up off my knees and heading for the door by now—if there was a door. I didn't need anyone's hand to help me get up. Touching after sex was not my thing. Once I came, I was out of there. I always got off on pleasuring my partner, but that's all it was. Once the orgasms were done, I didn't care to stick around. Not for any more touching and certainly not to talk. Fuck no.

But with Damien, I didn't want to leave.

You are so screwed and I'm not talking about sex.

I wanted to take his hand. So, I did.

He helped me stand up and it was a good thing since my legs were shaky. In fact, I was trembling all over. Eye to eye, I was waiting for him to suddenly change his mind. To tell me he was done.

Go. Get lost.

It was a mistake.

It never happened.

Instead of words filled with regret, he leaned in to kiss me. But before he could make contact, I put my hand on his chest.

"Are you sure you want to do that?" I asked. "I just had your cum in my mouth."

Damien cupped my jaw, his grip possessive, as he brushed his lips against mine. "I know. And yes, I definitely want to kiss you."

He silenced any further comment by taking my lips again. This time, the kiss was slow and sexy, like we had all the time in the world. Like his mouth was made for mine.

"I need to clean up."

"The bathroom's past the kitchen, first door on the left," he offered.

"How about you join me?" I replied, wanting to see the full Damien Banning in all his naked glory.

"I… think I need a minute, or more like twenty, to recover." He offered with a tentative smile, a dimple in his left cheek popping out. "This thirty-year-old doesn't have your stamina."

"I didn't mean for that," I started to backtrack. "You're right, I'll—"

Damien, whose hand was still in mine, ignored my rambling and pulled me into the house.

"Look, maybe it's best if I go," I muttered.

"Is that what you want?" He paused and stared at me, his eyes filled with a vulnerability that hit me right in the chest. "To leave?"

"No," I replied and kissed him, reassuring him in the only way I could. I wanted to kiss him again and I wasn't sure I'd be able to stop. And I sure as fuck wanted to stay. "But I want you to be comfortable."

He gave me a knowing smirk and kissed me soundly.

"Hurry up and get in my shower."

Bossy Damien was back, and I couldn't help but smile.

We wandered through the house, down the hallway, and

into a large bathroom with a walk-in shower. His thumb rubbed against mine and that strange fluttery feeling in my stomach took flight.

Holy fuck, I sucked off my coach.

It was the hottest sex of my life, but maybe it was better if I left. Things between us would probably get awkward now that the sex was done.

So, why wasn't I rushing for the door? Why was so I desperate to keep touching him?

Damien let go of my hand, and surprisingly, I wanted to protest. Instead, I leaned against the counter and watched as he turned on the shower, then shoved his jeans and briefs down his legs and stepped out of them. He had more chest hair than I did, and the dark treasure trail that led directly to his cock had my mouth watering again. I liked the fact that he didn't shave or wax. And who cared if he was thirty years old? He was fit as fuck and gorgeous. All over. A typical hockey boy with broad shoulders, defined pecs, and solid thighs that were the stuff of my dirtiest fantasies.

My gaze roamed lower, to his dick and balls, and Christ, no wonder my throat was sore. His cock was a monster, even when it wasn't fully erect. Unlike me, he didn't have a single tattoo on his rangy body, but I did notice the large scars on his right knee. The scars from his injury and operations. I couldn't even imagine. Seeing them and knowing what had happened to his hockey career, it hit me like a punch to the gut.

"Silas, are you okay?" he asked.

"Great," I croaked and cleared my throat, meeting his gaze. "I'm taking a moment to appreciate the incredible man before me."

"I think that's my line."

I shook my head and pushed my jeans down, mirroring his movements.

"Commando?" he raised one dark eyebrow.

"Of course." I smirked and stepped closer until our hips collided, nothing but hot, naked skin between us.

I felt a tremor run through his body. Or was that me?

It wasn't long before my cock was half-hard again.

"You were talking at practice about manifesting what we want," I whispered, giving him a slow, sexy kiss. "Mission accomplished."

"But it seems like you being naked under those jeans is more about what I want than what you want," he replied with a wicked grin.

And that right there is why I was getting in deep with Damien. His smile kickstarted my heart something fierce, but it was everything else that had me craving more. His ability to meet my sarcasm with his own, his passion for hockey, his drive to be the best. Did he realize how fucking amazing he was? If not, it was going to be my mission to show him.

"I'd say we're both winners."

I punctuated that comment with another kiss, this one longer, deeper, until we were so caught up in each other that we forgot about the shower. Damien hugged me tightly to him while I slid my hands up to grip his biceps, loving the fact that he was as consumed as I was by this heady chemistry between us. He walked me back, manhandling me until my ass hit the counter. Sliding one knee between mine, he ate at my mouth, and I moaned, wrapping one leg around his hip.

When we finally came up for air, he rested his forehead against mine, his breath hot against my lips.

"Kissing you is—" Damien paused and playfully nipped my mouth. "Fucking addictive."

"Damien."

I didn't even care if we did anything else tonight. Kissing him was more satisfying than any sexual act I'd experienced with any other partner. And I'd done plenty of fucking.

"Yes?"

"Let's take that shower before you run out of hot water," I suggested.

Damien nodded, and with one hand possessively squeezing my waist, he guided me into the shower. He gave my shoulder a teasing kiss as the steam swirled around us. I stood under the water first, letting it soak my hair and washing away the remaining cum off my face. He joined me under the spray, and the sight of his naked body, wet and all mine, had me rocking another hard-on that wouldn't quit.

While Damien turned and reached for the shampoo, I reached for him, sliding up behind him and notching my cock between his tight ass cheeks. He let out a filthy moan and dropped the bottle, gripping my forearms with a strength that was just shy of painful. The tight clench told me he was as gone as I was.

"How does this feel?" I whispered, canting my hips and rubbing my dick against his ass while my mouth trailed wet kisses over his shoulder.

"Do you need to ask?" he replied.

He took my right hand and placed it around his cock. My sexy hockey coach was getting hard again. And it was all for me.

"You're not freaking out yet," I murmured.

"You're not the first man I've ever touched," he confessed. "There was a player I roomed with, back when I was in college—"

The thought of anyone—man or woman—touching Damien like this had me holding him tighter. I didn't want to hear about his past. No fucking way. I was the one with him now. Me. Not that I could even express that in words at this point. I'd never had a desire to claim a guy I'd fucked around with, but Damien? It was all too natural.

Instead of telling him how I was feeling, I bit down on the skin of his neck, sucking hard, marking what was mine, as his groans echoed around me.

"He and I... we would... jerk each other off," he panted, writhing in my arms. "One time, we had a threesome with a woman."

"I don't want to hear about it," I snarled, jealousy and passion fighting for dominance.

I turned him around until his back hit the tiled wall and ravaged his mouth in a punishing kiss. When I finally let him up for air, his bright blues were molten.

"You asked. I'm trying to explain."

"I get it," I whispered. "You're not completely new to sex with a guy. But I don't want to hear the details. Not about him, and not about anyone, including your wife."

"Ex-wife," Damien clarified and raised one eyebrow. "And the same goes."

"I've only had casual sex. It didn't mean anything but a release."

"And this? Am I the same?"

I shook my head. Damien didn't look convinced.

"Do you get what's going on here with you and me? I wouldn't risk my career for a quick fuck. This is more than that. At least, it is to me," he pronounced boldly, his gaze locked on mine. "If you don't feel the same, that's fine. Done is done. We can walk away like nothing happened."

No fucking way.

"I can't do that," I replied and kissed him again. "I'm not walking away. Not that I know what I'm doing when it comes to a relationship, but that's what this is, right? I don't want to be with anyone else. This, us, it isn't casual, Damien. I need you to know that."

He finally relaxed against me.

"We gotta be careful, though," he admitted. "If anyone finds out I'm having sex with one of my players, there goes my entire career."

"We agreed this is more than sex, but I know what you

mean. It's better for everyone if we keep this private. For now."

Damien swiped an agitated hand through his wet hair.

"Why does everything have to be so fucking difficult? After years of being single, I finally find someone I connect with, but I have to hide like I've got a dirty secret."

"It's *our* secret." I leaned in and kissed him. "And dirty can be fun."

"Si, I'm serious."

"I know, baby, but let's take it one day at a time, all right? We're both under a shitload of pressure."

"Baby?"

"Too much?" I asked.

I wasn't a fan of nicknames, but like everything with this man, I was breaking all my rules.

"No," he stated and pulled me into his arms. "I like it."

"Well, enjoy it because that's about as romantic as I get."

"Romance, eh?"

Instead of replying to that, I turned around and placed my hands on the wall.

"Scrub me down, baby."

"Are you always going to be this demanding?" Damien quipped and swatted my ass.

I gave him a leering look over my shoulder.

"Oh, Coach, you haven't seen anything yet."

CHAPTER 22
DAMIEN

After we showered, Silas wanted to relax in bed but unfortunately his stomach had other ideas. And I could only ignore the loud growling for so long. Typical hockey player; food always came first.

"Sorry," he muttered, his cheeks unusually pink.

"I guess I better feed the beast."

He retaliated by pinching my ass and kissing me senseless.

When he finally let me go, I rummaged through my closet and threw him a pair of my basketball shorts and a T-shirt. He only took the shorts. Not that I was complaining. Having him wander around my home half-naked was a memorable sight.

We headed for the kitchen, hand in hand, like we did this every night. I grabbed a pepperoni pizza from the freezer and popped it in the oven. While that was cooking, I located a bag of tortilla chips and a container of guac, which Silas promptly finished in record time. Okay, I was starving too, and I did my share of eating. We kissed and flirted in between bites of salty chips and when the pizza was ready, I cut one slice for myself and gave him the rest. Silas insisted we split it in half, but I refused. He needed the calories more than I did.

Afterwards, I snagged a couple of beers, and we made our way out to sit on the deck. Silas couldn't have more than one beer, since he had to drive home later. Not that I wanted him to leave tonight. We'd only started seeing each other and I was ready for an overnight. If that didn't tell me how far gone I was for him, nothing would.

"Do you like living in Vermont?" he asked me as we sat in front of the firepit, his fingers interlocking tightly with mine.

The only time we'd let go of each other was to get changed.

Holding Silas's hand felt heady, incredible. Even with Eloise, holding hands was something I could take or leave. She often complained that I wasn't attentive enough as a lover. Not in bed, not out of it. I didn't touch her enough; I was always lacking in affection. Maybe she was right.

Or maybe it wasn't me, but me with her.

"I do. Even when I move on from this job, I think I'd like to keep a home here. A vacation escape."

He nodded. "You want to coach pro, right?"

I didn't see any sense in holding back.

"I do. That's my dream. Don't get me wrong, I've loved every minute of coaching at Sutton, and I've learned a lot. But I miss the excitement of the professional league. To put it bluntly, nothing compares."

Silas gave me an eager smile. "Can you tell me about it? The games, the traveling, the media. Did you love it? Do you miss it?"

"I loved most of it. When things were good, they were very good. Playing with guys at that level and for huge crowds gave me a kind of high that's difficult to explain. It's very addictive. A total rush." I paused, thinking about my past. "The traveling wasn't my favorite, to be honest. I liked visiting cool cities, but by the end of the season, all you want to do is stay in the same bed for a month. Plus, I'm a light sleeper and depending on who you room with, it can be fine or a total nightmare."

"No kidding. Ethan snores like a chainsaw. Even with headphones, it's freaking loud."

"Yeah, I don't miss that. Or the media attention. They love it when you're doing great, but they also pounce on you when things get rough. You gotta develop a thick skin and have a dedicated agent who has your back. And yes, sometimes I miss it fiercely. Being on that ice, the rush, the freedom. When my accident happened, well, I had to start everything over, rebuild from scratch." I sighed and met his gaze. "Sorry, that sounds dramatic."

"It's not. I can't even imagine."

I gripped his hand tighter.

"It wasn't the shock of 'one day I was on the ice and the next day I was in the hospital.' Like I said, it was losing the day-to-day routine with my teammates and what I thought my life would be. It's taken me a while to come to terms with the fact that any career in hockey isn't linear or stable. Not hockey, not anything. Life is full of unexpected surprises, and you have to be prepared to pivot. Looking back, I wish I'd had the ability to play longer, but inevitably, a player's career is limited. At least I've found something that keeps me active in the sport I love."

"And I, for one, am so grateful that you're here. Your passion for the game is what resonates with every player on our team." Silas squeezed my hand. "You're the best coach I've ever had."

"Stop."

"It's true, Damien. I told you before, no one has ever pushed me harder or made me want to prove myself more."

Guilt made my stomach clench hard.

"I wasn't completely convinced you belonged with the

Cougars at first," I admitted. "It wasn't personal. I make calls based on what I see and my experience."

"I know that. I was coming back after a year off, and yeah, I was pissed that you didn't have faith in me, but you didn't know me. I had to earn your trust over time, and vice versa." He paused. "Although, sometimes it still feels like you're unsure about my potential."

One thing I admired about Silas, he didn't evade the tough conversations.

"It's not that. You're a great defenseman, and you're getting better with every game. But you're also dealing with a lot of family responsibility. And you're twenty-two. The odds of you being drafted at this age, or later, aren't great. I don't want to see you make the same mistake I did, putting all your hopes in making it pro. What if it doesn't happen? What then?"

"I know all that, Damien," Silas replied and nudged my shoulder with his. "I do. And your worry is appreciated but not required. I've already told you that no one and nothing will stop me from trying."

If Silas did make it, and I made it back to coaching in the league, where would that leave us? Jesus, I was getting way ahead of myself. But the fact that I was thinking about a future with him made me pause. What would be the point in starting something that already had a deadline? Then again, I knew that life was short, and you had to grab your happiness wherever you could find it. No one was promised tomorrow.

"How are we going to do this?" I whispered.

"What?"

"We have to step back into that rink for training and this —" I paused and pointed between us with my free hand. "This interplay is not happening when we return to campus. We go back to our strict roles; I'm the uptight coach and you're the smart-mouthed player."

"So, nothing's changed. You're still gonna ride my ass

hard," he added with a smirk. "Only, in addition to doing it on the ice, you get to do it naked. And maybe I can return the favor."

I let out another laugh. God, I was doing a lot of that around him.

"Fuck me, I'm in so much trouble," I replied and took a long pull of beer to cool myself off.

"That is, if you're interested in riding my ass. Or having me ride yours. Is anal something you want to explore?"

I choked on my beer and nearly showered the deck.

Silas lifted my hand and kissed the knuckles. "Too blunt?"

"No." I cleared my throat and stared at him. "I like your forthright attitude. It's honest and that's important to me. But I don't know how we went from a discussion about hockey practice to—"

"Anal."

"Yes."

My face was on fire. Silas leaned over to kiss me. This man incinerated my normally icy control and turned it into dust. I couldn't help but smile against his lips.

"That was quite the change in topic."

"Not really. I can't help but think of sex anytime I'm near my smoking hot hockey coach," Silas quipped and waggled his eyebrows.

"Seriously, are you going to be able to concentrate on the ice?" I asked. "Am I?"

"We can compartmentalize. We're professionals."

"I'm a professional," I corrected. "You're a student."

Goddamn it, Banning, you're fucking your student.

"I'm the oldest one on the team, and I've got more maturity than the rest of the guys combined."

"True." I chuckled at that comment.

"I have faith in us," he stated.

Something about the serious tone in his voice had a shiver racing through my body. Ignoring my deeper emotions, I gave him a sceptical look, and a hint of my usual glare. He kept grinning at me.

"Don't give me that Banning glare around the guys, Damien. It gets my dick hard."

"Fuck."

"Yes, back to sex, I prefer to top, but I'm vers," Silas admitted. "I've only bottomed a few times. It takes trust. But I'd like to explore that with you. If that's something you want."

"I've never bottomed. I've had anal but—" I paused.

"But you topped? With that guy, in that threesome?" he bit out, his eyes intense.

His jealousy, because that's exactly the reaction Silas was giving off, was hot as hell.

"I did."

Looking back, that night was exciting and wild, and yet the memory of it now didn't stir anything inside me.

Silas inhaled sharply. "All joking aside, I don't need anal to be satisfied. A lot of times I'm happy with handjobs or blowjobs or frotting. It's all good."

I nodded, relieved.

"Then we'll see what happens. I'd like to… try." I licked my lips. "But I don't want to make promises I can't keep. Or disappoint you."

Silas claimed my lips and silenced any further comment.

"You could never do that," he whispered.

"We've only known each other as coach vs player, not lovers. How do you know?"

"I just do," he insisted and punctuated the remark with another heated kiss. "I know the man that you are, Damien. Once you're committed to something, like the team, you're all in. I hear it in your voice, I witness it in your actions, and I see it in your eyes. I'm the same."

It was scary how well he knew me already. And that we were alike in so many ways. Suddenly, I was vulnerable like I hadn't been in years. That knowledge should've sent me running, fast and far. Instead, I wanted to slide onto his lap and kiss him breathless, right here under the stars.

"Do that," he demanded.

"What?"

He tugged my hand. "Get on my lap and kiss me."

Holy shit, I'd said that out loud?

Without pause, I got up and straddled his waist, and Silas, in turn, gripped my ass in his hands and pulled me in as close as we could get. I wrapped my arms around his neck and leaned in to take possession of his mouth. One steamy kiss led to another, and another, until our moans filled the quiet night air.

Staring down into his eyes, the puzzle that was my personal life, the one I'd been trying to figure out for years, finally clicked into place.

"So, it turns out I'm bisexual," I whispered. "Wow, I think that's the first time I've ever claimed that out loud."

He smiled and clutched me tighter.

"Welcome to the Sutton U Queer Club, baby."

CHAPTER 23

SILAS

I wanted to stay with Damien, but it was past eleven, and I had to get home.

I texted Jo to let him know I was on my way back, then used the bathroom and got dressed, and Damien met me in his foyer.

Truthfully, I'd trade sleep for sex any day, but Damien insisted I get a move on because we had training tomorrow and I needed to be well-rested. The man was a total hard-ass, but I had no complaints. The fact that he was more concerned with my training than his sex drive was yet another reminder of why I found him irresistible.

While he came off as brusque and demanding, which he was, he also cared. A lot.

We spent nearly ten minutes on one goodbye kiss, stopping only so I could grab my backpack. I leaned in again for one more taste, but Damien put a hand to my chest.

"You kiss me like that again and you'll never leave," he teased.

"And your point is?"

Damien stepped back and shook his head.

"Go home. Get some sleep and be on time tomorrow," he warned me. "Or else."

"Or else what?" I bit my lower lip and chuckled when I saw the heat in his eyes. It only made leaving that much harder. "Ooh, what kind of punishment do I get? Does it involve edging?"

"Go on, get," he ordered and stepped back, leaning against the doorframe, crossing his arms, clad in nothing but those sexy shorts.

His raven hair was mussed, his eyes were bright, and the smile on his face had me struggling to move.

"What are you doing Saturday?" I asked.

"Hopefully spending it with you," he returned.

"How about I come here and cook dinner for you? Nothing fancy, burgers on the grill. Jo's staying at his friend River's for the weekend. I don't have to pick him up until noon on Sunday."

Damien reached for me, slipping one finger in the beltloop of my jeans and tugging me closer. "Stay overnight?"

I smiled and nodded. "It's a date."

"Text me when you get home."

Then Damien swatted my ass and let me go. I finally stepped out of his house and got in my truck. As I drove away, I stared at him in my rearview mirror. He was standing in the doorway, his arms crossed, that intense look on his face. I was tempted to hit the brakes. No, more than that; I was tempted to turn the truck around but my rational brain said no.

The drive back home took no time at all, and I thought about how funny it was that Damien lived so close all this time and I never knew. The porch light was on and when I entered the house, I checked on Jo, who was already in his room, fast asleep.

I wandered into the kitchen, ate a protein bar, downed a huge glass of water, and then got my breakfast prepped for tomorrow. Once I checked the alarm on my phone—twice—I padded down the hallway to my bedroom, plugged in my phone, and slipped into the bathroom to wash up.

When I finally hit the sheets, I was tired but not sleepy. It was like the night before a big game when nerves and excitement battled it out. Only, I wasn't obsessed with hockey, but with Damien.

I grabbed my phone and sent a quick text.

Silas: Home safe. I had a great time tonight.

Damien: Me too. Now go to bed.

Silas: Yes, Coach.

Damien: Don't start...

Silas: Next time we're naked, I want you to wear that whistle around your neck LOL.

Damien: Kinky.

Silas: Fucking right.

Damien: Stop flirting. We've got a full day ahead. I expect to see your best.

Silas: You'll get that and more. And take your own advice and stop teasing me.

Damien: Me? I didn't do anything.

Silas: You made it very difficult for me to leave tonight.

Damien: You made it difficult for me to let go.

My phone buzzed again, but this time it wasn't a text, but a picture. Damien was clearly sitting on the deck again, but all I could see were his long legs. The focus of the image was the lake, or, rather, the shimmering reflection of the moon on the water.

Silas: Gorgeous. And no, I'm not talking about the lake.

My cock chubbed up thinking about Damien wrapping those stunning legs of his around my waist. Soon. Very, very soon.

Despite his warning, I reached for the tube of lube I kept stashed under my pillow and began to stroke myself off.

Damien: Saturday feels like a long time away. I'm not going to wake up tomorrow and find out this was all a fevered dream, am I?

I snapped a pic of my hand wrapped around my dick and typed out a reply.

Silas: Not a dream, baby.

Damien: Stop.

Silas: What???

Damien: I'm ordering you not to come. You're going to save that for me. For Saturday.

Silas: Fuck, Damien.

Damien: Yes, soon. Stop touching yourself.

I did as I was told and removed my hand from my dick, rolling over onto my stomach. Shoving my face into the pillow, I let out a groan of frustration.

Silas: You being all bossy is such a fucking turn on. I stopped. Satisfied?

Damien: Not hardly. But think of how good it will be when we finally get our hands on each other again.

Silas: Four days feels like forever.

Damien: Go to sleep. I'll see you at eight.

Silas: I'll be there at seven.

———

When my alarm buzzed at six-thirty, I all but bolted out of bed. I didn't fall asleep until well past midnight, but who needed eight hours? I was so hyped from being horny and *not* rubbing one out that I could probably skate for two days straight. And who knew that Damien Banning was such a freaking tease? I had all kinds of dirty plans to get back at him on the weekend. Oh yeah, I was going to edge him until he lost his goddamn mind.

He thought he could play this game, but he'd met his match.

I shoveled in my breakfast—overnight oats with protein powder and blueberries, drank one cup of coffee and put another in a to-go cup.

When I was ready to leave, Jo stalked into the kitchen. He looked more rested today.

"Hey, you're looking better."

"I'm feeling okay," he muttered. "You, on the other hand, look like you hardly slept."

"Yeah, late night." I coughed into my fist. "Are you working today?"

"Noon to six. River's picking me up at eleven. Also, I've got a follow-up with my doctor on Thursday to talk about my medication."

"What time?"

"Nine."

"I'll take you before I go to work."

I plucked my phone out of my pocket and added the appointment to my calendar with a reminder. Then I texted Hen to make sure she was okay if I came in to work an hour late. I promised to make up the time next week.

"Thanks." Jo yawned and ran a hand through his curls. "So, what did you do last night?"

Man, where would I even start?

"I was, you know, out."

"Hot date?" he quipped.

"You know I don't do that."

"Maybe you will someday."

I thought about Damien. God, I couldn't stop thinking about him.

"Maybe."

"Are we going to stop by and see Dad on Sunday?"

"Of course."

My phone pinged with a reminder.

"You better get going. You don't want to be late for camp. Again."

"No, I don't." I chuckled. "Damien made it very clear that I was to be on time or else."

"You seem different," Jo commented and gave me a curious look. "Happier."

"I'm playing hockey today, of course I'm happy."

"That's not it," Jo replied.

I rolled my eyes, and he waved me off.

"Don't worry about it. You'll tell me when you're ready."

"There's nothing to tell, Jo."

I couldn't. Even if I wanted to tell him, I couldn't. Damien and I had too much at stake.

"Don't work too hard," I added as I walked towards the front door. "I'll be back around five, so I'll cook dinner."

"See ya."

I left the house and hopped in my truck. It was another sunny, hot day. Taking full advantage, I lowered all the windows and enjoyed the warm breeze washing over my skin. It was a nice change from six months of ice and snow. Not that I'd be basking in the warmth or the sunshine for long since I was heading for a cold, badly lit rink.

Summer? Beaches? That was for everyone *but* hockey players.

Besides, I'd take an icy rink any day, every day, over anything else.

The drive took a bit longer than usual since there was a decent amount of traffic in town. Tourists flocked to Vermont for the summer camping season and every other vehicle had kayaks and bikes on their racks.

Fifteen minutes later, I parked, unloaded, and walked into the rink. It was after seven, which was perfect. I wanted to be the first one there so I could get dressed, get on the ice, and get my head in the right space. More than anything, I needed to feign indifference when faced with Damien again.

I thought about the way I reacted every time I was near him. Or heard his voice. The way my heart pounded, and my stomach dropped out. Shit. Maybe I ought to look up an acting class, because hiding my intentions was going to take skill.

The locker room was freezing, no surprise, and quiet, with none of the usual chatter to greet me. I quickly changed, slid my pads on, my jersey, and helmet, and tied up my skates. By the time I grabbed my stick and headed for the ice, I was calm, centered. The ice was freshly flooded, perfectly smooth, reminding of the lake last night. And me and Damien, sitting under the stars.

No. Head in the game, remember?

I did a few practice laps to clear my mind, get my muscles heated up, and then I started my stretches. Halfway through my warmup, and I knew I wasn't alone anymore.

But it wasn't Damien.

"Extra early, eh?" Finn quipped as he joined me on the ice. "Show off."

"Hardly. I'm eager to get the day going. I'm doing what you suggest, trying to get in the right mindset."

I was trying *not* to think about Damien…

"You mean, you don't want to get on Coach's bad side?"

I chuckled. "That too."

Not that Damien had one. Fuck, everything about him was appealing to me. I had it bad. So bad.

"You're early yourself," I retorted.

"I guess we're all a bit eager." Finn skated past me and stopped short. "You look different today."

Not him too.

"Wait." Finn nudged my arm. "Holy shit! Si, what's that on your face? Are you… are you actually smiling?"

"Fuck off," I grumbled.

"Ah, I get it. I know what this relaxed vibe is all about. You got laid last night."

"No comment."

"Come on. I'm your friend, you gotta spill the deets. Who was the guy?"

"It was nothing. A casual one and done. The way it always is."

Lies, lies, and more lies.

"Well, it must've been good because you, my friend, are glowing."

"As if," I scoffed and shook my head.

"Someone's got a crush," Finn said teasingly.

"No."

"Who's got a crush?" a voice interrupted from behind me.

Fucking Ethan. How'd he get the drop on me like that? So much for getting my head in the game.

"No one," I bit out.

"It's Silas," Finn explained. "Look at him."

Ethan gave me a once over and then glanced at Finn.

"You're right, Finntastic. So, who's the guy, Rufus? Give us the dirty deets. *All* of them."

"You two are so freaking nosy. There is no guy and there will be no deets," I insisted. "Now, can we get back to our warmup?"

I sighed and pushed off, turning around to find Damien standing at the far end of the ice, his tablet in hand, looking entirely too hot for a man in sweats at this hour of the day. Before, I was always able to push my naughty thoughts about my hot coach aside and move on with my practice. Now? All I wanted to do was skate towards him, yank him into my arms, and kiss him senseless.

I got his trademark warning glare, which only made my pulse beat faster.

Determined not to fuck up in front of Damien, or, worse, have my teammates figure out what was up between us, I skated to the other end of the ice to get my focus back. It didn't matter. I felt his gaze tracking me, and I shivered in anticipation.

This was going to be the longest day of practice in the history of ever.

CHAPTER 24

DAMIEN

No one knew anything, right? They couldn't tell?

Normally, I walked into the rink, confident and calm, with a plan and a purpose. Today, however, I was like a nervous rookie with an itchy jock, pacing and fretting. When I spotted Silas on the ice, it took every measure of discipline I had to ignore him.

And I was successful.

For a good five minutes.

Until I overheard Ethan's comment about a crush, and I nearly choked on my coffee.

A crush? Why did that word make me run hot all over?

Instead of letting my dick rule my brain, I got out my tablet and got to work. In fact, I'd spent half the sleepless night preparing for today. I added to an already full schedule to ensure there would hardly be any time for me to break with the guys. And I was going to have lunch in my office this time, by myself, and then join them for our strategy session later. A little bit of distance was required, especially when a certain blond defenseman was within reach, distracting me like nothing and no one else.

I managed to keep myself in line throughout the morning,

but it wasn't easy. Especially when Silas made a stunning pass that was worth praising. I worried that I was somehow giving myself away. It felt like a light had switched on inside me and now that I was seeing Silas, and me with him, I couldn't dim anything. I watched him, intently, and despite his acting cool, I noticed he did the same.

When I paused the game they were playing to offer advice, Silas, of course, gave me attitude. I wanted to silence his smart replies in a way that wasn't fit for this rink or my job. And I had to keep reminding myself that he was my student, one of my players. That should've been warning enough to put an end to this insanity, but the truth was, it felt too damn good to stop.

It didn't matter that I appeared unaffected on the outside, on the inside I was a fucking mess. My body was hyperaware of Silas in a way I hadn't been with previous lovers. Not even Eloise. What that meant, I didn't even want to think about.

I'd skated over so many professional lines that I had no idea where I was going.

After lunch, I met up with the guys in the lounge for our strategy session and two hours later, we headed for the ice again. By the time four o'clock rolled around, everyone was played out. Me included. I called an end to the day and headed back to my office to take a breather and check my messages. And to get advice. I picked up my phone and texted the only person I knew I could count on, the one who would never reveal my secret.

> Damien: I'm in trouble here. BIG.

> Selwin: What's going on?

> Damien: I crossed the student-teacher line.

> Selwin: You mean you and Silas??

Damien: He came to my house last night. We kissed and then he… well, let's just say that I can confirm I'm bi and not curious. It was incredible.

Selwin: First of all, congrats on your bi awakening. Or reawakening. Second, tell me EVERYTHING.

Damien: This is serious, Sel. I shouldn't be proud of the fact that I did this. I could lose my job if word gets out.

Selwin: How's anyone going to know? Silas won't tell, will he?

Damien: No.

Selwin: And? You both got what you wanted. He's a consenting adult.

Damien: I'm his coach. That puts me in a position of power, so I think I'm in the wrong here. But you know what's worse? It wasn't a one-time thing. I'm seeing him Saturday. I can't help myself.

Selwin: Whoa, wait. You two are, like, dating? Ugh, bud, I don't have any advice for that.

Damien: Are you kidding me? You're the one who encouraged me to do this.

Selwin: Oops?

Damien: When you're here in three weeks, I'm going to make you run drills until you pass out.

Selwin: My agent won't like that LOL. But, in all seriousness, this sounds like more than sex. You like him. Silas likes you, too?

Like wasn't a strong enough word for how I was feeling.

> Damien: I've never felt like this about anyone. Not even my ex. I'm throwing away the rulebook without thinking twice. Me.

> Selwin: Be discreet and let this thing run its course. As long as you're both mature about it, who are you hurting?

> Damien: No one. I guess.

I put my phone down, but I didn't have any more clarity about the situation I was in. This was more than one and done, and more than complicated. Somehow, someway, my stupid heart was involved. I swore the damn thing froze when Eloise left, and I thought for sure it would never thaw again. But lo and behold, it was beating again. All it took was one ruthless defenseman…

Shaking off my unease, I forced myself to work on administrative tasks. With two professional hockey players visiting our training camp this summer came a mountain of related paperwork, including contracts and NDAs.

By five, I was ready to pack up and head for home when there was a sudden knock at my door. Was it Silas? Not that I was expecting him. Clearly, he was respecting our boundaries, and I was grateful. Grateful and frustrated. Then I reminded myself that Saturday, we'd have the night to ourselves. We could talk, and maybe I'd finally figure out what the hell I was doing.

"Come in!" I yelled out and closed my laptop.

When the door open, it wasn't Silas standing on the other side, and I couldn't help but feel totally disappointed.

Jesus, listen to yourself.

Finn stepped into my office and paced back and forth in front of my desk, shoving his hands in his pockets. Something was obviously troubling him.

"Hey, Finn, what's up?" I asked.

"Um, I just got a phone call from my folks. I'm going to have to skip camp on Friday and fly back home to Nebraska," Finn replied.

"What's going on?"

"So, my mom's having surgery." Finn shook his head, his face pale. "It's kind of… unexpected. They found a lump in her neck."

Oh shit.

"Family and health always come first," I replied. "You're only missing one day."

"They don't want me to fly home at all and miss any of my hockey training. But I want to be there."

"Of course. And if you need to skip next week, let me know. We can work something out. You can make up the days when you get back."

"Thanks, Coach." Finn exhaled, looking a little calmer. "I appreciate it."

"Of course. Have a safe trip home. Let me know what happens and when you're returning, all right?"

"Will do."

Finn quietly left, and I sat back in my chair. Fuck, I hope to God his mom didn't have cancer. My dad passed from leukemia when he was fifty-one, going from diagnosis to terminal in only eight months. I'd been twenty-six at the time, rebuilding my life as a new college coach in Washington, when he died. I was starting to get back up on my feet when grief knocked me right back down again. Only, his loss was worse than any physical pain I'd endured.

I was so caught up in my memories of the past that I didn't even hear the knock on my door. Or the door opening again.

"Hey."

Silas suddenly appeared before me, his anxious expression revealing that he too had heard Finn's news.

"I talked to Finn," Silas stated and closed the door behind him. "Can I sit down for a sec?"

"Of course."

Silas sat in the chair across from me, and I noticed that his hands were shaking. Instead of staying where I was, I got up and rounded the desk, taking the chair beside him.

"You all right?" I asked as I drew close, our knees brushing.

"No. Finn's news brought back memories of my mom," Silas admitted. "She went so fast. She had inflammatory breast cancer that was misdiagnosed. Within a matter of months, she was gone."

"I'm so sorry."

"I feel for him, Damien. If his mom has cancer—"

"I know," I whispered. "I lost my father to leukemia when I was twenty-six. It was horrendous to watch him go through that battle. And it went downhill fast. Trust me, I know."

"I'm sorry, too."

"All we can do is hope for the best when it comes to Finn's mom," I added. "And we'll support him whatever the outcome."

Silas nodded and reached for me, cupping my face. I didn't have the strength or the heart to pull away. Shivers wracked my body, my breath quickening.

"I've been wanting to do this all day," he admitted, his callused thumb tracing my lips.

Was I worried someone would come barging into my office?

"Everyone else is gone," Silas offered, as if reading my thoughts.

I turned my face into his palm and kissed it. He inhaled sharply and the flare of heat in his eyes was unmistakable.

"It took every molecule of control I have to stay professional out there," I confessed. "And I don't know if I pulled it off."

"I think we both deserve a trophy for our performance today. No one suspects a thing."

"That being said, Saturday can't come fast enough."

By way of agreeing, Silas pulled me close and took my lips in a scorching kiss, his tongue seeking mine, sucking on it, teasing me until I forgot where I was and why this was a bad idea. But I couldn't stop. Kissing him was now my complete obsession.

"Let's not wait another sixteen hours to do that," he whispered against my lips.

"It's been seventeen, but who's counting?" I replied with a grin. "Still, we need to be careful on campus. There's always the risk that someone could catch us. Even in the quiet of summer."

Silas nodded and leaned back, licking his lips. "Thank you."

"For what?"

"For listening. For talking. And most of all, for that sexy kiss."

"I should be thanking you."

"There's always Saturday."

He gave me a knowing grin, and I was about to say fuck it and reach for him, when there was a third knock on my door.

"What was I saying?"

I shot up and quickly rounded the desk to sit back in my chair. Silas, however, didn't move or look concerned in any way. I motioned for him to get going but he sat there and shrugged. There was another knock, louder, and then I heard my friend's voice on the other side of the door.

"Damien, it's Dave."

Dave? What was he doing here? I thought he was on vacation.

"Come on in," I called out.

I licked my lips, and I could taste Silas. Holy fucking hell. Were my lips swollen? Were Silas's?

"Oh, hey," Dave said as he stepped inside. "Didn't realize you were talking to a student. I can come back later—"

I felt a flush of heat creep up my cheeks and hoped like hell no one would notice.

"It's fine, I was leaving," Silas replied and stood up. Before he left, he turned to me. "Thanks again, Coach. I appreciate the… extra time you give me."

"No problem," I offered, my voice hoarse. "My door is always open."

And my lips were already anticipating the next time.

With a final nod, Silas was gone. I turned to Dave.

"What's up?" I asked, surprised at how composed I sounded.

Like I didn't have my tongue down my player's throat thirty seconds ago.

"I wanted to talk to you about Selwin's visit," Dave replied. "Him and… shit, who's the other player coming?"

"Aleksi Halko from Tampa. Do you mind if we walk and talk?" I suggested. "It's been a long day, and I was about to head home."

"Of course."

I closed my laptop and stuffed it in my backpack, tidied up my desk, and grabbed my keys.

After locking up the office, Dave and I walked down the narrow hallway to the exit.

"I thought you were supposed to be on vacation."

"I am, technically, but you know how it is." Dave sighed. "I never shut down. And Nora is keen on making sure we get as much PR from these visiting hockey pros as we can. I've revised the media schedule, and I wanted to review it with you before finalizing. We can also discuss your role when it comes to the interviews and related photo ops."

Dave pushed open the door and the blast of hot summer air greeted me.

"Do you want to grab a bite in town?" he asked.

"Sure. We can at least enjoy a patio while we work," I replied. "Or you can pass everything over to me and actually take your vacation?"

Dave shook his head. "I think it's best if I continue to act as the intermediary between you and the school's press office. They can be a bit much. Fuck, you've been copied on all those emails. You can see that it's a lot."

"They've been intense since the championship win, that's for sure. But I get it."

The college world wasn't that different from the pros. Money was always at the top of the agenda and more attention meant more funding.

"They're amazing, but the questions never end." Dave chuckled. "No, I can't do that to you, D. You're busy mentoring those players, like Silas, and that's enough."

I couldn't make eye contact with my friend. If Dave knew about me and Silas, he would kick my ass for sure. Suddenly, I had no appetite for dinner anymore.

"I knew what I was getting into," I admitted, and I wasn't talking about camp. "Besides, I can deal with the media stuff as long as it's about hockey. It's not work; it's an obsession."

There was that freaking word again. Obsession. All or nothing, that was me.

"Let's talk about it over a beer," Dave replied and nudged my arm. "And you're buying."

Dave was right about one thing; one way or another, I was going to pay.

CHAPTER 25
SILAS

Finn kept telling me he was okay, but I knew he wasn't. There was no way in hell he was all right. Not after receiving that kind of news about his mom. While I tended to deal with things internally, Finn was the kind of person that needed to talk.

So, I let him.

I invited him back with me to the house and we set up in the kitchen making dinner. Finn asked again about my "crush," and what was I going to say to that? God, the word was ridiculous, something that teenagers would use. Still, the idea that I was crushing hard on Damien made my stomach somersault.

"I can't, Finn. I wish I could, but it's complicated," I admitted. "To start with, he's not out."

Which was partly the truth. Finn, being the sweet guy he was, understood. He didn't push me to say anything else. Even though I knew he wanted to ask more questions, and to be honest, I was anxious to talk about Damien. Huh. That was a first for me. While I had no problem talking about sex, talking about my feelings for my coach was a no-go. For so many reasons.

By the time the tacos were ready, Jo had arrived home, and all three of us chowed down while watching a movie. Afterwards, I got busy cleaning up while Jo and Finn played video games. I couldn't help but laugh at their competitive trash-talk and one-upmanship. Hockey players never liked to lose, at anything.

I joined in on the games an hour later until Finn started to yawn.

"I better get going," Finn announced and rubbed his eyes. "I've got to get my shit packed tonight."

Finn said his goodbyes to Jo, and then I drove him back to campus around nine. He was about to step out of my truck when he paused.

"I can take a rideshare tomorrow if you're busy," he insisted.

"It's all good, Finn. I've gotta take Jo to a doctor's appointment before I head to work anyway."

"Thanks. I appreciate it. The ride, dinner, and the company. It was much-needed distraction."

"Of course. Anytime." I offered my fist, and he bumped it. "Now catch some sleep, bud, you have a long travel day ahead."

"You sound like my oldest brother," Finn quipped.

"I've had a lot of practice. Night."

I waited until I saw him head inside the dorm and then I pulled out of the campus parking lot.

When I got back home, I sat in my truck for a while, staring at my phone. Debating. Second guessing. It wasn't like me. When I decided, I was done. But what was going on with me and Damien, I didn't know how to deal with it. I'd seen him this afternoon, only a couple of hours ago, and already my fingers were itching to text him. More than that, to touch him.

Fuck it.

> Silas: Are you at home?

> Damien: I just got in. I was out with Dave. A work dinner, discussing the visiting pros and all the related media the school is pushing. They've even hired a photographer.

> Silas: Please tell me they're not going to follow us around all day.

> Damien: Not the whole day. But longer than I'd like. Is Finn all right?

> Silas: I dropped him back at the dorm. He had dinner with Jo and me. I think he's okay, but anxious to get home.

> Damien: I don't blame him.

> Silas: He was asking about you. I mean, not you directly, obviously, but he knows something's up with me. I feel like shit lying to him.

I got out of the truck, locked it, and then headed inside the house. Jo was sound asleep on the couch, so I covered him with a blanket, then made for my bedroom.

> Damien: I know. Same with Dave. Not that he suspects anything between you and me, but I know he'd be upset if he learned the truth. The only person I've told is Selwin.

My phone tumbled out of my hand and hit the floor with a clatter. I quickly picked it up, thankful it wasn't broken, and flopped down on my bed.

> Silas: What?

Damien: When we were in Chicago, I told him that I wasn't straight. And, not just that, he noticed the way you looked at me. And the way I look at you.

I had so many questions, but I was too overwhelmed to think, let alone ask.

Silas: Oh shit.

Damien: I know. But he won't say anything.

Silas: I'm not worried about that, but the fact that he noticed. Is it that obvious? Then again, I'm in over my head with you, so why am I surprised?

Shit, had I confessed all that to Damien?

Damien: I feel the same.

My cock got so hard, so fast, I was dizzy. Thank fuck I was lying down.

Silas: It's only been a few hours, and I already miss you.

Damien: I miss you too. Only two more days.

Silas: Can't wait. And speaking of which, I'm going to grab my dildo and prep for Saturday.

I saw the three dots pop up, then disappear, then pop up again.

Damien: Thanks a lot, now you've given me a hard-on that I can't do anything about. You better not come either.

Silas: I'm not. I made a promise to you, and I'll stick to it. But I will give my dildo a thorough workout LOL. Kind of like when we warm up on the ice. Gotta make sure the hip flexors and glutes are ready for all the action, right?

Damien: Goddamn it, how am I supposed to go to sleep?

Silas: All I can think about is you fucking me. So many possibilities. On the deck, in the shower, in your bed.

Damien: Oh God, I'm heading off take a cold shower. Or maybe jump in the frigid lake. Whatever works.

Silas: I'll send you some visuals to get you excited for the weekend.

Damien: I'm not sure I'll make it that long.

Silas: You will. You're a man of your word. And I'll see you Friday at the rink.

Damien: I'll be the first one there.

Silas: Better lock your office door.

I put the phone aside and yanked open my nightstand drawer to search for my dildo. Since I hadn't been fucked in over two years, and when the need for a good railing hit me hard, the toy always satisfied. But it wasn't a warm, real cock. It wasn't Damien's. And having his dick in my ass was becoming more than a want. It was a need that was getting stronger. More than that, I had to have him all over me, and me over him. I wanted to tumble around in his bed, wreck him, possess every part of him, until we were both to sore and too satisfied to move. Then we'd do it all over again.

I reached under my pillow, pulled out the lube, and poured a generous amount on my fingers and then the dildo. Spreading my legs wide, I took my hard cock in one hand, giving myself long, firm strokes, while my other slid over my hole. Thinking about Damien like this, lying on top of me, his cock teasing my ass, his hands tormenting my nipples, fuck, I wasn't sure I'd be able to hold on to my control.

I pushed the tip of my slick middle finger in my ass and groaned at the initial burn of penetration. Man, I loved that line between pleasure and pain, but then again, I was a hockey player. We were gluttons for punishment.

Pushing deeper, I got all the way in, then added another finger, until I was fucking myself. Panting and so turned on I could barely breathe, I withdrew my fingers and rolled over, getting up on my knees. I positioned the dildo behind me and leaned back, sinking down on the toy one slow inch at a time until it was all the way inside me. When the tip of the dildo nudged my prostate, I bit my lip to keep from crying out at the sheer enormity of the pleasure that washed over me.

I began to ride the toy, levering up and down, my hips pumping hard, but oh shit, this was a bad idea because my climax was building fast and furious.

No. Stop.

I didn't want to break my promise to Damien.

But I want to show him how far he's pushed me. How badly I want him.

Without pause, I reached for my phone with my free hand and held it back near my ass, snapping a pic. The angle was awkward, so I wasn't sure how it would turn out. I dropped the phone on the bed and took a deep breath to try and calm down.

Shaking from wanting to come so badly, I gently eased off the dildo and my bed, stalking into my bathroom for an icy cold shower. My cock slapped hard against my stomach, red and leaking pre-cum, and like Damien, I needed to cool down. Fast.

The shock of freezing water had my dick deflating just in time. I was so close to the edge, one tug, one more stroke, and I was done for. Instead, I scrubbed up fast, dried off, brushed my teeth, and called it a night. But not before I picked up my phone again and tapped on the photo I'd snapped. I had to admit that my ass looked pretty good fucking that dildo.

It would look even better when I was fucking Damien's cock.

Horny and frustrated, I sent the photo to Damien and told him just that.

> Damien: Are you trying to kill me? I'm going for a midnight run AND a dunk in the lake.

> Silas: I was a good student; I listened to your instruction, and I didn't come. I'm saving it all for you, Coach. And it's always smart to be prepared, right?

> Damien: I don't think anything's prepared me for you. Now stop flirting and go to bed.

> Silas: Yes, sir.

It took me nearly two hours to fall asleep. I didn't mind one bit.

———

The next day, surprisingly, I woke up before my alarm. I'd only managed five hours of sleep, but it didn't seem to matter. It wasn't easy to ignore my morning erection, and because of that, I was revved up. I didn't even need caffeine to get moving; I was running on hormones and heady anticipation.

And all because I was one day closer to Damien.

"Whoa, what's with the major smile first thing in the morning?" Jo teased when I entered the kitchen. "Who even are you right now?"

"Hey, I smile plenty."

"Only on holidays and special occasions."

Instead of replying to my brother's smart-ass comment, I offered my middle finger and set about making my breakfast. Such as it was. I chugged down an iced coffee and ate a protein bar. I'd have time to grab a snack when I got to Verdant.

"Are you good to go?" I asked Jo. "You have your meds with you?"

"Yep."

"Cool. I've got a list of questions for the doctor."

"Me too."

Then we hit the road. First stop, campus. Finn was waiting in front of his dorm, his bag by his feet. With his headphones and sunglasses on, he didn't even notice us pulling up to the curb until I honked the horn. He shoved his phone in his pocket and sidled up to the truck.

"Morning, guys," Finn offered as he slid into the back seat.

"Morning, Finn." Jo turned around. "Hey, do you notice anything different about Silas?"

I pulled out of the parking lot and made my way down Main Street, which was busy with tourists. Finn leaned forward between the front seats and stared at me. I kept my eyes focused on the road instead of their antics.

"Oh my God, he's smiling again." Finn nudged me. "It's like a Christmas miracle, but in the summer."

"You two are freaking hilarious," I offered.

"I think he's in love," Jo stated.

I hit the brakes hard at the next light. Shit.

"He didn't deny that he had a crush," Finn added. "But he's keeping his man a secret."

I sighed and floored the accelerator. In a few minutes, we were on the highway headed to Burlington.

"I'm going to leave both of you at the airport if you don't stop," I warned.

"I know that Silas has a thing for athletic guys. Maybe it's one of your teammates? Or a guy on another hockey team?" Jo continued.

"Since I play with him, I'd say nada to all that. In fact, Silas talks more to Coach Banning than any other player." Finn chuckled.

"Okay, guys, you've had your fun," I interrupted, panic washing over me. "That's enough."

"Is Banning single?" Jo continued.

Where the hell did that come from? Ignoring the comment, I gripped the steering wheel like a lifeline.

"No clue," Finn replied. "But his ex-wife showed up at the rink the other day and he wasn't happy about it. I'd say he's vehemently single. I've never seen him with anyone or heard him talking about a girlfriend. Silas, what about you?"

"What do you mean, what about me?" I bit out.

"Do you think Banning is single?" Finn asked.

I let out a long breath.

"I think Damien has a right to privacy."

"Damien?" Finn and Jo said at the same time.

Against all my willpower, I began to blush. Fuck. Please let this conversation be over now.

"Holy shit!" Finn exclaimed loudly.

"What? Did you forget something back at the dorm?" I asked him.

"Uh, no. No. I, um, realized something about, uh…. my flight. It's nothing."

"Okay."

Weird, but okay.

Finn and Jo were quiet after that, with Jo busy typing away on his phone and Finn staring a hole in the back of my head. Could he tell? Did I fuck up? By the time we arrived at the airport, I was ready for another coffee.

Or a plane ride out of here…

"Uh, Si, could you help me with my bag?" Finn asked as I drove up to the departure gate.

"Sure."

After I pulled into a temporary space, I parked and hopped out to help Finn. Only, by the time I rounded the truck, he was already out of the vehicle with his bag in hand. Odd.

"Thanks again for the lift," Finn offered.

"No problem. And text me when you know more about your mom."

"I will." Finn suddenly lowered his sunglasses. "And be careful."

"About what?"

My stomach tightened as I caught the knowing glint in my friend's eyes. Did he suspect about me and Damien?

"Training camp. Don't overexert yourself. You pushed hard yesterday but you don't want to get injured or worse. Be careful."

Oh, that.

"No worries," I replied calmly. "I want to keep my body in top working order."

For once, hockey was the least of it.

CHAPTER 26
DAMIEN

SATURDAY

Friday was a bust. Since Finn was gone and Ethan called in sick, I cancelled the training session. I figured I'd let the guys get a long weekend in and then we'd get back to it full force on Monday. I was also thinking of myself when I decided to cancel. This way, I didn't have the temptation of Silas around me all day.

Bad enough I could barely sleep or eat.

There were times when I wanted to text him and cancel our plans for tonight, but every time I picked up my phone, I couldn't do it. Was Selwin right? Would this thing between me and Silas burn itself out? If so, was there any point in worrying? It would probably be over in a few weeks, like summer, and then everything would go back to the way it was.

I didn't believe that, but I was clinging to any rationale.

I'd already stressed cleaned my entire house from top to bottom, made my bed with fresh sheets, and scrubbed out the grill. Silas hadn't texted me at all today, which was making me even antsier. Yesterday, he'd sent me more sexy pictures and each one had me so worked up, I was taking cold showers every couple of hours.

There was a snap of him lying in bed, showcasing all the tattoos on his chest and abs, along with that mouth-watering treasure trail. In another pose, he was standing in what I assumed was his bathroom, offering me a delectable glimpse of his broad back and that incredible ass. But it was the first pic, the one of him riding that dildo, that I couldn't unsee. I'd started jerking off to it, imagining my cock in his tight hole, fucking him deep and slow and then pounding it so hard I'd leave his ass red for days. It took every ounce of willpower I could summon to stop myself so I wouldn't climax. I didn't know how much more edging I could take, and it was all my own doing. My balls were harder than hockey pucks, and I was pretty sure I was ready to spontaneously combust even though that was not a real thing.

Or was it?

I was sweating so much it felt like I was standing in the desert in Vegas, instead of the mountains in Vermont. In the afternoon, I took a break, grabbed a sandwich, slathered myself in SPF, and wandered down to the dock at the base of my property. I sat down at the edge and slipped my feet in the water. The lake temperature was frigid but in another month it would be perfect. In my mind, I tried to picture what July would look like, and funnily enough, Silas was still there.

That told me a lot. More than I was prepared for.

After an hour, feeling more relaxed, I made my way back up to the house. It was nearing on seven. I picked up my phone and noticed one missed message.

Silas: On my way.

The nerves in my belly took flight and my pulse shot up.

Fuck, it was like the first time I ever hit the professional ice, overloaded, excited, in awe that this was happening.

Instead of standing by the door waiting like a lovesick fool, I made myself busy in the kitchen, grabbing a couple of beers and coolers and adding them to a bucket of ice. Then I pulled out the snacks, and when all of it was organized, wiped my still-sweaty palms on my shorts.

I was about to bring everything outside when I heard the knock at the door. I could've slipped on a T-shirt but decided against it. My heart took off running again, and when I opened the door, there was the reason.

"Do you ever *not* wear leather?" I quipped when I took in the sight of Silas, looking cool as ever in olive green cargo pants, a tight white T-shirt, and his motorcycle jacket. With his hair tied up, his sunglasses on, and the beard trimmed, he was giving off a sexy biker vibe that had my dirty imagination working overtime.

"Do you mean the jacket or something else?" He gave me a wicked grin and placed his hands on his hips.

My gaze followed his hands, lower, and suddenly I was dying to know what he was wearing underneath those pants.

"Are you going to flirt with me or are you coming inside?" I demanded, unable to hold back my grin.

"I'm definitely coming, and the flirting will continue," he stated and shoved his sunglasses up to rest on his head. "I want to kiss you right now but in case of neighbors—"

They were a good enough distance away but still, you never knew. I nodded and it was only then that I noticed the two bags at his feet.

"Instead of burgers, I grabbed a few steaks," he added and picked up the bags. "Steaks, salad, and dessert."

I offered to take one of the bags, but Silas refused.

"Let me help you."

"Nope, I got it," he insisted and carried the bags into the kitchen, placing them on the island. "I've got a few more things to grab from the truck. You unload the food while I do that."

"Wait," I replied, and Silas stopped to stand in front of me. "You forgot something."

I pulled him into my arms and took possession of his mouth, kissing him with all the frustration that had been riding me. I'd been aching to touch Silas, and now he was finally here. And given the passionate way he kissed me back, I wasn't alone in my desperation. His lips and tongue teased mine and we made out like horny teenagers, Silas pushing me up against the counter, taking control of the kiss. Fuck, I more than liked that.

"Don't move," he whispered and gave me one last kiss. "I'll be right back."

I grabbed the edge of the granite counter to steady myself as I watched him walk away, his hockey swagger in full effect. Taking a deep breath, I reached down and adjusted my aching cock, which was begging to be released from these shorts.

After taking a long, shuddering breath, I reached for the bags with shaky hands and began to unpack the groceries. The steaks needed to be seasoned, so I left them on the counter, then I placed the salad kit and the key lime pie in the fridge, and the bag of fries in the freezer. I wasn't hungry right now. Not for food. Cooking would happen later. Much later.

When I turned around, Silas was standing behind me, an uncertain look on his face. I wasn't surprised to see him holding his backpack, since he was, after all, planning to spend the night.

No, what shocked me was the bouquet of sunflowers he held in his other hand. That was a first. I'd given plenty of flowers to my ex, but I'd never in my life received any. Not that I expected it. Not that I needed that. Still, Silas's unexpected gesture made my heart clench in a way that I wasn't prepared for. He didn't a say a thing and I didn't either. Our eyes locked, and I swallowed hard, trying, but failing, to calm my runaway heart, desperate to put all these heady feelings about him into words.

Silas placed the flowers on the counter and the bag on the floor, and stalked towards me, crowding me back against the counter. He cupped my face and leaned in, resting his forehead against mine, his hot breath teasing my lips.

"Too much?"

I shook my head.

"No," I replied and slid my hands down to cup his ass, bringing him in closer. "Not at all. But you are one surprise after another, Silas Moss. There goes my playbook. I have no idea what to do next."

"Let's start with a kiss." He smiled against my lips. "Everything else we'll figure out together."

Silas

What possessed me to buy flowers for Damien? Who fucking knew. I'd never done that for a man before. To be fair, I never needed to. I was closeted for so long, and I had no desire to date. Also, it wasn't in me to make that kind of romantic gesture. I didn't need or want... romance. I had a hard time summoning the word, never mind saying it.

But then I found myself in the checkout line of the grocery store, and the bright sunflowers caught my attention. I reached for them before I even had a chance to question it. And driving to Damien's, the flowers on the seat beside me, I realized that I was behaving so out of character that I had to blink twice when I looked at myself in the rearview mirror.

Talk about a total mindfuck.

Damien wasn't the only one skating into the unknown; I didn't have a playbook when it came to him either. I was running purely on instinct. There was something about the man that kicked all my primal impulses into overdrive. I knew that I would do anything to get in his bed, and I'd be damned if he was going to look anywhere else but at me. It turned out, I was ruthless in this, too. I wanted to mark him all over because he was mine. And, even more shocking, I wanted him to claim me in return.

Which is why, not a second after I put down those flowers, I had my hands on him.

And my lips.

"Baby." Damien moaned when I backed him up against the island and ravaged his mouth.

We made out like we hadn't kissed in months, never mind days. There was a desperation to our coming together that I still couldn't wrap my head around. It reminded me of those nail-biting games when the clock ticked down, and there was only one goal that separated us from a win. You could taste victory, so heady, so close, and when it finally happened, it was the most incredible high.

When we lost, though, I didn't like the bitterness that lingered.

I thought winning and losing was always about hockey, but suddenly it was about Damien.

I knew one thing for sure: I didn't want to fuck this up.

"Hey," Damien whispered and cupped my face, staring at me. I had a feeling that he knew exactly what I was thinking. Probably because I was gripping him so tight I'd leave bruises. "You all right?"

"More than all right. You?"

"Never better." He smiled.

I couldn't resist this man or his gorgeous grin.

"I want to see your bedroom, Damien."

He licked his lips and swallowed hard, his Adam's apple bobbing up and down.

"This is real, right?" He groaned. I felt a shudder run

through his body, and yeah, he wasn't the only one asking that question. "Please tell me I'm not dreaming."

I kissed him soundly, then gently nipped his lower lip, teasing him.

"I'd rather show you."

Taking my hand, he guided me through the kitchen to the back of the house. His bedroom was as cozy as the rest of the place, with two skylights that flooded the room with sunshine, and a king-sized bed covered in a navy and white striped quilt. It was all too easy for me to picture the two of us in that bed. My cock grew so hard in my pants that it was almost painful to walk.

Suddenly, I was nervous as fuck. I wasn't new to sex, and yet I was sweating hard, like this was the first time I'd ever been with a guy.

Damien, observant man he was, turned and gave me a look I recognized from practice. The one that asked me if I was okay. Sometimes players pushed too fast, too hard, and that's when injuries happened. Mistakes that can't be undone.

Me and him? We were breaking the rulebook on so many levels.

No, not that. Rewriting it. There was no play for this and no going back.

But being here with Damien wasn't a mistake. I was anxious, but that was only because I wanted to please him. For once, it was all about his pleasure, not mine.

"We don't have to—" he started and then paused, seemingly at a loss for words himself.

Damien assumed my silence meant I was uncertain about him.

"I know," I whispered, feeling exposed, like I'd laid bare all my secrets. "It's not that. I got overwhelmed for a moment. This, you and me, it's fucking intense. Unexpected. Wild. Maybe a little crazy."

"A little?" He squeezed my hand. "If it's too much, maybe we should stop. Stop before it's too late."

"Do you want to do that?" I asked, terrified of his answer.

"No," he replied without hesitation.

I finally let out a long breath as I glanced at his bed and then back at him.

"Then I'm all in."

CHAPTER 27

DAMIEN

We stared at each other, neither one of us moving, the tension so thick that my fight-or-flight instincts kicked into high gear.

Fuck it. I couldn't say no to Silas. Not anymore.

"Kiss me," we both demanded at the same time, and then started laughing.

"Is this going to be a problem?" I chuckled, sweet relief filling my lungs as Silas reached for me, sliding his hands around my hips to cup my ass.

"What?"

"Me being bossy, you being bossy. I like to take charge, it's my comfort zone, but not always—" I paused, unsure how to explain how I was feeling.

I didn't always want to be the one who made the first move. Sometimes my need for control needed a break. I'd never said anything to my previous bedmates, but with Silas, I had no need to hide.

"But not always when it comes to sex?" Silas countered and took my mouth in a devouring kiss.

I completely forgot what we were talking about.

"I'm happy to take charge and also take turns," he continued. "There's no one way or right way, Damien. Not with you and me."

He squeezed my cheeks, distracting me, and suddenly I was powerlifted, Silas throwing me back on the bed. That move was no easy feat considering I weighed as much as he did. Fucking hell, I liked it. More than liked.

I bounced once and spread my legs, my cock so hard I was tenting my shorts.

"Being manhandled by you is the biggest turn-on," I groaned, cupping my dick.

"I haven't even started." He smiled as he whipped off his T-shirt, uncovering all those sexy tattoos, and miles of skin kissed by golden freckles. "Fair warning, I'm an even bossier bottom."

"All I hear so far is a lot of talk," I teased him. "You know me. I want action."

"Ask and you shall receive," Silas insisted as he pulled the elastic from his hair.

Fucking tease.

"Keep going," I urged. "I want to see you naked. Now."

My hands were aching to touch him.

He stepped forward, stopping at the edge of my bed, and finally, slowly, undid his pants.

Commando again…

I had nothing smart to say in response. All I could do was bite my lower lip and stare at his cock, curling up against his abs, a trail of pre-cum smeared across his skin. I was so freaking hungry to touch it, taste it.

That's all mine.

I watched as he cupped his balls in one hand, and his dick in the other, stroking off and letting out a deep, dirty grunt had my toes curling and my hips arching off the bed.

When I glanced up at his face, I caught Silas's smug grin. I couldn't help but smile back.

"My turn. Come here."

Silas gave his dick one last tug and stalked up to the edge of the bed. Every step closer had my heart thrumming harder, and my breath coming in fits and starts. He kneeled on the mattress, knees bracketing my hips, his hands reaching for mine, our fingers interlocking tightly. I was totally at his mercy in this position, and when our hips met, our hard cocks rubbing together, I let out a filthy moan worthy of any porn soundtrack.

"You make the most incredible sounds," Silas whispered.

"It's all because of you."

Silas bent down and brushed his lips against my ear.

"Baby, wait until your cock is in my ass," he growled. "You gonna fill me up with your cum, Damien? Take what belongs to you?"

When he turned his head, I answered his question with a frantic kiss, my tongue desperate for his taste. My blood pounded faster, hotter, my pulse thrumming with fiery need.

I had to have him; there was no other way.

"Yes," I whispered, my voice hoarse. "Mine."

"Fucking right I'm yours."

There was no denying the full-on shiver that raced through my body. I wrapped my legs around Silas's waist, holding on tight as he dropped to his forearms, blanketing my body, kissing me again, ravaging my lips and sucking on my tongue. But it wasn't enough. Not nearly enough.

I had to taste all of him.

Banding my arms around Silas's back, I canted my hips and rolled us over, flipping our positions, until Silas lay underneath me. His surprised grunt told me he liked that unexpected move.

"Damien."

"First, I'm going to lick every inch of you," I admitted, leaning down and punctuating my words with more heated kisses. "And every one of your sexy tattoos."

Silas gave me another one of those incredible smiles as he

slowly placed his hands behind his head, his veiny forearms and bulging biceps a sinful invitation that I couldn't—and wouldn't—ignore.

"Are you showing off?" I teased him.

"For you?" His gaze darkened. "Without question."

He let out a husky laugh, until I leaned in and gave his bicep a not-so-playful bite. His sharp inhale inspired me to keep going, and I did, trailing kisses on his shoulder, his chest, sucking on one nipple, then the other, lower, until I reached his *Ruthless* tattoo. I ran one hand over the letters, tracing each line, feeling his muscles quiver with every stroke. Then I followed the same path with my tongue, as Silas moaned and grabbed hold of my hair.

"Don't stop."

I let out a dirty chuckle and continued to tease him, tracing a path lower, along those tight abs and V-lines, until I was nuzzling his blond pubes. Fuck, he smelled so good, musky, and I knew that he would taste even better.

Instead of worrying about the fact that it had been years since I'd touched a man, I did what I always did and leaned into my instinct. I knew what I liked and figured I'd start with that. I spat in my hand and reached for his hard cock, giving it a firm stroke, all my senses eagerly mapping his reaction.

Like he could read my mind, Silas shook his head.

"It doesn't matter how you touch me, Damien. I'm going to love all of it," he insisted. "Don't stop."

The last tether I was holding on to—the one I used to guard myself from losing control, from getting hurt—snapped. I reached for Silas's legs, hooking my hands under his knees and pushing them against his chest, opening him up. Everything about this man was beautiful, and my eyes were hungry to take in all of it.

Not just my eyes, but hands, and my mouth too.

There was no hesitation when I buried my face in his ass. Determined to give Silas all the pleasure, I desperately ate at his hole, licking, sucking, then tongue-fucking it. I couldn't get enough, and I wasn't the only one. Silas pushed back, greedy for more, humping my face like this was the end game.

"Goddamn it, you… you go right for the goal, don't you?" Silas moaned.

"Always."

I licked a path from his hole to his taint, then slid my tongue around one of his balls and sucked on it. His taste was totally addictive, and the wild and sexy sounds coming out of Silas's mouth had my own throbbing erection begging for friction.

I ignored my needs in favor of his.

"So damn good," he groaned.

I gave his other ball the same attention, his musky taste and smell more potent than any shot of alcohol. My finger reached for his spit-slicked hole, rubbing, teasing, until I slipped the tip inside him. He was so tight and hot, and I knew that getting my cock inside him was going to completely ruin me.

"Damien, baby, give me more. More."

I ran my tongue along the base of his cock, tracing the long vein that ran along the rigid length. When I finally reached the fat head of his dick, I swirled my tongue around the underside, feeling him jerk in response.

"Enough," Silas growled. "I need your dick inside me."

Instead of heeding his demand, I lowered my head and swallowed his cock, sucking hard, taking as much of him as I could before I started to choke. Taking Silas all the way down was going to take some practice. A lot of it. But judging by his dirty moans, he was enjoying my effort. Fuck, everything about sex with him was already better than anything that had come before.

I pulled off his cock to take a much-needed breath, and before I could lean in again, Silas hauled me up in his arms.

We kissed fiercely, rutting against each other, my senses over-loading. I couldn't get close enough or kiss enough. And Silas was right. I needed to be inside him and right fucking now.

"Nightstand," I whispered against his lips. "Lube."

Next time I'd shove it under my pillow for easy access. Please God, let there be a next time…

I rolled off him and reached for the drawer, yanking it open so fast, I nearly toppled the table. I'd barely grabbed hold of the tube when Silas plucked it out of my hand and manhandled me until my back hit the mattress again.

"I'm gonna ride you until we break this fucking bed." He groaned as he kneeled above me, pouring lube into his palm and then reaching behind.

"Show me," I whispered, desperate to see him play with his ass.

Fuck that, I wanted my fingers inside him too. I wanted to be all over him, inside him, the need clawing at my chest.

"Let me—"

Silas shook his head.

"Next time." He panted and licked his lips. "I'm too keyed up. I don't want to come yet."

I took the lube from him and slicked up my erection, which was so hard at this point that with one or two strokes, I'd be a goner myself.

"Condom?" I asked before I totally lost my head.

"Only if you want," he whispered. "I told you, I'm tested regularly. I don't want the barrier. Not with you."

"Same. I mean, the last time I had sex was over a year ago, but I'm good too."

Silas groaned and dropped his head back, the muscles in his neck rigid as he rode his fingers.

"Please," I begged.

He reached for my hand and guided it to his ass, until my slick finger slid alongside his, taking over, breaching his hole.

"So hot," I whimpered and began to finger fuck him.

"Add another," he commanded, and I did just that, getting two fingers inside him, pushing in slow and steady, watching his face flush, sweat trickling down his hairline. "More, Damien. More. Give it all to me."

Silas's expression was as fierce as his words, his body primed to fuck as he hovered over me. I drilled my fingers in deeper, until Silas's ass clenched hard around them, and he cried out my name.

"I need inside you so badly," I whispered. "I need you now."

I withdrew my fingers from his ass, while Silas positioned himself over my cock, sliding down over me, taking me inside of him, one torturous inch at a time. Not using a condom was… the best thing ever. So intense. It was more than the physical sensation, it was what the lack of barrier meant. This was more than one time, more than casual sex. I was so far gone for Silas, for a man who was my student. I should've felt guilty, some kind of remorse. There was none of that.

"You ready?" he asked as he gazed into my eyes.

Despite the risks we were taking—all of them—I nodded.

"I am."

CHAPTER 28

SILAS

As I levered up and down on Damien's cock, I vowed to do what I'd promised.

We were going to break this fucking bed. Or die trying.

I knew that neither one of us was going to be the same after this. Fucking was always a good time, but this, us, was not fucking. Damien was mine and I was his, and we were staking our claim on each other. That's what was going on. A month ago, I would've rolled my eyes at the very thought of belonging to anyone. Now? It was all I wanted. I was caught up in my feelings, not just my body's reaction, and that's what made the rush of us coming together so electric.

There was nothing sexier than the man lying beneath me, his raven hair mussed from my hands, his ocean blues revealing more than words could say. Damien slid one callused hand around my cock and stroked me off, his other holding tight to my hip, pulling me in as close as we could get. I rocked my hips and Damien rutted in and out of me, his cock nailing my prostate with every thrust. God, the feel of him bare inside me was so fucking amazing that I couldn't contain the satisfied moans that rumbled out of my chest.

"That's it, Damien," I urged him. "Fuck me. Own me."

A dark flush stained his cheekbones and neck as we strained closer, our movements frantic as we fucked hard. I leaned in and took his mouth in a fierce kiss, wanting to be all over him, connected in every way.

"Silas, I need… need you," he whispered. "So fucking bad."

"I know, baby. I need you, too."

Heady emotions I'd tried to contain were rising to the surface and there was nothing I could do to stop them.

"Come for me," Damien insisted, his fingers digging into my hip, his eyes locking with mine, "Let go, Si. Trust me and let go. I'm here. I've got you. It's me, baby. It's me."

"Damien."

That wasn't the way. I had other people's back, but no one had mine. I didn't need them to. I was used to being the caretaker, not the one in need of caring. I couldn't let go. Not fully. Not ever. Who would be there to pick up the pieces when I shattered?

"Me," Damien replied. "I'm the one who's got you."

"No one's ever—"

"I know," Damien groaned, his voice hoarse. "Stop fighting it. Let go. I need you to let go."

My climax spiraled higher and higher as I lost all control, fucking him in a frenzy, every touch, every groan, every word pushing me to my absolute limit. I chased the hard dick in my ass and the rough hand on my cock, so much pleasure, all my synapses firing at once.

"That's it," Damien encouraged. "So fucking sexy. All mine. And I'm yours. Mark me with your cum, Silas. Do it now."

Damien's order pushed me right over the edge, my balls pulling up tight. I couldn't hold out any longer. Pleasure suffused my body as my orgasm unleashed, cum shooting out of my dick and hitting Damien's chest, his neck, even his face.

"Yes, yes, yes," Damien chanted as he fucked into me, every thrust like lightning striking inside of me.

Then his body went rigid as he came long and hard, the hot rush of cum filling up my ass.

Both of us were slick with sweat, gasping for air, and holding hard to each other. I collapsed on top of him, my stamina wiped out in the face of that incredible orgasm. I didn't care that my cum was sticky between us, or that we'd be glued together in no short order.

"I've never come that hard before. I think you broke my dick," Damien quipped as he wrapped his arms around me and clenched me tight.

Fucking hell, he better not let go of me. I was right where I belonged.

"Please God no," I replied and gave his neck playful nip. "We were only supposed to break the bed."

"The bed's still intact, so I'd say we need to try again," Damien replied and took my lips in a languid kiss. "And again, and again. Practice makes perfect."

I silenced his teasing with my tongue.

"You're not playing fair," he whispered.

"I'm not playing," I countered.

There were more kisses as we made out like horny teenagers. I didn't know how much time passed, an hour, two, as we lay there together, neither of us in any hurry to leave each other or Damien's bed.

Until my damn stomach growled.

Damien thought it was hilarious, and when I tried to swat his ass in retaliation, he laughed so hard he nearly rolled right off the bed and onto the floor. I caught him in time and proceeded to kiss the ever-loving fuck out of him, which made us both smile.

"You promised me steak," Damien insisted when I let him come up for air.

"So freaking demanding." I chuckled. "Anything else?"

"Don't put a shirt on."

"I wasn't planning on it."

After we took a quick shower, I pulled on my cargo pants and Damien reached for his shorts.

"Damn shame," I admitted as I eye-fucked him.

"Don't worry, we'll get naked later."

I reached for him, my arm snaking around his waist as I guided him out of the bedroom and down the hallway to the kitchen. We paused every five seconds or so, unable to stop kissing, until we were both punch-drunk and out of breath.

By the time we made it to the kitchen, Damien and I were hot, the steaks were room temperature, and the beer was ice-cold. All around, it was… perfection. We worked in tandem as we prepared dinner, stopping only to trade kisses and lingering touches.

With the meat on the grill and the potatoes in the air fryer, we grabbed a couple of beers and sat down on the deck and watched the day turn into night.

A half hour later, everything was ready. We fed each other bites of food, and talked for hours until our voices turned hoarse.

But as the night grew darker, Damien's relaxed demeanor began to shift. I squeezed his hand, determined to find out why.

"What are you worrying about?" I asked him.

He turned his head, his eyes clearly troubled.

"You've got another year left at Sutton. So do I. And I don't know how we're going to manage to keep this"—he pointed between us—"a secret. I've got a pretty good game face, but it doesn't apply in this case. You've completely wrecked my ability to remain indifferent."

I couldn't help but smile at that. Knowing I was the only one who could get under his glacial armor? That was heady stuff. It did more than turn me on; it filled me with pride.

Damien shook his head. "You like that, eh?"

"Damn right," I replied and raised his hand to my mouth, kissing his knuckles. "And you're getting worked up for no reason. I know me, and I know you. We can play this cool. And if we slip, so what? Plenty of college students have relationships with their teachers. It's not like we're the only ones."

"I don't imagine that anyone at the school, or the board, would like to hear you say that."

"It's the truth."

"I know that it happens, but it doesn't look good for a coach to be involved with his player. Think of what your teammates would have to say." Damien sighed. "One, or maybe both of us, is going to get hurt."

"You don't know that," I insisted. "And fuck what other people think, Damien. You didn't pressure me into this relationship. I made my own choice."

"Other people won't assume that's the case. And maybe there's a warning in there. I've stepped over a line, and I should probably recuse myself before we both end up ruining everything we've worked hard for."

"No. Our team needs you."

Fuck it, I wasn't backing down. I leaned over and kissed Damien. Hard.

"More importantly, I need you."

"Baby." Damian cupped my face. "Think about what would happen if the situation were reversed, if you were in my role?"

Damien had a point; I didn't want to fuck up his life. But I didn't want to lose him. Selfishly, I couldn't give him up, and I didn't want him to give up on me either. For the first time in years, I wanted something that was mine, and only mine. Damien was so much more than a lover; I connected with him in a way I'd never felt with any other man. I could talk to him about anything and be myself with him. He was a man I respected and admired, a man that was kind and caring underneath all those sharp edges.

A man I loved… Holy fucking hell, I was falling in love with Damien.

The stakes weren't high; they were all or nothing.

"I get it, I do." I paused, looking away, trying to control the reckless feelings tumbling around inside me. I wanted to say "fuck everyone else" but that wasn't realistic. "I promise that we'll keep this between us. We can be discreet."

I glanced over at Damien again, and he nodded.

"Then there's another issue. Are you going to be able to take my direction on the ice and not take it personally?"

"Of course."

"Silas." Damien raised one eyebrow.

"What?" I chuckled and silenced him with another kiss. "We're still us, right? I'll take your advice, but that doesn't mean I won't try pushing back once in a while."

"Once in a while?"

"Relax, it's all gonna work out," I assured him.

"I hope so," he quietly admitted. "I want us. I'm sure from the outside looking in, this is completely wrong, a disaster waiting to happen, but nothing has ever felt so right. I can't explain it any other way."

We stared at each other, nothing and no one between us.

"I know," I whispered, wanting to say the words trapped in my chest. Not yet. But soon. "It's amazing."

"Best feeling ever."

"Better than playing pro?" I teased him, trying to lighten the mood.

"There's no comparison."

He smiled and squeezed my hand.

In that moment, I knew I wasn't alone. Damien was falling for me too.

CHAPTER 29
SILAS

At midnight, we took a dip in the lake and ran back to the house to warm up. We messed up Damien's sheets again, frotting until we were both too fucked out to move, and then we fell asleep wrapped in each other's arms.

I woke up early on Sunday, listening to Damien's soft snores. Even in that, he was freaking adorable. I kissed his temple and slowly extricated myself from the possessive grip he had on me, padding out to the kitchen to fix breakfast.

It was tough dragging myself away from Damien's bed. I'd never had that issue before, and yeah, it was a problem. I wasn't sure I was going to be able to sleep alone tonight. I stared at my reflection in the window over the sink, wondering who the hell was looking back at me. I looked… happy. The way I did before illness and death changed my family forever. Part of me wanted to grab my stuff and hit the road, forget last night ever happened, forget anything with Damien happened. He was right; it was safer that way. But the bigger part of me knew that I was home. I'd found something with him that was worth the risks we were taking, something worth fighting for. Ruthless was an attitude when it came to hockey and my family, but now it was about Damien too.

A half hour later, Damien stalked into the kitchen wearing jeans and nothing else, with sleep rumpled hair and marks all over his skin. My marks. God, he was so fucking sexy I couldn't breathe.

He bypassed coffee, and the omelets I'd cooked, in favor of reaching for me and kissing me senseless.

"Next time, wake me," he demanded.

"You obviously needed the rest."

"I'd trade sleep for time with you any fucking day."

Instead of offering him coffee, or breakfast, I got down on my knees and showed Damien the better way to wake up. Yep, I sucked all the tension out of his body through his cock.

His legs nearly gave out after the blowjob, so I had to help him get seated, which got me a warning look. Retaliation was coming and I couldn't wait.

I smiled and kissed him harder.

"Why don't you come with me this aft?" I asked him as we finally sat down to eat.

I didn't want to leave, and he didn't want me to go, but I had to pick up Jo and I was anxious to visit my dad.

"And there goes our attempt at being discreet," he countered.

"It's my family. Who're they gonna tell?"

Damien crossed his arms and gave me his coach's glare. "And you think your dad will approve of us?"

I winced. Dad would be shocked for sure that I was sleeping with my coach. Probably angry. Upset. He didn't need that kind of stress. Shit, this was complicated. On so many levels.

"Okay, maybe he'll be concerned," I continued.

"Silas."

"But he knows me, and he trusts my judgement. For

fuck's sake, I've been Jo's guardian for two years. I'm not one to jump and look later. I know what I'm doing."

Damien nudged my shoulder with his.

"I'll go with you because I'd like to meet your dad, but let's not say anything. I don't want to put them in a position to have to deny it later."

"So, what? We say you happened to be in the area and wanted to stop by?"

"Something like that. I've got errands to run anyway. I'll think of an excuse."

"All right. But my father and brother know me. I only bring friends like Finn to meet them. They're going to know something's up."

"Speaking of Finn, have you heard from him yet?"

"Nope. I texted him yesterday and again this morning," I replied. "No response."

"That worries me."

"I'm going to give him a call before we take off."

"Sounds good," Damien replied and reached for my empty plate.

"Leave that, I'll clean up."

"Nope, it's my turn. House rules," Damien responded and gave me a resounding kiss. "Go call Finn."

I headed off to the bedroom and grabbed my phone off the nightstand. I was relieved to see there was finally a message from my friend.

> Finn: She got through surgery okay and is back home. Call me?

I tapped on Finn's contact info and waited anxiously for him to answer.

"Hey, Si."

"How's your mom?"

"She's doing all right. The surgery went without a hitch,

and they released her this morning. But it'll take a week or two to get the biopsy results. We were hoping it would be sooner."

"Waiting's the worst part."

"It is." He sighed. "Anyway, I'm heading back to Vermont tomorrow morning. My parents insist on it. I feel guilty but right now, there's nothing else I can do for her. And, honestly, I'd rather be busy at practice than sitting at home driving everyone nuts with my nervous mouth."

I chuckled. "I'm sure they don't feel that way. But busy is always good. How're you doing?"

"I'm still… upset. But I'm hoping for the best. That's all I can do, right?"

"It is. Try to stay positive. And make sure your family keeps on those doctors. Don't hesitate to push if you don't get answers soon. Trust me on this. You've gotta advocate for her."

"I will," Finn replied. "What are you up to? How was camp on Friday? Did I miss much? Did Damien ride your ass hard?"

Yes, yes he fucking did…

Tell him about Damien.

"You didn't miss anything. Ethan called in sick, so Damien cancelled the camp."

"You're calling him Damien again. What happened to Coach Banning?"

"Well, see—"

"What's going on, Silas? And don't tell me nothing. I've known you long enough to know something was up on the ride to the airport Friday. Your voice sounds different. Are you okay?"

"More than okay," I blurted out. "There is something important, but you need to promise me you won't say anything to anyone. Promise."

"I promise."

"Not even if the news freaks you out?"

"I've got your back. Tell me."

"Damien and I… we slept together."

The silence on the other end of the line had me wondering if Finn had dropped the phone or hung up.

"Hello? Did you hear what I said?" I asked.

"You had sex with our coach?" Finn's voice was so loud, I had to pull the phone away from my ear. "I mean, I noticed the tension between you guys, and it made me wonder, but I—"

"Finn—"

"Having teammates that are dating is shock enough, but now this?" Finn continued. "Wait, you're not dating Coach. It was sex, right? It's done?"

"Ah, well not exactly—"

"Holy shit, it's more? You're seeing each other?"

"Yes."

"You have feelings for him? Like, the real deal?"

"As real as it gets," I admitted.

"I have no words. No words," Finn replied. "And yet I keep talking. Because if I keep talking, I can pretend I didn't hear what you told me. Because now, I have to keep something this big a secret. I mean, you dating a guy isn't a big deal. But dating our coach? That's major. Like, mind exploding major. I'll do my best, but you know I'm shit at hiding stuff, and what if—"

"Breathe, Finn."

"But you and Banning, this could ruin everything."

"No, don't say that. He's the best thing to happen to me."

I couldn't believe the words coming out of my mouth, but it was the damn truth.

My comment was met with silence.

"Finn? Are you still there?"

"I'm here. And I'm happy for you, Si. I am. But you can't

be that naïve. What happens when people find out? And trust me, someone always finds out."

"I'll deal with that when the time comes."

"Shit answer, my friend. And guess what? Coach is going to get the worst of it."

I wanted to throw my phone at the wall and scream out loud. This couldn't be the way. I finally find happiness and it's got to be tainted already? Or even worse, taken from me, if Damien decided that I wasn't worth the trouble.

"No one's going to find out. Not until we're ready."

"Si—"

"Please, I know what I'm doing."

"Do you?"

"Yes. And so does Damien."

"I trust you, but I'm worried."

"Not about me. You focus on your mom," I insisted. "I take care of myself. Always have, always will."

"What about Damien? Does he take care of you?" Finn asked.

"He does."

I could hear Finn sighing again. "Man, I hope it's worth it."

"He is."

"Then I've got your back. And don't worry, I'll keep my lips zipped. Even if I have to use duct tape to do it."

I chuckled at that image. "Thanks, Finn."

"But no more shocking news, all right?" he countered. "I need a breather."

"Got it. Go get some sleep."

"I need that too."

"You're not the only one. I was up all night."

"Ew, I don't want to hear about Coach like that. Just no."

I laughed at Finn's put-out tone.

"Damien's fucking hot."

"He is, but that's not the point," Finn added. "Wait, are you at his place?"

"Yep, I stayed over. I like him, Finn," I confessed. "More than like."

"I'm speechless. Without speech. Me. No words. None. Done."

"And yet, you keep talking."

"I've got to go. My dad's yelling for me. I'll text you when I arrive tomorrow."

"You need a lift from the airport?"

"You'll be at camp already. Tell Coach I'll be there but an hour late."

"Will do."

I hung up and headed for the shower. By the time I was nearly done, Damien joined me. Watching him walk towards me, all long lines and tight muscles, I shivered, despite the heat of the water.

"How's Finn?" he asked as he stepped into the shower.

"Okay. His mom's recuperating. Still a wait on the biopsy, though, at least a week or two. He'll be back tomorrow but an hour late."

Damien nodded and reached for me.

"I also told him about us. I couldn't lie to him."

Damien slid his arms around my waist and notched his head in the curve of my neck. "And?"

"He's pretty freaked out."

Damien gave my neck a teasing kiss and worked his way up to my mouth. He was gorgeous any day, but naked, and wet? If I didn't have the wall to support me, I would've fallen on my ass.

"Did you expect anything less?" he murmured.

"No, but I'm not sure I want to tell anyone else," I grumbled. "I don't care if other people think this is a mistake. It's not."

Damien's hands slid up my back, higher, then cupped my

face. The kiss he gave me was slow and sweet, hitting me right in my feels. I gripped his forearms, and I held on tight, unwilling to let go.

"Baby, I'm sorry," he whispered.

"For what?"

"You've got enough pressure as it is. I don't want to make your life harder."

"You're not." I shook my head. "Now stop distracting me and get washed up. We're going to be late."

A half hour later, we were dressed and headed out the door, taking separate cars of course.

I gave Damien the address of the nursing home and while he headed off to run errands, I drove to River's to pick up Jo.

"I guess I don't have to ask how your weekend's going," Jo teased as he hopped in the truck. "Are you finally going to tell me who put that smile on your face?"

I so wanted to tell him. Then, I figured I didn't need to. As soon as Jo saw me with Damien, he'd know.

"I had a good night," I offered. "What about you? How's River?"

"He's good. I mean, he's still upset about his parent's split, but we talked about it. Even if he moves, our friendship doesn't change."

"And you?" I asked as I pulled out of River's driveway and headed back to town. "How's the new medication?"

"Better. No dizziness."

I reached for my brother's hand and squeezed it tight. "I'm so fucking happy to hear that."

We pulled up to the nursing home parking lot a short while later.

Jo and I entered the home and found my dad sitting with the other residents in the lounge, playing bingo. The game was organized once a week, and every resident was an eager participant. There were prizes, like books and puzzles, and competition was surprisingly fierce. The desire to win, no matter the game, no matter the circumstance, was human nature. Several volunteers helped the residents with their cards, including my dad.

Jo and I grabbed a couple of nearby seats and waited until the game was done. No one interrupted bingo time; it was sacred.

After a half hour, Mandy, his nurse, wheeled Dad over to us.

"So, how many games did you win?" I asked.

My dad held up two fingers.

"Nice. You going to share your prizes with me and Jo?"

My dad shook his head slowly, and Jo and I laughed.

"You want to sit outside for a while? Get some sun?" I asked.

He nodded. I took over from Mandy and wheeled my dad out of the residence with Jo following.

Damien was waiting there, on the grounds, standing by the picnic table with our championship trophy in his hands. I guess that excuse was as good as any.

My heart was so full at the sight of him that it took everything in me to keep calm.

"Whoa, Banning is here," Jo remarked and patted my dad's shoulder. "Isn't that cool, Dad? That's Silas's coach come to show you their championship trophy. What a great surprise."

It was.

My father barely nodded, but I could tell by the look in his eyes that he was excited to see that trophy.

Jo nudged me. "When did you arrange this?"

"Yesterday." God, I hated lying to my family. I couldn't do this for much longer. "I told you that every player gets their turn."

"Yeah, I know. But I didn't expect your coach to come along with it," Jo replied as he stared at me.

I ignored my brother's perusal as best I could and kept

walking. Damien placed the trophy on the table as we ambled up to greet him.

"Pops, this is Coach Damien Banning. Damien, my father, Tobias."

Damien sat down on the picnic bench, so he was eye level with my father. My dad reached out a shaky hand and Damien took it in two of his. "It's an honor to meet you, sir. It's been a privilege to coach Silas."

"And often, a pain," I added, chuckling. "Don't deny it, Damien."

Damien rolled those gorgeous blues and then offered a smile at my father.

"He's stubborn, your son."

"Y-yes… n-n-nice… m-m-meet… y-yo… y-yo… you… t-t…" Dad paused, shaking his head, struggling to reach that last word. Damien sat patiently and waited. "T-t-too."

My dad could have used his phone to type out a response but the fact that he insisted on speaking told me a lot. There was no question that I got my resilience from him. I squeezed his shoulder in response and swallowed down my emotions.

"How about I take some pictures of you and Silas and Jo with the trophy?" Damien offered and stood up again.

I held Damien's gaze for longer than I should've and nodded.

"That'd be amazing, thanks," I replied, resisting the urge to lean over and kiss him.

Dad tapped on the arm of his wheelchair.

"Pops? What is it?"

Dad motioned to his pocket. "P-phone."

"Of course."

I took his phone and passed it over to Damien. Then I grabbed hold of the massive wood and silver trophy and rested it on my hip while Jo stood beside me, flanking Dad. Damien held the phone up and began to take photos.

"Perfect," Damien announced. "A few more."

"How about one with you, Coach?" I asked.

Damien nodded and slowly walked over, sliding in beside me, then raised up the phone for a selfie. When he showed me the shot, I nearly dropped the prize.

I wasn't smiling for the photo, but at Damien. And he was looking at me too.

And when my brother and father asked to look at the picture?

Our secret was no more.

CHAPTER 30

SILAS

Damien stayed, chatted, and took more photos. Of course, he charmed Jo and my father, and even the nurses who stopped by to check on my dad. Part of me wondered if that was due to his media training. Then again, he rarely smiled, even for school events. I was hoping his effort was all for me, and when he caught me staring and winked, I had my answer.

An hour later, he took his leave with the trophy.

I didn't want him to go, and my eyes tracked his every step until he got back in his SUV. Jo headed inside for the washroom, and that's when my dad began to slowly type on his phone.

Dad: What's going on with you and Damien?

I sighed, unable to keep myself locked up anymore.

"A lot, Pops. A lot is going on." I sighed and ran a hand through my beard. "I'm… I never told you before, but I'm… So the thing is, I'm gay."

My dad's gaze never wavered from mine.

"I'm sorry I didn't say anything sooner," I added. "I

figured you had enough to deal with given your stroke recovery and worries about Jo. I didn't want you to worry about me too."

Dad: Glad you told me. But him?

"Is it that obvious?"

Dad: To anyone that knows you.

I nodded. *Discreet, my ass.*

Dad: He's older and he's your coach.

"He's only eight years older than me. And we're both adults. I'm not going to stop seeing him. I don't care what anyone says."

Dad: It's serious?

"Yeah. I'm falling hard."

Dad: You know your own mind. Always have. The way he looked at you... I don't know if that makes it better or worse.

I glanced at the picture of the four of us and marveled at the way Damien was smiling at me. What we were to each other was right there for anyone to see.

"I'm happy," I reassured my dad. "Really fucking happy."

Dad: Language.

I started laughing, reaching for his arm.
"It's going to be fine. I promise."

Dad: Until the school finds out. What then?

"I'll worry about that later."

It was a shit answer, but it was all I had. I should've been more concerned about how my teammates might react to this news; probably freaked out, like Finn. And what about Damien's job? Why did I keep ignoring the warnings that were flashing in front of me? Before, the only thing I saw was my family and hockey. But now, there was Damien. All I wanted was him, and fuck anyone's opinion about it.

Dad: What we want and what's best can be two different things.

"I know. But I've never felt like this before. This isn't casual. Not for me or for him. And I know it seems impossible, but I'm good for him too. The man hardly laughed before and all I want to do is draw it out of him."

Dad: He better treat you right. Or I'll roll over his feet.

I chuckled at my dad's protectiveness. "That won't be necessary, but thanks for having my back."

Dad: You've had mine. Looking after Josiah. It's a lot for a man your age.

"I'd do it all over again."

Dad: You and Damien, it won't be easy. But I raised you to fight for what's right. If Damien's right for you, don't give up.

A lump the size of a puck lodged in my throat, and I tried to swallow past it.

"Yes, sir."

The door of the home swung open, and I glanced up. Josiah gave us a wave.

"They're setting up for dinner," Jo called out.

"We'll be right there."

> Dad: Have you told Jo?

"Not yet. But I think he already suspects."

> Dad: Next time, invite Damien to join us for dinner.

"I'll make it happen."

———

Later that night, after Josiah had gone to bed and I was folding laundry, my phone buzzed. When I spotted Damien's name I headed for my bedroom and shut the door.

> Damien: It was awesome meeting your dad. To spend time with him and Jo. They're both great.

> > Silas: Next time, stay and have dinner with us.

> Damien: Did you tell them?

> > Silas: My dad knew. I guess we're shit at hiding.

> Damien: I thought the trophy was a perfect excuse and no one would be wise.

> > Silas: We'll need to work on our game day face.

> Damien: I'll go practice in front of a mirror right now.

> Silas: Do that, but take your clothes off first. Better yet, video call me, and we can get undressed together.

I reached for my nightstand, rummaging frantically until I located the dildo and the lube.

When Damien's face popped up on my screen a second later, I tapped accept, lowered the volume, and positioned the phone on the pillow between my legs.

"Hey baby, can you see me?"

"I can see all of you." Damien licked his lips. "This bed is too fucking empty without you."

"I wish I was there. Are you wearing anything?"

"This smile that I can't seem to get rid of."

I grinned in return.

"Prop the phone up so I can see you."

I held my breath and waited, my pulse jumping like crazy, while Damien set up his phone.

"Yeah, like that," I whispered when he lay down on the bed, his body on full display.

My eyes roamed over every inch of him, the powerful biceps, the slope of his abs, that delicious, dark treasure trail, and finally, his cock. He was hard, and all mine.

"Grab some lube and stroke yourself," I demanded. "Nice and slow."

"You do the same."

"I'm getting my dildo ready," I confessed.

Damien groaned. "Fuck, this is the first time I've ever been jealous of a fake cock."

I laughed out loud at that.

"No jealousy needed. I've named him Banning."

Damien's husky laughter filtered through the phone, and it made my already aching cock even harder.

"Fucking tease."

"You haven't seen anything yet," I warned him. "Stroke yourself off, Damien."

Watching him fuck his fist was so much more than hot. It was better when my hand was the one wrapped around him, but I'd take him anyway I could get him.

"Imagine I'm right there with you, baby, touching you, teasing you."

Damien's deep groan had me reaching for the lube, slicking up both my hands. I slid one around my cock and gave myself an experimental tug, reaching for my balls with my other, teasing my taint, then my hole. I watched Damien jerk off, my movements mirroring his, both of us stroking harder, faster.

"I want to see your hole," Damien growled. "Show me."

I spread my legs and pushed one finger in my ass. The burn was so good, so heady that I added another finger, and fucked myself. In and out, over and over, while my other hand frantically stroked my dick.

"I want you inside me," Damien confessed. "I want you in every way."

I glanced at my screen, mesmerized by the sight of Damien teasing the rim of his hole. When he pushed one thick finger into his ass, my hips came off the bed, and both of us let out a dirty moan at the same time.

"You want me to fuck you, Damien? You want my cock in your ass?"

"Yes."

"Watch."

I withdrew my fingers, grabbed the dildo, and pushed it into my hole. Inch by inch, my ass swallowed the whole thing, the tip of the toy nudging my prostate.

"Damien! Shit, that's good."

"I'm right there with you, baby. Don't stop."

I fucked the dildo, and fucked my fist, all while watching

Damien do the same. My rhythm faltered when he added a second finger, his hands working as fast as mine. My climax couldn't be contained, all the pleasure washing over me.

"Come for me, Damien. I need you to come for me."

Damien's grunts and moans grew louder, and his hands moved faster. Both of us were making a sexy mess of ourselves with lube and pre-cum, and I wished like hell I was with him. Watching was a turn on but touching him and tasting him couldn't be equaled.

"Baby, I'm so close… Oh fuck, oh God, I'm gonna come."

Damien's hips pumped faster as his groans grew louder.

"That's it. I wanna see it," I moaned. "Next time, I'm gonna pump your ass full of my cum and eat you out."

"Fuck!" Damien screamed as his body jerked.

Ropes of glistening cum covered his dick, his balls, his hands. The sight of his release pushed me over the edge. My balls pulled up so tight, it was damn near painful, and when I tapped my prostate with the dildo, I was done. My thighs locked up, the orgasm obliterating what was left of my control. I released so hard that my vision wavered, my hips coming off the bed, and I unloaded cum everywhere. So much cum.

"Look at you," Damien whispered. "So fucking hot."

"Holy shit." I panted. "That was incredible."

"You better be at my place tomorrow after work," Damien demanded. "We need to reenact this in person."

"Only if I can rim you. I want to suck on your hole and fuck you with my tongue."

"Jesus, the filthy things that come out of your mouth," Damien muttered, his legs lax, his face flushed. "I think I came again."

"Lick it. Taste yourself."

Damien slid his hand up his chest, higher, until he reached his mouth. He made a big show of sticking his tongue out, licking his fingers.

"Now slide that wet finger back over your hole, and tease it real good," I encouraged.

Damien did as I asked. The sight of his finger sliding over his pink hole, the hole I was going to fuck soon, had another spurt of cum leaking out of my dick.

"I can't wait until I can suck on that tight hole of yours," I confessed. "I'm going to rub my beard all over your skin too, until I redden those gorgeous thighs. You gonna ride my face, baby?"

"Yes."

"You gonna let me fuck your ass, Damien?"

"Yes, yes, yes," Damien chanted. "I need it. Want you all over me, inside me. Jesus, I need you so fucking badly."

"I'm gonna give you everything you need. Face-to-face. I want to watch those incredible blue eyes of yours when I pull your sexy legs over my shoulders and make you mine. Then I'm going to pound your ass until you come so hard you won't remember your own goddamn name."

Damien's body jerked again, more ropes of cum covering his abs. Another spurt leaked out of my cock, my erection half hard.

"I don't think I'm going to make it until tomorrow," he moaned. "After coming twice in a row, I feel like I'm going to pass out."

"Good thing you're already in bed," I teased. "We're going to wreck it tomorrow. I can't fucking wait."

"Wish you were here now. I want to kiss you so badly."

"I want to kiss you too," I admitted. "I need that more than anything."

I was completely addicted to this man, and there was no going back.

"I should let you go," he replied. "But I don't want to."

"So, don't. Talk to me."

"About?"

"Anything," I replied. "Hockey, sex, dreams, goals, life—"

"We could be on the phone all night," Damien replied with an irresistible smile.

"Exactly."

CHAPTER 31
DAMIEN

THE FOLLOWING NIGHT

Silas was supposed to be here an hour ago. Where is he?

Maybe he'd changed his mind? Maybe he wasn't coming? I wanted to text him, but hesitated, realizing that I was acting like a possessed fool. Instead, I paced my living room, trying to calm myself down. That didn't work, so I sat down and turned on the TV for distraction. My knees bobbed up and down like I was sitting in the sin bin, waiting for that glorious moment of freedom, ready to hit the ice.

He'll be here. He wants this as much as I do.

Still, waiting on him had me unsettled. I was never obsessed with anyone I was having sex with, not even Eloise. Sex was a good time, but nothing more than that. Our entire relationship always felt... comfortable. She seemed like a perfect fit for me. At least, on paper. There was no intense push and pull, no magnetic spark, no raw discovery. Nothing like I was experiencing with Silas. A year into my relationship with Eloise and I suggested she move in with me. Her response was "Not until I'm your wife" and I said "Okay, let's get married." That was it. But even that was more about convenience than a need. Which didn't say much for my self-awareness at the time. And probably why our relationship unraveled so quickly after my injury.

There was nothing to fight for.

But Silas? Nothing prepared me for him.

For a connection that rocked my entire world to the core.

I was taking risks like I hadn't done in years and loving every minute. That phone call last night? Bar down, the hottest sex of my life. And if I didn't get my hands on him in the next thirty minutes, I was going to get in my car and go looking for him. That's how far gone I was, counting down the seconds like I had in that championship final, anticipation riding me hard.

I heard the rumbling of an engine and vaulted to my feet, racing for the door.

Eager much? Jesus, Damien, calm yourself. You're acting a fool.

A fool about to get fucked…

The very idea had my cock chubbing up in record time.

I watched as Silas's truck came to a stop in my driveway. He turned the engine off, slipped out of the cab, and stalked up the entryway. He glanced up and spotted me, his expression feral. I'd never been on the receiving end of such heated determination before. Every nerve ending in my body lit up. It was like Silas could see all of me, everything I needed, without me having to say a word.

Next thing I knew I was backed against my door, and we were kissing like our lives depended on it.

Forget the phone sex last night. This, Silas's mouth on mine, this was the best sex of my life.

"You're late," I whispered.

"No." Silas punctuated the word with another possessive kiss. "I'm right on time, baby."

"Cheesy."

"But true."

I smiled at him, and he moved suddenly, manhandling me until we were inside the house. I heard a door slam but don't ask me if I was the one who closed it. I was too wrapped up in getting my hands all over Silas, pulling at his jacket, urging him to get it off. I needed him naked. Now.

"Too many clothes," I growled as we stumbled down the hallway, unable to keep our hands off each other.

"Look who's talking."

"How about I give you a key for next time?" I suggested. "I'll be ready and waiting in bed."

Silas's grip around my waist tightened.

"I can drop by anytime I want?"

"Anytime."

"Fucking hell, Damien."

"Is that a yes?" I teased.

"What do you think?"

Silas rocked his hips against mine, and when I felt how hard he was, I let out a filthy moan. His hands squeezed my ass, then slid under the denim, cupping my cheeks. God, his callused hands on my skin felt amazing.

"Commando?" he chuckled.

"I'm taking a play from your book."

His finger teased my crease, making me shudder, and I pushed my ass back, eager for more.

"Mmm, I like this role reversal. What else can I teach you?" Silas asked, his hot breath teasing my lips.

So close and not close enough.

"Everything."

"Cheesy," he quipped and gave me a wicked grin.

"But true," I repeated.

"Take these sexy jeans off."

I reached for my zipper, undoing it slowly, then pushed the jeans down my hips, until they puddled on the floor. I stepped out of them as Silas kneeled in front of me. My cock slapped against my stomach, so fucking hard that it was painful.

"Turn around," he demanded.

I shifted to face the wall, my hands meeting cool wood, as I spread my legs and offered my ass to him. I'd prepared for tonight, googling everything I could find on bottoming for the first time. And when Silas's warm hands slid up my thighs, making me quake all over, I was so fucking grateful for the prep.

"Do you have any idea how fucking beautiful you are?" Silas rasped, his hands cupping my ass, spreading my cheeks. "I have to keep reminding myself that this is real."

There was no mistaking the raw hunger in his voice. I felt the exact same way.

"Silas, please—"

"Please what?" he asked, rubbing his beard over my skin.

"Touch me."

"I am."

He massaged my cheeks, spreading them apart. I began to shake with need, dropping my forehead to rest on the wall.

"More. Please."

"Tell me," he demanded. "Tell me what you want."

I all but screamed in frustration.

"Get your tongue in my ass."

There was no hiding the passion in my demand. I needed this, I needed him.

"Go on," Silas urged, giving my skin a teasing lick.

It was so much and yet, not enough. I pushed my ass back, desperate to feel his tongue all over me.

"Suck my hole."

I'd never been so vocal about what I needed when it came to sex. Or so in tune with my body. There was no hesitation. Every sexy, dirty scenario I could think of, I wanted to explore with him.

Silas's tongue slid over my taint, and my legs locked up.

And when he licked a path over my hole, shoving his face between my cheeks, I started to shake all over. There was so much pleasure, almost too much, as he licked and sucked, then pushed the tip of his tongue inside me.

"Damien, you taste... Fuck, you're all mine. You know that, right?"

"Yes."

"You only give this to me."

"Yes, yes," I croaked. "Please, don't stop."

Silas ate at my hole, licking, sucking, then fucking me with his tongue. My balls ached and my cock leaked pre-cum all over the wall. I locked my arms and rocked my hips, pushing back, riding his face with abandon, hardly recognizing the husky groans and pleas coming out of my mouth, floating in a pleasure haze that went beyond fucking.

I looked over my shoulder, and seeing Silas on his knees, his face buried in my ass, was too much. My climax was about to unleash.

"Silas, please. I need—"

"What, baby? What do you need?"

"You. I need you inside me. Fuck me."

Silas snuck a hand between my legs and began to stroke me off. No. Too soon, I was going to come.

"Bed," I moaned. "Bedroom... lube."

Silas gave my hole one last lick and pulled back, leaving me aching, empty. Part of me wanted to protest, but then he swatted my ass, hard, and ran off towards my bedroom. After the initial shock, I pushed off the wall and chased him down the hallway.

"You better finish what you started," I called out.

I turned the corner, and he was there, standing at the foot of my bed, like he'd always been there. It wasn't only my dick that ached like a motherfucker, but my heart too.

"You know that I always play hard, Damien. Right to the end."

He stepped out of his jeans and threw his T-shirt aside, and fuck, I mapped every inch of his sexy body with my eyes. I reached for him, cupping his face, claiming his lips, tasting myself on his tongue.

We moved in sync, towards the bed, and I found myself flat on my back, legs in the air. Silas pushed my knees to my chest and lowered his head again.

"Fuck," I whispered.

"Fuck is right," he replied, flicking my hole with his tongue. "I'm not going to eat your hole; I'm going to fuck it full of my cum."

"Oh God, Silas."

I pushed my ass up, desperate for him. His responding chuckle hit me right in the balls.

"Lie back, baby," Silas whispered. "It's gonna be so good, I promise."

I reached for him, sliding my hands through all that silky hair. He grabbed my ass cheeks, spread them wide, and feasted on me. I'd never been consumed like that before. He licked the rim of my hole, then speared me with his tongue, fucking me with it. All I could do was ride the intense wave of pleasure, and when he slid the tip of his callused finger over my hole, I wanted more.

"Yes, do it."

I heard a click, the snap of the lube cap. Silas worked one slick finger inside me, and the burn of penetration felt so good.

"Did you play with your ass today?" he asked.

I nodded. I'd taken a drive to Burlington, to a store on the outskirts of town, so I could make some purchases including a dildo and more lube. There was no way I could take Silas's monster cock for the first time without prepping.

"Check out the nightstand."

Silas yanked on the drawer and pulled out my new dildo. Maybe next time I could ride it while sucking him off...

"You're not the only one who likes toys," I added. "I'm calling him Rufus."

Silas's sudden bark of laughter had me smiling so wide my face hurt.

"You know about that ridiculous nickname?" He chuckled, leaning back in to kiss my thigh.

"Of course. I pay attention when it comes to you."

Silas gave me a wicked grin. "Aw, Coach, does that mean I'm your favorite?"

"No question."

It didn't matter that he was my student, my player. Off limits. I didn't care. There was no doubt that he was mine.

Silas put the toy back in the drawer and crawled up over me, until we were face-to-face, his lips hovering over mine, connected head to toe. So close, but too far away. I reached for him, the kiss long and deep, his tongue sliding over mine, the taste of passion so heady I was trembling again. And when his hard cock brushed against mine, I knew that I couldn't wait anymore.

"We go slow, all right?" Silas whispered.

"Not too slow."

"Damien."

"Stop teasing me. I know what I want."

Silas leaned back and reached for the lube. I spread my legs, holding onto my knees, offering my hole to him. Silas stared at me for one hungry second, then closed his eyes, like he was fighting for control.

"Baby?" I asked.

"Give me a sec, Damien," he bit out and reached down, gripping the base of his cock. "Christ, I almost came."

I was the one he wanted, the one who pushed him to his limit. Me.

"I like that," I whispered.

He shook his head and licked his lips. "You're the one who's trouble."

Silas reached for the lube, pouring a generous amount into his palm. With his hand slicked up, he traced a finger over my hole and damn, I was greedy for it.

"Do it. Please."

Slowly, he pushed the tip of his finger inside me. There was pain mixed with the pleasure, but pleasure won out. I moaned so loud I didn't even recognize myself. I'd never felt so full, and yet it wasn't enough.

"Keep going," I urged, wanting so much, wanting more.

Silas slid another finger inside me. He moved in and out, fucking me like we had all the time in the world. It was so damn good that I couldn't help but writhe and beg for more.

"I'm ready."

"Not yet."

Silas added a third finger, and that's when the burn became intense. Leaning forward, he slid his free hand around my cock and stroked me off. I didn't know what I wanted more of: his hand on my dick or his cock in my ass. When he crooked his fingers and pressed on my prostate, I had my answer.

All of it. I was greedy for *all* the pleasure.

"Yes, fuck yes."

"Baby."

I wasn't going to last long. Silas was going to wreck me, that I knew for sure.

"Fuck me now," I moaned. "Please."

He withdrew his fingers, and I protested the emptiness. I watched as he slicked up his dick and fought like hell for my control.

"I'm gonna make you mine, Damien."

I shivered in response as his promise became my reality. He took hold of my legs and draping them over his shoulders, pressing his cock to my hole. The entire time we stared at each other, unable to look away, like neither of us could believe this was happening.

Inch by inch, he worked his big cock inside me. I was so full, and yet it wasn't enough. Silas pumped his hips and pushed all the way inside me, and my eyes rolled back in my head.

"Oh God," I moaned as I dug my heels into his back. "Don't stop. Please."

"Damien."

He was shaking hard as he pushed all the way inside me, holding on tight to his control.

"I'm good. I swear," I pleaded. "Don't hold back."

Silas gripped my ass cheeks and thrust into me, slowly at first, letting me adjust. I clawed at the bedsheets and rocked my hips, trying to take more of him, showing him that I was ready for all the fucking.

"Bossy," Silas teased.

"Fucking right."

He dug his knees into the mattress, and lifted my ass, rutting into me, harder, faster, taking complete ownership of my body. I was totally at his mercy in this position, and when every thrust of his cock nailed my prostate, sparks of pleasure raced up and down my body. All I could do was hold on and ride the incredible wave.

"So good," Silas panted. "You're mine. Only mine."

"Yes."

"You belong to me."

"Yes, baby, yes."

He snuck one hand around to tease my cock, stroking me off in time with his thrusts. He was all over me, inside me, and I couldn't get enough. The room echoed with the sound of our moans and grunts as we clawed at each other, desperate to come. The bed groaned and I wondered if the whole thing would collapse underneath us.

My climax was building so fast and sharp that I knew I wasn't going to last.

"You ready?" He groaned. "I'm gonna fill your tight hole with my cum."

"Give it to me."

Silas finally let loose, gripping my thighs and pummeling my ass, fucking me like a man possessed. I was as gone as he was, trying to get him as deep inside me as he could get.

"Oh fuck, I'm coming." Silas's body locked up tight, his neck and forearms rigid. "Damien!"

Hot cum flooded my ass as he continued fucking me. All it took was one more thrust and I slipped over the edge and joined him, the orgasm completely annihilating me, every nerve ending firing at once. My legs finally slipped off his shoulders, and I wrapped them around his waist.

"You okay?" Silas asked me.

"The... bed," I panted.

"What about it?"

"Still... not... broken."

Silas chuckled and kissed me.

"Is that a challenge?"

"Are you a hockey player?"

CHAPTER 32
DAMIEN

TWO WEEKS LATER

Selwin was due to arrive any minute now, and I was pacing the ice.

The photographer was already here, and so was Dave, acting as the school's PR rep. But hopefully not for long. A couple of hours, tops. Having outside people observing my players wasn't exactly conducive to a full day of training camp. Not for my players or for me. I needed everyone focused, not distracted.

And speaking of major distractions, I glanced over at Silas, who stood near the net, talking to Finn, Dane, and Ethan. My gaze never strayed far from him. Not today, and not for the past two weeks. Outside of camp, we stole every spare moment away together and it still wasn't enough. The sex kept getting hotter, and more than that, what blew my mind every time, was that the conversations between us had no end. It took us forever to end any text exchange or phone call, and when we were together, there was always one more kiss that we had to steal.

I didn't want to let go. I couldn't.

There was no doubt about my feelings; I was in love with Silas.

But falling was one thing, sneaking around was another. We couldn't hide forever. I wanted to hold his fucking hand and not just in the privacy of my home. I knew he wanted the same, but how? When? I was trapped in a maze of my own making, with no clear exit in sight. There was no one I'd rather be confined with than my sarcastic defenseman, but damn, I wanted to stand with him in the light.

"Damien!"

I turned to find Selwin staring at me from the other side of the boards, suited up in his hockey uniform, giving me that shit-eating grin that told me today was going to be one for the records.

"You finally made it," I quipped. "I was about to call Aleksi to see if he could switch days."

"What? No way. No second best for Sutton U," Selwin returned with his trademark grin and stepped out onto the ice.

"I dare you to say that to his face."

"I'm silly, not stupid," Selwin remarked.

I skated over to my friend, and he brought me in for a hug.

"You look amazing, D," Selwin whispered, and then not-so-subtly glanced down the ice. "And one guess as to why."

"Later," I replied quickly. "For now, you've got players to mentor."

"Lead the way."

We skated off down the ice, and I watched as each player offered their hand to Selwin. Sel lapped up all their attention, making jokes and putting everyone at ease. Silas, who normally reserved his comments for snarky comebacks aimed at me, peppered Selwin with tons of questions about the upcoming season, while Finn, who was always talkative, stood there silently staring into space like he'd been hit by the

Zamboni. Meeting a hockey idol had a strange effect on players, and mine were no exception.

After almost ten minutes of talk, I motioned for everyone to get moving. Everyone but Sel and Silas headed off down the ice.

"I said, let's get to work."

I blew my whistle hard and Selwin covered his helmet with his gloved hands.

"Not in my ear, man."

"Then go get warmed up," I warned.

"How do you put up with him?" Selwin quipped as he nudged Silas's arm.

"It's hard, no doubt." Silas replied and gave me a grin that was way too dirty for a morning practice. "Damien's a total pain in my ass, but I have to say I enjoy it."

Selwin laughed at that comment, but thankfully, no one else heard our conversation.

"Enough shenanigans," I insisted, trying not to react to Silas's words. "Both of you."

They skated off together, my lover and my oldest friend. I watched the scene with a pang in my chest. We all knew, and yet nothing could be said. Or done. What was I going to do? Nothing. I couldn't do fuck all to change the situation I found myself in and I didn't like it one bit. For a guy who preferred his private life to stay that way, I was frustrated with hiding what was going on between me and Silas.

Instead of feeling defeated, I got *my* ass in gear and set up the scene for our first set of drills. The guys worked hard for over an hour, and by the time we were ready for our first break, the journalist slash photographer, along with Dave, had arrived.

I lost control of the narrative at that point.

There were posed pics of the guys with Selwin, interviews, photos of the guys in play, and more questions for me about the camp.

After an hour of media relations, I had a blooming headache and a desire to never smile again. Dealing with the press was always my least favorite part of the hockey job and that hadn't changed. I had a limited capacity when it came to peopling, and I'd hit it.

While the guys were still talking to the journalist, I scuttled off to my office to take a much-needed break. I shoved my headphones on, blocking out further noise, and grabbed my laptop so I could work on the afternoon strategy session.

I was ten minutes into enjoying my bubble of peace when I hear the knock on my door.

"Come in!" I shouted.

Silas entered the room, his helmet in one hand, his hockey stick in the other, looking disheveled and way too hot for me to be alone with him. He dropped his gear, slammed and locked the door, and rounded the desk before I had a chance to say anything, never mind "what are you doing?"

He grabbed hold of me, kissing me fiercely. I tasted his sweat and traces of orange Gatorade. Delicious.

"Couldn't wait any longer," he murmured, taking my lips softly this time.

"Baby, I was trying to be good."

He smirked and rocked his hips against mine. "Good's overrated."

"Do you think anyone, I mean, anyone other than Selwin, suspects?"

Silas licked his lips. "Finn knows. I told you that."

"Right." I nodded. "No one else?"

"Nope," Silas confessed. "But I'm sick of lying."

"Soon everyone's going to know. We'll be the worst kept secret at Sutton."

"Is that such a bad thing?" Silas asked.

I cupped his face, rubbing my thumb over his lips, tracing the curve of his smile. "I don't know anymore."

"My family knows, Finn, Selwin. I feel like I want to tell more people."

"More?"

"Like, everyone. Sooner rather than later."

I sighed and kissed him again.

"Baby, I love you, but that's a huge step."

Silas's inhaled sharply and crowded me back against my desk.

"You what?"

It was too late to take the words back and I didn't want to. I wasn't one to shy from the truth, especially when I was looking at him.

"Damien, say that again."

I stared into his eyes.

"I love you," I declared, my voice hoarse with emotion. "You stole my fucking heart, Silas."

He smiled against my lips.

"Told you I was ruthless," he teased. "And fair's fair, you took mine."

"You want to know what else?" I whispered, happiness surging in my veins. "I don't want it back."

Silas's husky laughter filled my office.

"Even better, because I'm keeping it," he countered with another kiss. "I love you, too, Damien. So much."

Shivers wracked my body, and I clutched tightly to him.

Was this the ideal time for us to confess our feelings? Fuck no. Did either of us give a damn in that moment? Nope.

"We'll celebrate tonight. Right now, we've got training to continue."

Silas gave my ass a playful swat. "I'm so going to show off this aft."

"Focus on the game, remember. Not me."

"Yes, Coach."

"Now get your ass back out there."

Silas slowly stepped back, and much as I didn't want to let go, I braced my shaky hands on my desk.

"Meet at your place after?" he asked.

I nodded.

Silas picked up his gear and headed for the hallway. I dropped back onto my chair and ran a hand through my hair. Yup, I was still shaking.

I told Silas I love him. And he loves me.

Giving myself a minute to process, I reached for the water bottle on my desk and took a big gulp to wash down my fear. Loving Silas meant I had a lot more to lose if things came out and there was backlash. We were so caught up in each other that we forgot reality was right here. All around us. It wasn't easy having players that were dating on the same team, not for them, for their teammates, or for the school, especially when I had to explain to outsiders what was going on. And me being involved with a player? How would that go down? Not well. Not well at all.

I hated that I couldn't even enjoy this moment, too worried about all the what-ifs. It was like my last night as a pro player, the night my knee got fucked up. Once I was in motion, there was no stopping the collision. By the time I got hit, it was too late. Not that I could change anything; accidents happen. And I didn't regret my time on the ice.

I certainly didn't regret falling for Silas, but I *was* afraid for him.

I only wanted to protect him, not be the very thing that he needed protection from. And when word got out, a shitstorm would unleash. That, I knew. I'd been trying for weeks to find a solution, but I still had no answer.

Would it come to me? Hopefully, not too late.

Slipping on my jacket, I grabbed my tablet and made my way back to the ice.

There was already a three-on-three game happening, with Selwin acting as referee, critic, and coach. The journalist, a guy named Cillian—I couldn't remember his last name—was still here, still taking photographs, but he was seated in the stands instead of on the ice. I looked around but there was no sign of Dave anymore. He must've headed home.

I stepped out onto the ice in time to watch our captain deke around Finn and Colin, slamming the puck home.

"Yes!" Dane shouted.

"That's 3-1 for Dane's team!" Selwin called out. "Finn, you let him slip past you, again. What did we talk about?"

"Obviously I can't remember," Finn commented and skated off.

His posture slumped, frustration obviously setting in. I called Finn over, concerned.

"Is everything okay, Finn? How's your mom?"

"She's good. Her spirits, I mean. The results aren't back yet, but the doctor says a few more days. The waiting is taking forever."

"I'm sorry. If you need to skip a day of camp, let me know."

"I'd rather be here," he admitted.

"It seems like you're having trouble focusing."

"I'm having an off day, but I swear it'll pass."

"Rest up tomorrow. Wednesday will be better."

"Thanks, Coach."

They continued their game and Dane's team finished it off, 5-2. I called an end to the day, and while the guys took off, I stayed on the ice to chat with Selwin. Ten minutes later, he headed off too. But not before we'd agreed to meet in town at Boots 'n' Burgers for dinner. He told me to invite Silas along too.

Tonight was going to be interesting to say the least.

The rink was quiet again, almost too quiet.

I was halfway to my office, wrapped up in my head, when I was suddenly grabbed by a familiar set of hands and shoved against the wall.

"What the—" I startled and looked up. "I thought you already left."

Silas chuckled and held me tighter.

"Nah. But everyone else has. It's just you and me."

He leaned in and kissed me, stealing my breath and making me forget everything except how right I felt in his arms. I don't know how long we stood there, seconds, minutes, his tongue teasing mine as we made out.

Until I heard what sounded like a door slam.

"What was that?" I asked, reluctantly pushing him away.

Silas shrugged. "Probably the ice machine in the lounge."

"No, it sounded like a door closing," I replied, my heart pounding hard. "Let's take this to my office."

"It's a little late for that," a voice echoed in the hallway.

I turned my head, and fucking hell, the journalist, Cillian, was standing at the exit, his camera in hand, aimed at us.

"With the exception of meeting Selwin Kirkland, today was boring as hell. I didn't even want to stay this afternoon, but the dean insisted, and what do you know?" Cillian replied with a smug expression. "Now I've got a real story, one that's going to make actual headlines. The public loves scandal, and a coach and his player fucking around? I couldn't have asked for anything juicier."

My heart dropped along with my stomach.

"There's no scandal," I insisted, stalking down the hallway and getting up in the journalist's face. "And nothing to report on."

"Are you kidding me? I caught you sucking face with your student. It's news all right."

"What it is, is none of your business," Silas barked behind me. "And if you took a photo of us now, you better delete it."

"Why? This is a public space."

"The rink is private property," I corrected. "School property."

"I was invited."

"The camp is over for the day, and we didn't consent to that photo. Besides, there's nothing to report," I interrupted, Silas standing by my side. "So go ahead and write whatever you want. It doesn't matter."

"Of course it matters," the reporter countered and stared at me like I'd lost my mind. "Why wouldn't it?"

"Because—" I glanced at Silas.

No matter what, I'd protect him. There was no other way.

"Because… Silas and I are married."

CHAPTER 33
SILAS

ARRIED?

The word pinged repeatedly in my brain, sounding off loudly, like a slot machine winner in Vegas.

Ding, ding, ding, you've won the jackpot!

It was a brilliant improvisation on Damien's part, and one that might salvage my epic fuck-up.

I should've known better than to grab him in the hallway, but it was too late for regrets. What was more surprising than the suggestion we were married? I more than liked the sound of being Damien's husband, fake or not.

Do you take Damien to be your husband?

I do. I do. I do.

"Married?" the reporter scoffed. "You two are claiming to be husbands? Seriously?"

"Yes," I replied, amazed at how calm I sounded, and how easily the lie slid off my tongue. My heart was racing faster than ever. "We are."

The reporter's widened gaze bounced between me and Damien.

"How old are you again?" he asked me.

"I'm twenty-two. And as my husband stated, we're none of your business."

The reporter narrowed his eyes at Damien. "How come no one said anything about this when I arrived today?"

"It didn't apply," Damien replied calmly.

"A college coach is married to one of his players and that's not important enough to mention? Right. I'm going to Dean Chancer to verify this information."

"Go for it," Damien bit out. "Now I'm telling you again, it's time for you to leave."

The guy shoved the camera in his carrying case and stomped off down the hallway. I waited and watched until he exited the building.

I turned to Damien. "I'm so fucking sorry."

"It was only a matter of time, right? We knew that," Damien whispered. "Still, what the fuck did I do?"

"You solved our problem."

"Or, I made it ten times worse. Because now everyone's going to want proof. The only thing left is for us to do is to actually—"

"Get married?" I offered.

"Jesus."

"I'm in."

"Silas—"

"You heard me, Damien. Let's get married. For real."

He stared at me. "Baby, this is crazy."

"Not as crazy as things will get when Dave finds out about us."

"Fuck! I have to warn Dave—"

Damien pulled out his phone, tapped it, and held it up to his ear. He paced the floor.

"Hey, are you at home?... Oh, okay... I need to talk to you... No, it can't wait until tomorrow... Your place, at nine? Yes, that works. But listen, whatever you do, do not take any calls from that reporter that was here today, okay?... Why?

Just don't, not before I talk to you. Promise me? ... Okay, thanks, bye."

Damien shoved his phone back in his pocket. "He's going to rip me a new one."

"You're not going alone. I'm going with you," I stated.

"Probably best that I go see him alone."

"No, baby. I got us in this mess. I'm not letting you take the heat."

Damien sighed, his eyes filled with resignation. "I'd say we're both to blame. I'm so sorry. I don't know why the fuck I blurted out that we're married. I thought it was the only way to protect you. But I'll have to come clean with Dave. I know what I have to do."

"No! There's no blame. And I'm sick of feeling like we've done something wrong. You and I are not wrong. And you're not falling on your sword or some other dramatic bullshit."

Damien finally smiled and reached for me, silencing my words with a soft kiss.

"Tell me how you really feel," he teased.

Despite the drama that was about to unfold, I was steady, centered. I reached for his wrists, holding on tight.

Damien was my rock, my home. He hadn't lied. We were in love, and we were committed to each other.

"I love you, and I want to be with you openly," I whispered before giving him another kiss. "So, let's make a stop before we head to see the dean."

"Where?" Damien asked.

"Come on, *husband*, you're a smart man," I quipped. "You can figure it out."

I didn't need to say anything else. Awareness dawned in Damien's vivid blues.

"Silas—"

"You know I'm right," I insisted. "I've got your heart now, remember? And I'm gonna take good care of it. Always."

"This is crazy—" Damien paused, licking his lips.

"This is us. It feels right. Doesn't it?"

Damien stared at me and nodded. That was all I needed.

I was done hiding.

I took Damien's hand and pulled him towards the exit. There were no cars remaining in the parking lot, save for my truck and Damien's SUV. I guided him to my pickup, and he got in, no hesitation. I floored it out of the campus parking lot, turned down Main Street, and drove another seven blocks, until I spotted city hall.

Neither of us said a word as I parked.

We got out of the truck, and as soon as I rounded the hood, Damien reached for my hand. In public. There was no fear, no trepidation, no question.

We stalked into the building as a couple. I'd never been prouder or surer of anything in my life.

An hour later, we emerged, still hand in hand. But now, it was official.

Damien Banning was my husband.

Fucking hell, this was beyond wild. Hockey players don't do anything by half measure, and we were no exception. We stood for a moment on the steps and locked eyes, then both of us burst out laughing.

"All or nothing, baby," I said as I squeezed his hand.

"Our worlds are about to implode, you know that?" Damien replied. "What's your family going to think?"

"They'll be happy for me. You've already charmed them. What about yours?"

"They'll be... surprised. I haven't even told them I'm bi yet," Damien added.

"Is that going to be an issue?"

"No." Damien paused. "At least, I don't think so."

"What about your ex-wife?"

"Ugh, don't even mention her." Damien sighed. "She'll be fine. Except, she'll probably accuse me of stealing her wedding spotlight."

"And Dave?"

"He's going to be more than pissed."

We arrived at Dave's around nine, and yes, Damien was right. As we stood on the porch, Damien wouldn't let go of my hand, and even though we didn't have rings yet, there was no mistaking the possessive way we held onto each other.

Damien didn't have to say anything as his friend ushered us inside and completely lost it.

Dave was angry. More than angry. Thank fuck we were in his house and not on campus…

"No, no, no!" Dave shouted as he looked between us. "Are you shitting me? Damien, what the fuck is going on here?"

"I think it's obvious what's going on with me and Silas. I was going to tell you sooner but—"

"You're sleeping with one of your players? Have you totally lost your mind?! Throwing away your career for a fuck?" Dave yelled.

"Calm down, Dave," Damien warned, his glare in full effect. "Silas is my husband, so watch your mouth."

I didn't think Dave's jaw could drop any lower, but it did.

"This is a joke, right? You can't be serious?"

Damien shook his head. "Not a joke. Not at all. And we're coming out. That reporter who was on sight today? He caught me and Silas kissing in the hallway—"

Dave made a strangled sound, like he was choking.

"Anyway," Damien continued. "I wanted to warn you. The reporter wants to verify my claim that Silas and I are married."

"For real?"

Damien nodded.

"I can't believe you've done this," Dave repeated, his voice hoarse. "It's like I don't know you at all."

"Dave, listen to me," Damien insisted, letting go of my hand to step in front of his friend. "Silas and I are married, okay? This is not a fling. We're both adults and we chose each other. We're in love."

Dave started walking back, until he slumped against the wall.

"How do you want me to react to this, D? As your friend, I'm upset you didn't confide in me. I mean, I didn't even know you were queer." Dave sighed and ran a hand through his hair. "And as your boss, I have no choice but to put you on administrative leave as of right now."

"No!" I shouted. "That's bullshit."

"You don't get a say in this, Silas, and don't think you're off the hook either," Dave warned, pointing at me. "You're also going to face disciplinary action for your behavior."

"For what? Being married?" I spat out. "I don't think so."

"This is such a clusterfuck," Dave muttered. "I have to inform Nora, our media team—"

"Do what you need to do," Damien bit out. "I'm sorry you had to find out like this, but how was I going to tell you? I knew how you'd react. But I won't apologize for how I feel. Whether you like it or not, Silas is a permanent part of my life."

"Your life is about to unravel," Dave hit back. "You hit rock bottom before, Damien. You know how hard it is to get back up. But I don't know that your career can survive this. What then?"

An overwhelming sense of panic, a fear I hadn't felt in two years, not since Jo's surgery, suddenly washed over me. If Damien lost his coaching career, lost hockey for good, what would happen? It was the one constant in his life.

This was all my fault. All of it.

"Damien—" I started, feeling like I was going to throw up.

He turned and recognized the look on my face. I didn't need to say a word.

"I'll take my leave," he said and turned back to Dave. "You can find someone else to run the camp or cancel it."

I thought about my teammates, and how all of this was going to impact them.

Fuck. Too late.

"Give me your work phone and the keys to your office," Dave requested as he held out his hand.

I watched as Damien passed over his stuff, his hand visibly trembling. Then he reached for me.

"Let's go."

I took his hand again, both of us shaking, and we headed back outside.

"Baby, are you okay?" I asked.

"I was going to ask you the same thing."

"Did I ruin your life?" I whispered, my voice cracking. "Your job, the team, your friendship with Dave—"

Damien shook his head, his lips pressed together.

"No. It's going to be all right. Dave will come around once the shock wears off. It might take another apology, or several, but personally, he'll forgive me. Professionally, I don't know what's going to happen. But the camp and the team will continue on, and so will you, whether I'm on leave or not. As to my job, I don't know. Right now, I'm more concerned about you."

"You say that now, but—"

"We made a promise to each other, and I meant every word. Did you?"

"Of course I did." I cupped his face and brought him in to seal my words with a kiss. "Baby, I did. I do."

"Then whatever happens next, we figure it out. Together."

He kissed me soundly, and my fears subsided.

"We need to talk to your family, and I need to call mine," Damien added. "Then I'll get on the phone with my lawyer."

Jo was finishing his shift at the driving range, so I called him to let him know I was on the way to pick him up. Damien, meanwhile, texted his brother and sister to arrange a video call for tonight. He also texted Selwin to tell him what happened since they were due to meet up in town for dinner.

We broke the news to Jo on the ride to the nursing home to see Dad. My brother wasn't surprised. Well, being married, yes. At me and Damien as a couple, no. Apparently, I was shit at hiding from him too.

"What's going to happen next?" Jo asked. "I mean, where are we going to live?"

I glanced at Damien. Just before we'd said our vows, I'd reminded him that me and Josiah were a package deal.

"I'd like us to move in with Damien, but we have time to work it out. We can either keep the house and rent it or sell it. I think I'd be more comfortable renting it for now."

"Cool," Jo replied and patted my shoulder. "Now I can relax about heading off to college in a year."

"What?"

"I was worried about you, Si. You're always at school, or working, and you never let anyone help you. I always worry, who's going to look after you? Now, with Damien, I don't have to."

"Jo—"

"Plus, when you go pro, Damien can help you navigate all that. And best of all, he makes you smile."

I got choked up and couldn't speak for a moment. Damien reached for my thigh and gave it a reassuring squeeze.

Despite Jo's approval, I was worried.

"It's not going to be easy, Jo. A lot of people will talk when word of my relationship with Damien gets out."

"So what?" Jo shrugged. "After losing mom and almost losing dad, I know what's important. If you're happy, I'm good. I don't give a crap what other people think."

"Spoken like your brother." Damien chuckled.

"I thought of something else, Si. You need to change the name on your jersey," Jo continued. "Given that you're *Silas Banning* now."

"I like the sound of that," Damien replied and leaned over to kiss my cheek. "What do you say, husband?"

I glanced at Damien.

"I think it's more than changing my jersey. I need a new tattoo to celebrate."

"Maybe we could both get one?" Damien offered.

"What would yours say?" I quipped.

Damien's grin was lethal.

"Taken."

CHAPTER 34

DAMIEN

The shit wasn't hitting the fan; it was multiplying.

The shock had worn off on the drive back to my house while my phone buzzed like mad. I'd texted Selwin, of course, to let him know what was up. There were more messages from Dave, and a phone call from Nora that I was ignoring. Not that I could ignore my friend or the college president for long. Plus, that fucking reporter was hounding me, requesting a formal comment for his story.

A statement from me *and* my husband.

Fucking hell, Silas and I were *married*.

If it weren't for the certificate in my pocket, and his possessive grip on my leg, I'd have assumed we'd dreamt up the whole damn thing.

As we pulled up my driveway, I spotted Selwin waiting by the front door, a couple of takeout bags by his feet. We got out of Silas's truck, and my friend rushed over to greet me with a hug. No matter what, I knew I had at least one friend in my corner. Then again, Sel knew the whole story. I'd blind-sided Dave. The guilt about that wasn't going away anytime soon.

"Damien, you dirty dog." Selwin chuckled. "Getting married and not inviting me?"

I gave him my best finger.

"Dave is *never* going to speak to me again," I admitted.

"Nah." Selwin waved me off. "I know him. He'll get over it."

"I lied."

"Yeah, but anyone in your situation would." Selwin shrugged. "Shit, I've done it."

"You're not involved with a student."

"No, but I'm still not honest about being queer," he replied. "Fuck knows, I'm lying to everyone."

I heard both Silas and Josiah's audible gasps.

"Okay, maybe not everyone."

"Sel, meet Silas's brother Josiah," I offered. "Jo, my friend and former teammate Selwin—"

"—Kirkland, oh my God," Josiah whispered. "It's an honor to meet you, sir."

"You too, Jo," Selwin replied with a grin. "So, what do you think of your new brother-in-law?"

Holy shit, I was married...

"He's cool. Silas is happy, so I'm good."

"See?" Selwin grinned at me. "It's not complicated."

"It's not simple either. I got put on leave."

I glanced at Silas, and he slid his arm around my waist and pulled me in tight to his side.

"They won't fire you," Selwin replied. "You won them a college championship for fuck's sake. Plus, this isn't a dirty secret. You two are married."

"Yes, but—"

"And watching you and Silas together, there's no doubt it's legit. You're welcome, by the way."

Silas grinned. "So, this is all your doing?"

"Let's just say I noticed the chemistry in Chicago and offered some words of encouragement." Selwin admitted with a shrug. "And you know what, you two have inspired me."

"What? How?"

"I'm coming out, baby!" Selwin shouted with both arms in the air.

"Am I hallucinating?" I asked my husband.

"No." Silas smiled at me. "But this day keeps getting more and more interesting."

"And we haven't even got to the honeymoon yet," I quipped.

The heated look Silas gave me had me wishing we were off together at some private hotel, just the two of us.

"Soon," he whispered, reading my mind.

When he leaned in and kissed me, I finally settled.

"Wow, you two are insanely hot together," Selwin remarked.

This time, both Silas and I offered up our favorite finger.

"Ew, stop," Jo muttered. "You're talking about my brother."

Selwin chuckled and clapped his hands. "Come on, guys, I've ordered dinner. You look like you need it."

I nodded and passed over my keys. "Make yourself at home. We'll be right there."

Jo followed Selwin, helping him with the bags, the two of them talking over each other.

"So, our life is crazy right now." I sighed.

I was scared that I'd fucked up, but also, deliriously happy that I'd chosen Silas, and best of all, that he'd chosen me.

"Are you still in?" I whispered.

"Baby, don't even ask me that."

Silas pulled me in tight, until our foreheads touched and we shared the same breath.

"I'm sorry, my head's spinning in a million different directions right now," I admitted. "First, I've got to deal with all these messages. Can't wait to see how the school administration is going to deal with us as a couple. I'm probably going to get fired. Selwin has a point about the championship, but the optics aren't in my favor."

"I think life will be a bit of a shit show when word gets out, but eventually the news will die down," Silas replied and squeezed me tighter. "And no, I don't think they'll fire you. But a lot will depend on the team's reaction. I'd say you better call Dave and Nora back and figure out a plan to tell the guys before they hear about it online."

His voice was steady, and I gazed into my husband's beautiful eyes.

"How are you so calm?" I asked.

"I don't fucking know," he blurted out, and his blunt confession made me chuckle. "No, that's not true. I do know. I know me, and I know you. This is our life, no one else's. If other people don't like it, fuck them."

"I hope you feel that way a month from now when I'm climbing the walls from boredom."

Silas grinned. "Baby, my gut instinct tells me that the team will have our backs. Don't ask me how I know, I just do. The guys respect and admire the hell out of you."

"They did—"

He kissed me again and silenced my worries. "Have some faith, all right?"

"That's my line."

"We can share it." Silas cupped my face. "Let's go make those calls."

I nodded. "I'm on it."

"*We're* on it. You and me. Teammates for life."

Silas

Damien and I held off on dinner, and settled into his office, replying to Nora's message with a video conference call that included Dave. The reaction of the school's president was much like Dave's, shock at first, until her media training kicked into high gear.

"We need to get our PR people on this now," Nora insisted. "I want photos, interviews, you name it. The two of you need to sell this HEA and sell it hard. You're a winning hockey duo, champions in sport and in love. We keep the focus on the fact that you're happily married, and we're good."

The shocks kept on coming...

"Nora, what are you—" Dave interrupted.

"This doesn't mean that I'm pleased about this turn of events," she interrupted and gave us an icy glare. "A heads up would've been appropriate given the seriousness of this situation."

No shit.

"But I've also been around long enough to know that this isn't the first student-teacher relationship at Sutton, or any other college for that matter, and it won't be the last. I'm not condoning it, but you're both adults, and given that you're committed to each other, legally, what else can I say? Except that I'm overturning Dave's decision."

"What?" Dave shouted at the same time as my husband.

I stared at Damien, wondering what the fuck was going on.

"If we put Damien on leave and suspend Silas, it looks like something's wrong and that will make this journalist even hungrier for blood. No. No way am I putting the school's reputation at risk like that. It's business as usual. We confirm the story, and then we sell the hell out of it. The camp goes on."

"What about informing the team?" Damien asked.

"PR will write an email for you ASAP. The sooner the team knows, the better."

"And if there's backlash?" Damien added.

I gave my husband's thigh a reassuring squeeze.

"You know your players better than I do," she countered. "How do you think they'll react?"

"With a lot of swearing," Damien quipped.

Nora glared at us. "It's too early for jokes, Banning."

"I think they'll be as stunned as everyone else," he admitted. "At first."

"I agree. They've witnessed the intense... I mean, the way me and Damien... The fact that we..." I glanced at my husband, unable to find the right words.

That was a first. *Help me out, baby.*

"They've witnessed the tension between us," Damien offered.

Thank fuck my husband found the discreet word for our smoking hot chemistry. I was going to say "eye-fuck each other," but it was doubtful Nora and Dave would want to hear *that*.

"Once the initial shock wears off, though, I think the guys will be okay," Damien continued. "As long as we make it clear that nothing changes when it comes to the game. That's the priority."

"Exactly. When we're in the rink, we're focused, professional," I confirmed, then turned to smile at Damien. "But I'm still gonna mouth off and that means you're still gonna ride my—"

This time, it was Damien's turn to squeeze my thigh.

"Okay, I think we have enough information for now," Nora interrupted. "Let's get the media plan rolling. And I want to see you both in my office first thing tomorrow morning. You too, Dave."

"I'll be there," Dave replied. "Damien, I'll be in touch later."

We closed the call, and Damien sagged against me with a sigh of relief.

"Holy shit, I wasn't expecting that."

"Me neither, but Nora's plan makes sense."

I kissed his temple.

"It's clear that her concern is about the school's reputation, not ours, but things could be a lot worse."

"Shit's getting real."

"It is." Damien reached for my hand. "Selwin isn't the only one coming out. I better call my family next."

"I'm sorry you have to come out like this. Back at the rink, I didn't pause to think. It's all my fault."

"Hey." Damien lifted my hand and kissed my knuckles. "It was happening anyway. I told you; I was tired of sneaking around. Baby, I'm ready."

"Are you?"

"Unequivocally. I love you."

My heart clenched hard.

"I love you, too," I whispered. "So fucking much, it's kind of scary."

"But in the best way."

I nodded, feeling overwhelmed.

"And the haters?" I added, staring into his bottomless blues. "Because they're going to come too, Damien."

Damien leaned in and claimed my lips in a heated kiss.

"What's the number one rule of defense?" he whispered.

I grinned.

"Always back up your partner."

He confirmed my answer with another kiss.

"That's me, baby. I might be a coach, but in my heart and in my soul, I'll always be a defenseman. I protect what's mine. That's you. And fuck everything and everyone else."

"Love it when you talk dirty," I quipped.

Damien's sudden burst of laughter filled me with a happiness that I still couldn't believe. Thank fuck I was sitting down because his gorgeous smile totally wrecked me.

"That's coming later."

"Once the chaos calms, we're planning a honeymoon," I stated.

"Oh yes."

I kissed him again.

"Let's call my family and then we need to eat."

"If Jo and Selwin left us anything."

"Did I mention that both my siblings have hockey careers, too?"

"You did. Olivia's a coach in Europe and Trent's a physiotherapist for the league, right?"

Damien nodded.

"That's pretty cool."

Oddly enough, I was more nervous about this call than the one with the school president. Meeting the family and all that. But it turned out all right. In fact, Damien's brother and sister weren't shocked that he was bi, that he was married, or that he was married to a man. The fact that I was eight years younger, however…

"How did you manage to marry someone so obviously out of your league, Damien?" his sister Olivia teased. "Like, way, way out."

Damien offered his middle finger in response. "So funny, Liv."

"Actually, it's the other way around," I replied. "I'm the lucky one."

"Aw," Olivia gushed.

"Whatever the case, I've never seen my brother smile so much in all his life," Trent added. "It's kind of freaking me out. What happened to your trademark glare?"

"Hey," Damien started.

"Oh, the glare's here to stay," I reassured them. "It's my favorite."

Then I kissed the pout off Damien's lips.

"Payback's coming later," he whispered to me.

"Can't wait."

"Aaaand that's our cue to go." Olivia chuckled.

"Are you guys taking any vacation this summer, D?" Trent asked.

"In early August. Hopefully."

"Definitely," I replied.

"Come to the cottage in Algonquin. Liv's flying over. I'll be there for the entire month of August. Bring some friends, you know there's plenty of space."

Damien glanced at me, and I nodded.

"That'd be great. Silas and I will be heading for our honeymoon first."

"We'll see you then."

We said our goodbyes, and I was about to suggest we break for dinner when Damien's phone pinged.

"It's the email from PR," he muttered and passed me his phone.

I quickly read through the note they'd prepared for the team. It was brief but said everything that needed saying. I passed the phone back.

"Looks good."

"Here we go." Damien began typing. "Let's see what the team thinks."

Nothing could've prepared us for the response.

CHAPTER 35

SILAS

t took less than two minutes for Damien's email to garner replies.

While my husband headed for the kitchen to grab us a couple of beers, I stayed behind in the office. My phone began to chime with notifications. The first one, no surprise, was from Finn. He'd group texted almost half the team.

Finn: WTF???!!! WE NEED DETAILS!!!

Dane: Moss, IS THIS REAL?

I forwarded a selfie of me and Damien kissing.
No, not a naughty one. The one at the courthouse…

Silas: It's OFFICIAL. And it's Banning from here on out.

Jace: Holy fuck!! And I thought dating a teammate was dramatic.

Axel: Drama? Us? Honey, what are you talking about?

Ethan: He's talking about your constant eye fucking, bickering, the sexual tension that's so thick I'm always choking on it.

Jace: Didn't know you liked the kinky stuff.

Axel: Come on, Walrus, don't be jealous.

Ethan: As if. And FYI, I win the bet about Si and Coach. Pay up pronto. I accept Visa, PayPal, cash.

Silas: The fuck?

Ethan: I said sexual tension, didn't I?

Kayden: OMG I snorted half a can of soda… damn…that is…fucking painful.

Silas: What?

Maddox: Kay was so shocked by the "Silas and Coach are married" email that he inhaled his drink up his nose and sprayed it all over the kitchen.

Kayden: A hundred percent do not recommend. The snorting, that is. But Si, bro, give us some warning next time, please.

Silas: There won't be a next time. Damien's it. Speaking of which, my HUSBAND is waiting on me.

Finn: Husband, holy shit, it's going to take a while to get used to that. Hey, can we see the rings?

Silas: Don't have them yet. Soon. But first, I'm going to get a new tattoo.

Ethan: Rufus & Damien forever LOL.

Silas: Better watch out the next time we party, Ethan. You might wake up with a hangover AND a tatt in a very unusual place.

Ethan: You wouldn't dare…

I laughed out loud. It would be a fun prank to pull on Ethan. He didn't like needles at all. The joke had merit, and payback was due, so I stored that away for future use.

Silas: So…are you guys okay with the fact that Damien and I are together?

Three dots appeared and then disappeared. I waited, holding my breath.

Dane: Hockey-wise, if you and Banning are focused on the game, in the game, I'm good. And I know that you will be. Personally, I'm happy for both of you. You two make a formidable team.

Finn: I agree with Dane.

Ethan: Me too.

Kayden: Same.

Maddox: Yep.

Jace: We've got your backs, Si.

Axel: And we've got a championship to defend next season!

Relief washed over me. I didn't assume that every player on the team would be okay, but knowing that the guys I respected and hung out with the most were supportive, meant a lot.

Kayden: So, when's the massive party?

Silas: Seriously?

Jace: Yes! We have to celebrate this! Ethan, get organizing.

Ethan: Me? I'm not a wedding planner for fuck's sake.

Finn: He said party, not wedding.

Ethan: You want me to invite Banning to my frat house??

Axel: God, no. Silas and Damien need something way classier than beer kegs and couches that smell like cum.

Ethan: Hello, you're responsible for those couches. You and Honey.

Axel: Damn right and proud of it.

Finn: Back to the party...

Ethan: I'll get it going, but I need help.

Dane: I know someone. We'll get it done.

Silas: Any other questions? And yes, before you ask, I'm going to change the name on my jersey.

Jace: That's so freaking hot.

Finn: So, the party is a yes? Silas?

There was a knock at the door and Damien appeared, two beers in hand.

"Am I interrupting?" he asked.

"Nope. Come see this."

He sat down beside me, and I showed him the group text. Damien chuckled and rolled his eyes.

"The team organizing a party for us is scarier than facing any reporter," he admitted as he passed me a bottle.

We raised our beers and clinked them together.

"No shit. God knows what they're going to come up with."

"I think you better add your input before it turns into something from a reality TV show."

I set my beer down and began typing again.

> Silas: The party's a go, but like Axel said, let's keep it classy. Only the best for my husband. And now, it's time for me to say goodnight.

> Jace: Wait, you didn't get to experience a bachelor night either. We can combine the two events? We start off the party with a stripper (or two) and then end with champagne and cake?

"Now they're talking about strippers," I added.

Damien's bottle almost slipped from his grip. "Oh my God. No. Unless… unless that's what you want?"

"Are you kidding?" I shook my head, then leaned over to take his lips. "The only stripping I want to see is you, now."

Damien chuckled and deepened the kiss, his tongue teasing mine.

"Hold that thought," I whispered.

> Silas: That's a hard no to the strippers. I'm trusting you guys to do this right. Night.

I silenced my phone and set it aside, reaching for Damien.

"Now, where were we—" I whispered.

"I was about to strip for you."

"Yes, please."

Damien stood up in front of me and reached for his shirt. I

leaned back against the couch and watched him, palming my dick as it grew hard. Suddenly, like I'd poured the cold beer over my head instead of down my throat, I remembered that we weren't alone in the house.

"By the way, Jo said to tell you goodnight, he's gone off to the guest room," Damien offered. "And Selwin's asleep on the couch."

"Perfect."

"But we still need to be quiet."

Damien straddled my lap, and I gripped his thighs, holding on tight.

"I can only think of one way to do that," I whispered, licking a path up his neck, over his jaw and finally, to those lips I couldn't get enough of. "Fuck my mouth, Damien."

"God, yes."

"Better yet, I want you to fuck mine at the same time as I fuck yours."

"Keep talking like that and you're going to make me come in my jeans," he admitted.

I ran my hands up his thighs and around his hips, cupping his ass, and there was no mistaking the shudder that ran through his body.

"Don't you dare," I insisted. "That cum is all mine."

I moved quickly, flipping Damien until his back hit the couch and I was staring down at him.

He smiled wide, and when that dimple in his left cheek popped out, I was a goner. My husband was gorgeous, sexy, an incredible man, inside and out.

And all mine.

"Ever have sex in here?" I asked.

He shook his head.

"Well, then, let's get this honeymoon started right."

Damien

I woke up the next morning with a swollen mouth, a sore throat, and a satisfied grin. Wrapped tightly around my gorgeous husband, I soaked in the moment of total contentment. After last night's playful round of sex in my office, Silas and I snuck back through the house and made our way to my bedroom. Our bedroom. Both of us crashed hard.

Despite what I knew was going to be a long and difficult day ahead, with Silas by my side, I was happier than I'd ever been.

The house was quiet, so I assumed it was early. I rolled over and glanced at my phone; it was shy of seven a.m. I shut off my alarm before it started chiming.

"Where do you think you're going?"

I turned back to find Silas blinking at me with slumberous eyes.

"Nowhere. I was checking the time," I whispered. "It's seven. We need to get up soon."

"Not yet," Silas grumbled and reached for me. "And it's too damn early to get out of bed."

"I'm not arguing that."

Silas silenced me with a devouring kiss. "Good morning, baby."

"It most certainly is."

We didn't kiss so much as consume each other, sleep and alarms all but forgotten as we hungrily made out. I rolled on top of my husband and pinned him to the mattress, relishing in his husky groan of approval. Silas wrapped his legs around my waist, his morning wood brushing against mine, setting off a million fireworks in my belly. I didn't know how we were going to make it out of this bed... *our* bed. Fuck, I liked the sound of that. I couldn't think about anything else, never mind getting up, getting dressed, driving to campus, and making intelligible conversation with others.

I wanted at least a week, just the two of us, no distractions, no interruptions. My new life was in my arms, and I wanted to revel in him.

But reveling, and spending all day in bed, would have to wait.

"Quick and dirty, baby," I groaned.

I spat in my hand and reached for his stiff cock, stroking him off with an urgency that made my own dick leak like crazy. All the while, I stared into his beautiful brown eyes, my heart pounding fast and furious, my emotions rising to the surface. For a man who used to shut down, I was not holding back with Silas.

"Love you."

"Love you more," Silas moaned, and when I teased the head of his dick on the upstroke, his head dropped back against the pillow, his neck muscles rigid. "Oh God, Damien, like that. Don't stop."

"You are so fucking incredible," I whispered. "I still can't believe you're mine."

"All yours. Only yours."

My hand grew slippery with Silas's pre-cum as I stroked faster, and he began to fuck my fist, both of us rutting together. Watching this strong, sexy man give himself over to me had my climax barrelling towards the finish line in record time.

Until the loud knock on our bedroom door rudely interrupted us…

I froze. My good mood, and worst of all, my erection, was fading.

"Dave's here!" Selwin yelled from the other side of the door. "Save the hot morning sex for another day!"

"Fuck," I blurted out, removing my hand from my husband's dick and all but collapsing on top of him, burying my flushed face in his neck.

Silas chuckled, cupping the back of my head and kissing my temple.

"We'll be out in ten!" Silas called back.

"I'm never inviting him to our house again," I grumbled.

"You don't mean that."

"No," I admitted and let out a frustrated sigh. "I guess we better get up and get showered."

"We can finish our husbandly duties in there," Silas quipped and squeezed my ass cheeks.

I chuckled and gave his lips a teasing nip.

"You're so dedicated." I chuckled.

"What can I say? You've rubbed off on me."

"I was going to," I muttered sarcastically.

After one more kiss, I rolled off Silas and we padded into the bathroom.

After a quick, but satisfying, mutual shower, Silas and I got changed and headed out of the bedroom to find Dave, Selwin, and Josiah seated around the kitchen island, eating breakfast.

Dave hadn't called me back last night like he said he was going to, and it worried me. I didn't want to voice my concern that he'd never talk to me again, but Silas knew what I wasn't saying. Even after we headed for bed last night, I'd been unable to fall asleep right away.

"He'll come around," Silas insisted as he held me tight. "He needs time."

The fact that Dave was here now gave me hope. Hope that I hadn't completely fucked up our friendship for good. Silas and I held hands as we walked into the kitchen and Dave stared us at with bemusement.

"I still can't believe that you're married. To one of your players," Dave announced and shook his head. "What the fuck, Damien?"

Did I regret not telling Dave about my relationship with Silas? Yes. Would I do the same thing over again? Probably. My reasons for staying silent were valid; I wanted to protect Silas from the judgement we'd face as a couple. Dave's initial response proved that. And while our families were on board —as well as many of his teammates and Selwin—not everyone would approve of me and him as a couple. Even if we were married.

Silas let go of my hand and instead, wrapped his arm around my waist. The move was protective as hell.

"If you're here to yell at my husband again, you can show yourself out," Silas announced.

"What he said," I added.

Dave worried his bottom lip, staring at the two of us. "I'm not going to do that."

"I'm sorry that you had to find out that way," I replied. "And that I didn't give you any warning about what was going on. But I'm not sorry for falling in love with Silas."

"You really do love each other," Dave stated.

I nodded.

Dave slipped off the bar stool and stood in front of us, offering his hand to my husband.

Silas slowly took it, shaking my friend's hand.

"You know that Damien's more than a grumpy pain in the ass in the morning, right? It's like, an all-day thing," Dave quipped, breaking the tension.

"Hey!" I started.

I could feel the tension in Silas's body release as he laughed at Dave's comment.

"I love every single one of his moods, and I'm not exactly Mr. Sunshine either," Silas admitted.

"That's right." I smiled at him. "You're Mr. Banning from here on out."

CHAPTER 36

DAMIEN

After a quick breakfast, Silas and I followed Dave as we headed to campus for the meeting with Nora and the school's media team. We arrived at the president's office at nine, and that's when reality hit.

Last night we told the hockey team, today the press release about my relationship with Silas was a go; our marriage was officially public news.

There were discussions about scheduling interviews, how to answer questions from reporters, and when to comment on socials going forward. Cillian Wexford, the journalist hired for the write up about the hockey camp, the one who caught me and Silas kissing, was back for a formal interview. Unlike the media team, who knew him, Silas and I greeted him with cool politeness. When it came time to sit down with us, Cillian was just as reserved, probably because we didn't give him the college scandal he was so keen to write about.

"Why don't you guys wear rings?" Cillian asked us.

"Hockey players don't wear jewelry for the most part, even in our off time," Silas replied. "It's a safety thing and then it becomes a habit. We save it for special occasions."

I was more than impressed with how calm and cool my

husband was the entire time. Not only that, but he was protective of me too. Whether that was a word, a look, or a touch of his hand. It worked both ways. Being in the spotlight wasn't easy but he seemed to take the questions, and everything else, in stride.

The longer I sat with him, the more I realized that while our wedding might have been impulsive, my decision to choose him wasn't.

I knew, without a doubt, that this man was right for me. I'd never felt surer of anything in my life.

But after two hours of meetings and question after question, my head began to throb. The reporter left, and Silas and I were dismissed. Thank fuck. I needed to move; I had to do something, anything. Whenever I was faced with a difficult situation, I didn't sit and wait for the answer to come to me, I acted. Whether that was on the ice as a player, on the bench as a coach, or when it came to my personal life, like eloping with Silas, I didn't talk about it; I did it. It was the reason I vibed with hockey, and it was how I built my life back up after my injury.

Silas and I were so alike in that way. We didn't let life happen to us; we shaped our life.

When we stood up to leave, I could feel the eyes of the entire office on us. Most of the attention seemed friendly, or at least, polite, but not all of it. Not that any of the staff would say anything while Nora was in the room. Her stance was clear, and she wasn't one to be questioned. But while I was used to the spotlight in my playing days, this perusal felt different. With my ex, I never thought twice about taking her hand in public. No one noticed or cared.

Not anymore. Not that I'd waste any time on what other people thought.

Fuck that.

There was only one opinion that mattered, and that was Silas.

We stepped into the elevator and when the doors shut, I breathed out a long sigh of relief. I turned to my husband, and only then noticed the tense expression on his face.

"Are you okay?" I asked him.

"Yeah, I'm good. But it was a lot of talking. Like, a lot. I'm not used to being the focus of everyone's conversation. My head's spinning in a hundred different directions."

"You were amazing. I'm so damn proud of you."

"Same, baby."

I squeezed his hand and pulled him into my arms. He notched his face against my neck.

"You know what we need right now?" I whispered.

"A beer?"

I chuckled. "That too. But I'm thinking something much colder."

Silas leaned back and stared at me.

"Let's hit the ice," I explained.

Silas grinned and kissed me. "I like that idea, but first, we need to head into town. There's something I'm missing."

I shook my head. "But all your equipment's in the locker room."

My husband held up his left hand and pointed to his ring finger.

"Not all of it."

Silas

"Wow. Just... wow."

Damien chuckled and pulled me in close.

"You've said 'wow' ten times in a row, are you sure you're okay?"

"Yeah, I—" I paused and studied my left hand. "I can't stop staring. It's so real. We're married. It's right here on our hands for everyone to see. I love it."

"Me too."

We'd entered Sutton's one and only jewelry store—a tiny but elegant shop named Kismet—and it took no time at all for us to decide on our ring choice; classic gold bands with a hammered finish. The owner, Erik Kismet—coolest last name ever—ran the shop with his husband, Sam.

"If you'd like them engraved it'll take two weeks," Erik informed us. "Or you can decide on that later. There's no rush."

I looked at Damien and he nodded.

"Let's do the engraving," I replied. "We can wait."

We slid the rings off and passed them back to Erik.

"After all, hockey players don't wear jewelry," Damien quipped, sliding his arm around my waist.

"I said on special occasions," I returned and kissed him. "And we'll have plenty of those."

"You two are so cute together," Erik announced. "Is that how you met? You're both hockey players?"

Damien groaned and I bit back a laugh.

"We did meet because of hockey, yes."

The PR training this morning was kicking in…

"I sense a bigger story going on here," Erik replied as he pointed between the two of us.

I chuckled. "I promise, we'll tell you the whole thing when we pick up our rings."

Erik nodded. "So, back to the engraving—"

We settled for simplicity: *Taken*.

Was it usual? No, but then nothing about our relationship could be called that. It was perfect for us, and that's all that mattered.

Once we were done at the store, I texted Finn to let him know about the press release.When he asked what I was up to, I mentioned that Damien and I were in town but headed for the rink. It didn't take us long to drive back to campus.

While Damien headed to his office to grab his skates, I walked to the locker room and got changed.

I met him back on the ice a few minutes later and we warmed up together. Damien took his time, and then he watched as I ramped up my workout.

Suddenly, Finn and all the guys from the camp appeared, ready and eager to join us.

"I guess we're doing an extra day of camp this week," Damien quipped.

Finn skated up and offered his hand to me. "We had to see the newlyweds for ourselves."

I shook his hand, and he pulled me in for a hug.

"Congrats, Si. I still can't believe it, but you look so fucking happy."

My face flushed as I glanced over at Damien. "I am."

"They're both smiling like crazy, so I know the news is real," Ethan added with a smirk.

After all the guys offered Damien and I congratulations and hugs, we got right into our drills. But I was clearly still reeling from the events of this morning because next thing I knew, Dane whizzed by me and scored.

"He got the drop on you, Banning! Follow the puck, remember? Run the drill again."

Damien's words gave me a weird sense of déjà vu, but at first, I didn't even realize that he was talking directly to me. Until everyone in the camp came to a stop and looked my way.

"What?" I asked.

"He's talking to you, bud." Finn chuckled.

"Holy shit," I exclaimed.

Everyone started laughing, Damien included.

"Now it hits you?" Finn replied and nudged me.

"Now it's fucking real. Even more than the rings."

"Rings?" Finn asked. "Where? Let's see them."

"We're having them engraved so it'll take a few weeks," I added.

"Okay, less talking, more working!" Damien called out.

An hour into our practice and I was in the zone. And it was clear to me, and the guys, that nothing on the ice had changed; I was back to playing hard and Damien worked me harder.

When we took a break to hydrate, Damien skated off to the boards and pulled out his phone. The relaxed expression on his face from earlier was replaced by a glare I knew all too well.

I skated over to him. "What's going on?"

"Lots of comments on the press release," he whispered. "And some of it is nasty. As we expected."

I yanked my gloves off and motioned for him to pass me his phone. "Let me see."

"I don't think that's a good idea."

I gave that glare right back at him.

"Don't do that, Damien. Don't try to protect me from *this*. You know I can handle it."

Damien nodded and reluctantly passed me his phone. There was our photo along with the college's official announcement. My first thought was *damn, we look hot together*. Then I read through some of the comments, which I refused to give voice to, and my stomach dropped out. Was I surprised by the hate? Not at all. It was the reason so many queer students and athletes hesitated to come out, me included. I remembered when Dane came out, along with Jace, the first guys on our team to do so. While most of the people in our circle and at the school were supportive, there were always haters. Always. The only thing we could do was stand tall and refuse to back down.

Getting hit on the ice was one thing, but off it? It took a whole other level of courage.

Did I give a shit what anyone else thought? No.

I gave Damien's phone back and skated to the bench to grab mine. I tapped on my socials, opened my photo app and began posting pics.

"What are you doing?" Damien asked as he slid up to me.

I selected the photo of us in the jewelry store with our wedding bands on. And another pic of us at his house, sitting on the deck, and one of us kissing too. If people wanted to talk, we'd give them something to talk about.

"I'm doing what we planned. I'm making it known that I'm proud as fuck to be your husband." I showed him my posts and kept scrolling for more pictures. "And anyone who doesn't like it can screw off."

Damien's tense expression finally eased. "Get in your opponent's zone and don't let up."

"Exactly."

"If we weren't surrounded by your teammates right now, I'd kiss you so hard," he whispered, his husky confession making me shiver.

I stared into his eyes, and I saw… everything.

His love, and his vulnerability too.

"We can't let these haters win," I replied. "This is our life, not theirs."

"It's going to be rough for a while and I… I'm worried you're going to question your decision to be with me," Damien admitted quietly.

This man… he totally wrecked me. This wasn't only about us, but about the past. Damien's ex left him when he was at his lowest point. And he was all up in his head that it was going to happen again.

"No, baby," I whispered. "I'm not going anywhere. I'm with you and that's final."

I slid one hand to his back to reassure him. It wasn't a kiss, but it was the best I could do for now.

"Stubborn as always," he quipped, his smile making a comeback.

"That's right."

"I'm so damn lucky."

"It goes both ways," I admitted. "And remember, I'm new

to being out too. But we don't win by easing off, right? Or letting these stupid comments divide us. We win together, or not at all."

"So, you *do* listen during practice."

"I remember every single word you've ever said to me. Every word, every argument—"

"Discussion," Damien corrected.

"That too." I smirked.

"Hey Rufus!" Ethan suddenly called out from across the ice. "Are you gonna play with us or what?"

"You heard him." Damien chuckled and crossed his arms. "Get back to work, Banning."

"You got it, Coach."

EPILOGUE
SILAS

"Baby, have you seen my jersey?"

My question went unanswered. No surprise there since this morning was total chaos.

It was, after all, the first day back at school.

Jo was already out of the house by the time I woke up and Damien fixed breakfast while I hopped in the shower. Now I was rummaging through a pile of laundry, searching for my shorts and my jersey. Where had Damien put them? I had five minutes to get my shit and get out the door. I had a full day of classes, a hockey practice, and a soccer game to get ready for.

We'd been running around like crazy for the past week getting ready for the new school year. The Banning household was always busy, sometimes messy, often loud, and at times, chaotic. More than anything, it was filled with love, laughter, and family. Our family and friends.

Our home became the go-to summer hangout for the hockey camp crew, notably Finn and Ethan. Finn's mom was diagnosed with lymphoma, but since they caught it early, and she'd started treatment, she was doing well and her prognosis was good. Despite that stress, Ethan always managed to get Finn laughing, and he stayed positive. Everyone in our camp became a tight knit group of friends. So much so that in August, Finn, Ethan, and Dane, along with Dane's boyfriend, Jackson, kindly offered to stay with Jo while Damien and I took off for our honeymoon.

Where did we go? Toronto, of course, because we had to visit the hockey hall of fame. We got razzed about our choice, but for me and Damien, it was exactly what we wanted. After three days of exploring the city, Damien and I drove northeast to his brother's cottage in Algonquin. We had our own tiny cabin in the woods; one of three that Trent built on the property. The main cottage, where we gathered for meals, had a view of the lake that rivaled our home in Vermont. The days were sunny, hot, and humid, and the nights surprisingly cool. Halfway through our stay there was a wild thunderstorm with lightning like I'd never seen, and it knocked the power out. Damien and I more than enjoyed our night together in the dark. Being alone with my husband, no phones, no lights, no distractions, was primal, sexy, and unforgettable.

All in, it was an amazing two weeks. Best of my life.

And falling in love with Damien meant the most incredible change of my life. I never imagined that being with one person, having *my* person, could even be possible. But every day with Damien showed me what I'd known from my very first encounter with him a year ago; he expected nothing but my best, and I was never going to stop giving it to him. Team Damien forever. Was my husband still a hard-ass? Yes, about a lot of things, hockey included, and I loved him for it. He was my biggest supporter, challenging me when it came to the game I loved and the life we were building together.

Not that our marriage was without growing pains. I was used to being hyper independent, and so was Damien, and we were still learning to lean into each other. Not to mention, the homophobic comments on socials and in person when we came out as a couple. Thankfully, the hockey team, as well as our family, supported us. Even Eloise, Damien's ex, and her fiancé, Rick. Damien was right; she was more annoyed that he'd remarried first rather than the fact he'd married me.

We'd also talked a lot about what would happen when—not if—I got drafted. Damien was determined to get a coaching job in the pros, but with the caveat that he'd only accept an offer for a team on the same coast. It wouldn't be easy, no matter where we ended up. It would mean long-distance for a good part of the year, but we'd find a way. I knew that we would. Plenty of couples juggled busy sports careers and made it work.

Jo was headed into his last year of high school. His medication was improving his symptoms, and he'd even gained ten pounds. He'd also been given the all-clear to return to hockey on a regular basis. I'd resisted at first, worried that he was pushing too hard, too fast. Until I played one-on-one with him, and realized that yes, Jo was ready.

My dad was still working hard on regaining his speech and mobility. In addition to our weekly visits, we were able to bring Dad home for a weekend, which meant everything. Damien and my father always got along since they shared the same dry sense of humor. Not to mention, my husband's hockey stories, past and present, were the highlight of my dad's week.

No surprises there. Damien had a magnetic charisma that drew people in.

And me? I was undeniably, completely, head over skates in love with Damien. And the way he loved me back? That man had me wrapped around his glove.

Now, if only I could locate my man, and my laundry…

I wandered into the kitchen, only to find Damien leaning against the counter, holding my jersey in his hands.

"I've been searching for that," I commented. "Where was it?"

"In my bag, by mistake." Damien grinned. "Along with those tiny athletic shorts you tease me with."

He held the jersey up, and I smiled when I saw *S. Banning* in bold, gold letters.

"Are you sure you want to wear this?" he asked me. "This isn't like summer where only a handful of people will see it. The entire campus will know."

I took the jersey from his hands and shook my head.

"Of course I want to wear it. I'm damn proud to be your husband. And if the jersey doesn't say it, the tattoo will."

He stepped up to me and slid one hand up my chest, over my heart. I'd had Damien's initials tattooed there, along with our wedding date: July 20. It was only later that I thought about the significance of the date. My mom wasn't here to meet Damien, but I had a feeling she'd wholeheartedly approve.

I wrapped my arms around his waist and gave my husband a long kiss.

"What time does your soccer practice start?" he asked me.

"Seven."

"You ready?"

I shook my head. "Let's just say that I'm not nearly as coordinated running on grass as I am skating on ice. It feels like I'm going way too slow on that field. Plus, it's fucking hot out there in the sun."

"Do the Cougars proud." Damien smiled and playfully squeezed my ass. "It's not a hockey game, but you still play to win."

I grinned. "Yes, Coach."

"What about a T-shirt?"

"Ethan's got them," I explained. "He insisted on creating custom shirts."

"Why?"

"Probably because they say something raunchy."

"Oh fuck." Damien shuddered. "Like the invitation

heading he so helpfully suggested for our upcoming reception; *Congrats to the Banging Bannings*."

I bit my lower lip, trying not to laugh. "He's ridiculous, but he means well."

Damien raised one dark eyebrow. "And putting him in charge of our wedding reception?"

"It's all under control," I insisted. "Dane got one of Jackson's rowing crew buddies to work with Ethan on the party. To supervise. It's fine."

I hoped.

"It's a week away," Damien replied. "Do we have any other details? I mean, besides the inappropriate tagline that we said no to. Like where it's being hosted?"

"I have no clue. Apparently, they want it to be a surprise."

Damien groaned and rested his forehead on my shoulder.

"I've got a bad feeling."

"It's going to be fun," I reassured him, rubbing his back. "Better than a stuffy black-tie event."

Damien lifted his head, pinning me with those gorgeous eyes of his. "If I didn't love you more than anything—"

I let out a laugh at his put-out tone. "I love you, too."

"But this party—"

"Our wedding reception. And you're not going to miss out on it, even if I've gotta drag you there myself."

"So ruthless," he whispered, kissing me. "First, you take my heart, and now this. I married one determined man."

"So did I."

Like always, Damien's stunning smile knocked the breath right out of me.

"I'm ready for anything, baby. As long as you're beside me."

"You and me, Damien. You and me."

———

Thank you for reading Heart Taker! Click here if you want to find out what happens at Damien and Silas's reception. Plus, there's more college romance coming soon in Catch, Sutton U Crew 1, Jett & Ethan's story!

Want more of my MM romances? Check out all my books here.

BONUS STORY

WEDDING SHAKER

"Are you almost done? Our ride is here and it's a stretch hummer!"

I stared at my reflection in the mirror and bit back a grin at Damien's comment.

"Are we picking up the entire team along the way?" I called back and continued to trim my beard.

"I hope not. And FYI, the guy driving the car *isn't* wearing a shirt."

My hand fumbled as I started to laugh. Thank fuck I was using an electric razor.

"Are you joking?"

"Nope."

Damien stepped into our bathroom with his arms crossed and his dark blues set to maximum intensity. He was dressed up in a custom three-piece charcoal suit, a crisp white button down, no tie (my request). He'd let his hair grow out this summer—longer on top, shaved on the sides—and the undercut emphasized his gorgeous features. Add to that,

Damien stopped shaving this week (also my request) and his sexy scruff was irresistible.

But what had my undivided attention was the gold ring on his left hand. I was still pinching myself that Damien was my husband.

"I have to wonder, is this going to be a wedding reception or a bachelor night?" Damien asked, raising one eyebrow.

"Knowing Ethan, probably both," I chuckled and set the razor down, turning to face Damien. "And I promise you, no matter what crazy shit he has planned, we're going to have the best time."

Damien growled and reached for my bicep, hauling me into his arms, and the towel I'd wrapped around my hips slid to the floor.

"You promise, eh?" he whispered, leaning in to kiss me.

"It's going to be a night we'll never forget."

"That's every night with you," Damien confessed, his hands sliding down by back to cup my ass. "Why don't I get out of this constrictive suit, and we can—"

The doorbell interrupted us, and Damien let out a growl of frustration.

"That's probably the driver," I chuckled. "We better get a move on."

"Let's hope he's at least wearing pants," Damien quipped and gave me another kiss. "I'll get the door, you get dressed."

"Yes, Coach," I smirked.

He swatted my ass in retaliation.

"We'll continue that later." Damien grinned. "Sneak away early?"

"Hell yes. Let's fuck in the back of that limo."

"I don't think the driver's prepared for that kind of road trip."

The doorbell rang again. Damien gave me one last kiss and let me go.

I slowly stepped back, until my bare ass hit the counter.

Damien stalked out of the bathroom, the Banning swagger in full effect. The sight made me weak in the knees, every damn time. I never imagined I'd fall for anyone, much less Damien, my coach, and yet, here we were, getting ready to celebrate our marriage in front of family and friends. So, what if the reception was a few months after the actual event? It was well worth the wait.

I turned back to the mirror, washed off my face, and added some styling crème to my hair. Then I reached for the garment bag hanging on the back of the bathroom door. Unlike Damien, I wasn't wearing a traditional suit tonight. I hadn't said anything though, because I wanted to surprise him.

Once I finished changing, I walked into the bedroom to find my dress shoes. After I slipped those on, I grabbed my phone and keys.

"The driver's ready when you are and yes, I can confirm, he's wearing pants," Damien called out, his footsteps getting closer. "Baby, did you charge up your ph…"

The rest of Damien's question was all but forgotten as he stood in the doorway and stared at me, his eyes wide, his mouth open.

My husband was never short on words, so I took it as a good sign.

"You like?" I asked him, suddenly nervous.

"Like?" he exclaimed and stalked towards me. "Silas, you're so fucking sexy in that outfit. A kilt?"

I smiled back, watching his dark blues flare with heat.

"My mother's maiden name was Campbell," I explained. "I thought it would be a nice way to honor her."

The idea for the outfit came to me when I was visiting my dad weeks ago. I'd spotted the picture of my mom on her wedding day, my grandfather proudly walking her down the aisle, wearing his full Scottish attire, and inspiration struck. I drove to a tailor in Burlington to get fitted for the kilt, and it turned out better than I'd hoped. In fact, I fucking loved it. I couldn't wait to pair the kilt with my leather jacket and combat boots on my next date night with Damien.

For tonight, I chose a pale blue button down, and a navy suit jacket to go with the blue and green tartan. With knee length socks, my grandfather's leather sporran, and the dress shoes, I was ready to rock this reception.

Damien stalked up to me and cupped my face in his palms.

"It's amazing," He whispered. "You're amazing. Every day I wake up and I'm so damn happy that you're here beside me."

"Sometimes it feels like a dream," I admitted. "I love you so much."

"I love you too, baby."

We sealed our words with a long, deep kiss.

"We're not going to make it out of this bedroom if you keep that up," I warned.

"Tempting. Very tempting," Damien chuckled. "But I don't want to be late to our own party."

"I'm ready."

Damien ushered me out of the bedroom with a pat on my ass.

"What are you wearing underneath this kilt?"

I looked over my shoulder and smirked at him. "You'll find out soon enough."

"Are you commando? Because one gust of wind and it's game over."

"Don't worry, only you get to see the goods."

We locked up the house and when we stepped outside, I noticed that yes, the driver did indeed have pants on. Dress pants, loafers, and a plaid shirt. The guy was young, maybe my age?

"Evening gentleman," the driver replied. "You both look great."

"Thank you," Damien replied. "Braxton, this is my husband, Silas."

I offered my hand to Braxton. "Nice to meet you."

"You as well. And may I say, you're killin' it in that kilt. Kind of reminds me of Brodie James, the rockstar from Wayward Lane."

"I'm a big fan, so I'll take the compliment," I replied with a grin.

"Ethan told me all about you guys when I booked this job, so I feel like I already know you. Congrats on your wedding and I'm sorry about the lack of shirt when I arrived. I was running late from my other gig, and I spilled coffee on my dress shirt," Braxton explained. "Thank God I had a backup in my bag."

"No worries, shit happens. What's your other gig?"

"I'm a server, a dancer, and a soon-to-be student."

"You sound like me two years ago. Well, minus the dancing," I replied. "That's a lot of jobs."

"I'm a hard-working boy."

Braxton stepped over to the car and opened the back door, motioning for us to take a seat. There was room enough for eight people, never mind the two of us. Then I spotted the bottle of champagne sitting in the console and a wrapped box that sat on one of the seats.

Once we got settled, Braxton closed the door and Damien poured two glasses of bubbly.

"To us, baby." Damien announced as he passed me a glass.

"To us," I repeated. "You've made this the best year of my life."

"That's because I've got the best partner of my life," Damien added. "And we've got many more years to come."

I took a sip and marveled at the crisp taste of the champagne. Normally, I was a beer guy, but this was a special occasion.

The partition lowered and Braxton piped up. "I don't

mean to interrupt folks, but if you need me, press the blue button near the console. We'll arrive at our first stop in forty minutes."

"First?" I asked and took another sip of my drink.

"Yep," Braxton chuckled. "We got a whole night of stuff planned for you guys."

"Okay, thanks."

"You're welcome."

The partition closed and Damien and I had our privacy again.

Suddenly, I glanced around the luxury vehicle, and it hit me.

"Wait, I thought this was going to be a simple reception. I didn't budget for all this."

My husband poured more champagne into my glass and offered a wry smile.

"I contacted Ethan and told him to go all out."

I took a gulp of the sparkling wine to counter my shock. "Seriously?"

"You're not the only one who can plan a surprise," he whispered.

"Damien."

I was too choked up to say anything else.

Then I didn't need to. My husband silenced me with a heated kiss.

"It's my gift to you. Our marriage deserves a celebration. The biggest and best."

"Baby," I whispered.

"Open the gift."

I handed my glass back to him and he put it aside, then I reached for the box and tore off the wrapping paper in one go.

"Ruthless," Damien teased as he watched me.

"You know it."

Slowly, I opened the lid of the box and stared at the envelope that sat inside it. When I ripped the envelope open, I couldn't believe what I was seeing.

"You didn't," I whispered.

"I most certainly did."

There were two tickets for Chicago's opening game the first weekend in October. Not just an opener, but the best seats in the house. There were also two VIP access passes, which meant we would get a tour of the rink and get to meet the players after the game.

"Holy fuck, Damien."

"Are you excited?"

"Beyond," I replied, still in shock.

"Selwin helped me set the whole thing up. He's also arranged for us to have dinner with some of his teammates on Saturday night after the game."

What? Having an opportunity to watch a game, meet players that were my idols, and to sit down and eat with them too?

"This is unreal. I can't wait."

I reached for Damien, giving him a resounding kiss.

"And don't worry, Finn, Kayden and Maddox will be staying at the house with Jo."

My brother turned eighteen at the end of August, and he was getting more independent with each passing day. I felt comfortable leaving him on his own for a few days, but I still preferred that he had company, just in case he had a flare up and needed to go to the hospital. Not that he'd had one recently, which I was thankful for. I was thankful for that, and for my teammates, my friends, who were Jo's too.

"You've thought of everything. Thank you."

"You're more than welcome," Damien whispered. "But that's not all."

I looked down at the box in my hand and realized that there was another envelope sitting there. When I tore that one open, I started laughing.

"Six tickets to watch New York play Boston in December?"

Damien nodded. "I thought we'd make that one a family trip. I've arranged for a nurse to accompany your dad. And I know that Jo's missing River now that he's moved to the city, so he'll get a chance to meet up with him that weekend."

No lie, I started tearing up and shook my head to try and stop the flood.

"Si?" Damien asked me, cupping my face.

"You are…I…I can't believe you did all this for me."

"There's one more thing—" he started.

"It's too much," I shook my head. "I thought we agreed, no gifts. You've given me enough."

"Not possible. And I can spoil my husband if I want to, so I don't want to hear any arguments." This time, our kiss was slow and sweet.

"I got you something too. It's not tickets to a hockey game, but I thought the timing was perfect."

Damien kissed me harder. "Show me."

I reached into my sporran and pulled out my driver's licence, holding it up for Damien to see.

"Silas Banning," Damien read aloud.

"It's not only the name on my jersey. It's permanent."

The heated intensity in Damien's gaze told me that we were going to be late to our own party. Very late.

"It's the best gift I could ever imagine," Damien whispered, and this time, he was the one who was fighting back tears.

"I'm yours, Damien. Always."

We reached for each other, the kiss hot and deep, his lips and tongue teasing mine. We made out for ages, until Damien leaned back and licked his swollen lips. I was about to protest and pull him back into my arms but he slid off the seat and kneeled in front of me.

I was wrong. So wrong.

We weren't going to be late to our party because all the fun was happening right here.

"I can't wait any longer to see what you're wearing under this kilt," Damien growled as he slid his hands possessively up my thighs.

I winked at him.

"Don't say I didn't warn you."

Damien

We arrived at our first destination—which turned out to be Unicorn & Ale—completely disheveled but totally relaxed. I'd forgotten all about Braxton, our driver, until the car stopped moving. Shit, had he heard us?

I was too satisfied to worry about it. And judging by the smirk on my husband's face, he wasn't worried either. God, the sounds Silas made as he came in my mouth were so freaking hot. He reached for me afterwards, but I didn't want to come yet. I craved the edging, the heated anticipation, the desperation. Silas loved to tease me, and I loved his teasing.

Months after our first forbidden kiss, and I still couldn't believe that Silas Moss was mine.

All mine.

Correction, Silas Banning.

Fuck, I loved the way that sounded. It made my chest ache and my cock throb.

Falling in love was the start of our romance, a relationship that went way beyond sex. It was the way we fit together; we were partners and teammates in everything. The best part was that I had no filter with him, or him with me. We didn't avoid the tough conversations, not at home and not in the rink. After all, he was still my player, and I was still his coach. I'd never met anyone I could go toe to toe with, someone that I knew would have my back no matter what. Coming out wasn't easy either, but I always trusted in my gut.

In my gut, and now, in my husband.

I looked up at the rainbow flag that hung over the door of the pub and smiled, thinking back about the first time I was here. I'd come to the bar with questions about my sexuality and when Silas walked in, well, there was my answer.

We'd interlocked our lives and created something that was better than my wildest dreams.

And I knew it only got better from here.

With his hand in mine, we strode into the pub to find Ethan chatting with Kolt, the bartender.

"You guys finally made it!" Ethan called out and walked towards us. "Wait, Coach, stop smiling. No one will recognize you."

I gave him a rude gesture in response, but it only made him laugh harder.

"Cool kilt, Si," Ethan added. "Can I borrow it sometime?"

"Nope," Silas replied with a smirk. "It's like hockey equipment, you don't mess with someone else's."

"Come on! I've got great legs, and they deserve to be seen," Ethan remarked with a cocky grin.

Unlike most hockey players, Ethan looked like a runway model with a perfect grin and stylish dark hair, not a broken tooth or nose in sight.

"People saw enough at your birthday blowout last week."

Ethan's smile all but disappeared.

"I don't want to talk about it," Ethan bit out.

He ran a hand through his hair and tugged at the ends.

"Come on, it's not like you're shy."

"It was total misrepresentation, Si," Ethan replied. "I'd been in the lake for fuck's sake."

I glanced at my husband, confused, but Silas shook his head.

"Rowing crew party crashers," Ethan muttered.

"Don't worry," Silas insisted. "We'll kick their ass on the soccer field next week."

I'd heard all about the upcoming competition set to take

place between the university's hockey team and the rowing crew, but apparently, not all of it. Maybe the rivalry between the groups wasn't so friendly?

"I'll tell you later," Silas mouthed, and I nodded in understanding.

Suddenly, a member of said crew, Jett Hawthorne, stalked up to us. Several heads nearby turned, and it wasn't a surprise as to why; with short, dark blond hair, a wide smile, and deep-set green eyes, the guy had presence. Not to mention a unique sense of style, pairing flared pants and a striped button down with cowboy boots. He wore silver rings on every finger and sported several necklaces too.

It was only the second time I'd met Jett in person, but the rowing star seemed like a grounded guy. According to Dane, Jett was not only a great athlete, but top of his class, studying chemical engineering. Somehow, Jett had been roped into helping Ethan with tonight's planning. Or, as my husband told me, Jett was supervising…

"Si, how are you?" Jett reached for my husband and gave him the bro hug.

"And Damien." Jett offered his hand to me. "You guys set to get this party started? The crowd's getting restless back there."

"Hunger pains?" Silas quipped.

"You know it," Jett replied. "A room filled with athletes means food is a top priority."

"Where's that photographer dude?" Ethan asked, staring at Jett.

"The *dude* has a name," Jett snapped.

"Whatever, where is he?" Ethan prodded.

"Renner's here somewhere," Jett murmured and looked around. When his eyes suddenly narrowed, I followed his line of sight and looked over my shoulder. "There he is."

A man I didn't recognize, dressed in a tight suit with an

even tighter smile, headed towards us. He was holding a professional looking camera in his hand.

"Jett, sweetheart, why did you walk off like that?"

Jett reached up and tugged on his necklace.

"I said I'd be right back."

"No, you didn't."

"Not here," Jett snapped.

It was clear that an argument was about to erupt but I didn't want anything to ruin this night.

"I'm sorry," I interrupted and offered my hand to the stranger. "We haven't met. I'm Damien, and this is my husband, Silas."

"Of course, the guests of honor. I'm Renner Whitner, Jett's boyfriend." He held up his camera with his free hand. "And part-time photographer, ready to document your special night."

"Nice to meet you," I replied. "Are you also a member of the Sutton rowing crew?"

"Me? No way. I can't stand the water."

"You hate everything, Whiner," Ethan replied sharply.

"It's Whitner. And I can't stand the cold either," he sneered at Ethan. "Or understand why people would chase a puck around the ice. At least rowing requires skill and effort."

Whoa, there was nothing quite like being insulted at your own party…

"Did you really just say that?" Ethan hissed.

When I glanced at my husband, I could tell he was thinking the same. I had another five seconds before Silas launched a verbal attack to defend our sport, and I was right behind him.

Instead, I opted for the calm and mature approach. I clapped my hands together.

"I don't know about you guys, but we're ready for a drink," I announced, changing the topic. "And dinner."

"Of course, everyone's waiting," Jett commented and

stepped away from his boyfriend. "Let's head on back and join the others."

I took my husband's hand again, squeezing it tight. When I looked up, Renner snapped an impromptu photo, the flash startling me. I hoped like hell that my trademark glare wasn't recorded. Then again, Silas loved all my expressions, my glare included.

Ethan walked and talked alongside us as we headed down the narrow hallway towards the back of the pub. The closer we got, the louder the echo from the private dining room. When we turned the corner, I could see that the room was packed with all our friends and family. Silas's brother Jo and his dad Tobias sat at one end of the table with my brother, Trent, along with Finn, Selwin, Kayden and Maddox. Selwin, of course, was telling one of his dramatic stories and he had everyone hanging on his words. Dane, Jackson, Axel, and Jace were in conversation with my sister, along with Dave and the rest of the hockey team.

Selwin stood up and whistled when he spotted us.

"The guests of honor, Mr. and Mr. Banning, have arrived!"

Everyone cheered and clapped as Ethan ushered us inside the room.

Once we made our way around, greeting everyone, we took our seats at the head of the table. A waiter began to serve champagne cocktails, but the neon orange color had me pausing for a moment.

"What's the drink?" I asked Ethan.

"It's a Hat Trick; prosecco and Aperol, with an orange twist. I got to sample it earlier, it's so good."

"Are you of legal age yet?" Silas teased as he passed me a glass and took one for himself.

"As of last week. You were there, remember?"

"Right, at the party you don't want to talk about." Silas chuckled and offered me a wink.

Before I could take a sip of my drink, Finn stood up and tapped on his glass, getting everyone's attention.

The chatter in the room quieted.

"Hey, everyone, if I could have your attention please." Finn smiled and cleared his throat. "It's my honor and pleasure to be here tonight with you to celebrate Silas and Damien's wedding. On behalf of the Cougars, I want to congratulate my teammate—"

"And coach!" Selwin called out.

"Yes, and coach, thank you Selwin, I was getting to that—" Finn paused. "I want to congratulate my teammate Silas, and my coach, Damien, both of whom are not only my colleagues, but my friends. Silas and Damien's relationship changed their lives, and our team too. One of the many changes over the past year that has brought our group closer together. We're a tight knit family, one that's inclusive, strong, and ready to face anything. It's one that I'm proud to be a part of. So, please join me in raising a glass to Silas and Damien."

"To Silas and Damien!" everyone repeated.

"I wish you two every happiness."

Finn's heartfelt words had us smiling and raising our glasses in turn. I took a sip of my drink as I turned to look at Silas.

'I love you' he mouthed.

"I love you more," I whispered.

"A reminder, though," Ethan piped up. "For some of us, this is our first stop of the night so eat well, pace your drinks, and remember, everything's being photographed."

Ethan pointed over his shoulder to Renner, who in turn, gave him the finger.

The echo of laughter filled the room, as more servers appeared and brought in plates of appetizers. When everyone was served and seated, I took my glass and raised it.

"Thank you, Finn," I announced and glanced around the

table. "Thank you to everyone who's here tonight. Like Finn said, we're not just friends but family, and we wouldn't be here without your support. Silas and I are thankful for so many things in our life; for each other and for you."

"I couldn't have said it better myself." Silas agreed.

Josiah tapped his water glass, and the rest of our guests followed, chanting. "Kiss! Kiss! Kiss!"

Silas and I leaned towards each other, and when our lips met, I tasted his smile.

"Now that's what I call a hat trick," Silas whispered.

"It's one kiss."

"Not with you."

———

After an incredible meal that included rib eye steaks and grilled shrimp, there were more photos and more cocktails.

Our table grew louder, raucous, everyone was having a great time.

After dinner, the wedding cake was brought out. It was shaped like a hockey rink and topped with two figures facing off for the puck. I served my husband a piece of the decadent double chocolate fudge, and he did the same for me. Watching him slowly lick the icing from his fingers, though, had me aching to do the same. Silas made a big show of taking his time, and I cupped his face, kissing away the remaining frosting from his lips.

"Tease."

"You love it," Silas whispered.

"I do."

I'd almost forgotten that we were surrounded by other people. Until another flash hit my peripheral vision.

"Hold it right there," Renner said as he snapped away. "Perfect. Now one facing me."

I turned and wrapped my arm around Silas's waist as we posed for more pics.

When we were done cutting the cake, we sat down and finished our coffee. Josiah leaned forward and tapped Silas's arm.

"It's time I head out with Dad. He's getting tired."

Tobias used his phone to communicate with people at the party. His speech was slowly improving, and he was working hard, physically and mentally, but it was a lot. Still, having Tobias with us today was special. It meant everything to my husband, and to me.

"We'll come with you," I insisted.

"You can't leave yet," Jo replied.

"We're headed to Boots n' Burgers shortly for the afterparty," Ethan offered. "Why don't you take your dad home and meet us there in an hour?"

"That works," Silas replied.

"Can we get the rest of the cake wrapped up?" I asked.

A short while late, wedding cake in hand, we headed out of the pub and told Braxton we had one stop to make before going to Boots. I helped Silas get his dad in the truck, and Jo drove him home while we followed along.

The residents of the nursing home where Tobias lived were all gathered outside on the lawn watching a movie when we pulled up. Saturdays were movie marathon nights, a tradition from June until it was too cold to sit outside, usually October. Most of the residents were more interested in our car, and my husband's kilt, than the movie playing. The staff took photos of us, and we offered cake to share with the other residents.

An hour later, we said our goodbyes to Tobias and drove back into town.

Silas assumed we'd grab another drink with the guys at Boots, and then we'd head home.

Nope.

When I told Ethan to go all out, he went all out.

Boots n' Burgers was Sutton's busiest pub and the team hangout. Ethan booked the entire place for our private party, and it didn't disappoint. The team greeted us at the door with a line up worthy of a hockey game entrance, jerseys on, music blasting. Inside was all decked out for the reception too. Instead of wedding bells we had hockey sticks, a photo booth with masks of our favorite players (Silas picked me), and an icy drink created in our honor.

I glanced at the martini glass that Selwin set before me, and it had me thinking back to that trip to Chicago, the college championship win, and the bar afterwards; the revelation that brought me to this very moment.

This time, however, my drink wasn't an extra dirty martini, but it looked just as dangerous, the glass filled to the brim with crushed blue ice.

"And this is called what?" I asked, reaching for the glass and giving the ice an experimental lick. Sweet and strong.

"A Zamboni Crush," Selwin replied. "Vodka, blue curaçao, simple syrup, and lemon juice, over ice."

"Like a snow cone?" I asked.

"The adult kind," Ethan offered. "Drink up, guys. You gotta throw the jockstraps next."

I'd only take only one sip – or, rather, one bite – of the slushie drink when I started to cough.

Silas rubbed my back in soothing circles. "You alright, baby?"

"Did you hear that?" I turned to him.

"I did," Silas smiled and leaned in, brushing his lips against my ear. "But don't worry, my leather jock is only for you."

"Damn right," I replied and turned my head to kiss him.

He tasted sweet, like the drink, and suddenly I was punch-drunk.

"Okay you two, there's plenty of time for that later," Dave

called out. "Sel, crank the music up, man, I'm ready to get the dance-off going."

"Dance off?" I stared at my friend. "You?"

"Hey," Dave scoffed and stood up. "I've got moves."

"Yeah, on the ice, way back in college," I chuckled. "How many of these Zamboni drinks have you had?"

"Two," Dave paused and shook his head. "Yes, two, no… maybe three?"

"Given how blue your lips are, I'd say three," I quipped.

"Haha." Dave shook his head. "I'm still a better dancer than you."

"Oh, it's on."

Silas got up and offered me his hand. "The first dance is ours."

"First?" I replied as I stood up and pulled him into my arms. "Every dance."

"So possessive."

"Well, you are my husband, Mr. Banning."

I felt the shudder that ran through Silas's body. I was aching myself, filled up with so much love for this man.

"I will never get tired of hearing that," Silas confessed.

"No?"

Silas kissed me. "Never."

Everyone started to gather on the makeshift dance floor, which turned out to be the patio at the back of the pub. The evening air was cool, but with the outdoor heaters, the space was surprisingly warm. Blue paper lanterns decorated the awning above us, along with strings of white lights and glow in the dark hockey pucks.

Ethan grabbed a mic and a bag from the DJ's table and walked around to stand in the center of the room.

"Alright folks, we're going to shake up the wedding reception routine tonight. The happy husbands are going to… toss the jocks! That's right, Silas and Damien, get over here," Ethan motioned for us to join him.

Ethan opened the bag and pulled out two bright blue jockstraps.

"These are brand new, folks, I swear."

He passed one to me and one to Silas. It was only then that I noticed what was printed on the front. Mine said "Ready For The One" and Silas's said "Ready For Anything". We held the jockstraps in the air so everyone could see and of course, there were more claps, lots of laughter, and a couple of raunchy comments to boot.

"I need everyone to gather around!" Ethan continued. "Single or otherwise. Come on, I mean everyone!"

"That includes you, Ethan!" Kayden called out.

Claps and whistles followed, until the DJ walked around the table and motioned for Ethan to pass the mic back. Ethan reluctantly did so and joined the rest of our entourage.

"Are we ready?" I asked the crowd.

"Throw it hard, D!" Selwin yelled. "Just not in my direction!"

I turned around and threw the jock over my shoulder, unaware of where it might land.

A roar of cheers erupted.

When I looked back, I spotted Dane holding up "Ready For The One" proudly, his boyfriend Jackson by his side.

Silas, of course, launched his jock into the crowd like a slingshot. Unlike me, my husband aimed precisely for his target.

It hit Ethan's surprised face and landed in his hands. There were more jeers and flashes popped as he held it up and swung it around his finger.

"Put them on!" Jace called out.

"Model it, man!" Axel encouraged.

Both Dane and Ethan pulled the jocks on over their pants, and everyone had their phones out taking pictures. They looked completely ridiculous, and Silas and I were laughing so hard we were in tears. Ethan walked over and grabbed the mic again, pointing to us.

"Don't be jealous of how good Dane and I look right now, okay?" Ethan nodded at the DJ. "Alright, before we bring out the next round of drinks and games, it's time, lovebirds, for your first dance."

"You Shook Me All Night Long" blared out of the speakers.

I looked over at Ethan. "Really?"

"What? I told you we were gonna shake up this wedding," Ethan replied into the mic, and everyone heckled him. "I'm kidding folks. Just kidding."

The tune changed again, and this time "A Thousand Years" filtered out over the air.

"That's more like it," Silas whispered as he slid his arms around me. Both of us held on tight to each other as we danced slowly, in perfect synch. "Are you going to sing the words to me like you did in the shower last week?"

I gave my husband a warning glare, but it only made him smile harder.

"That secret stays between us."

"What'll you give me to stay silent?" he teased.

"Always so ruthless," I whispered admiringly. "How about my undying love and devotion?"

Silas shifted, dipping me low, kissing me soundly.

"I'll take it."

———

I hope you enjoyed Wedding Shaker, Damien & Silas's bonus story! **Do you want more college romance? Jett & Ethan get their story in Catch, Sutton U Crew 1.**

ABOUT THE AUTHOR

Ava Olsen writes steamy and dreamy MM romance with heartwarming characters, sexy banter, and ALL the romantic feels.

Sign up for my newsletter for the latest updates, cover reveals, and bonus scenes: http://avaolsenauthor.com

FOLLOW ME

ALSO BY AVA OLSEN

Sutton U Crew: MM Sports Romance

Catch

Bar Down: MM College Hockey Romance

Rule Breaker

Play Maker

Heart Taker

Stand Alone (enemies to lovers)

Happily Never After

Wayward Lane MM Rockstar Romance

PUNK-IN

B-MINE

4-EVER

Wayward Lane Backstage

Don't Fall For A Rockstar

Don't Fall For A Bodyguard

Don't Fall For A Dreamer

Voyagers Series

Oh Buoy

Starboard

The Cockpit

Endeavor

Nauti or Nice

Stand Alone (Voyagers spin off)

Co-Star

NY Nights

Novel Affair

Troublemaker

Unforgettable You

NY Nights Bodyguard Edition

Hate to Love You

Love Like Yours

Never Knew Love

Stand Alone (novella)

Long Time Coming